Lisa Dickenson is the pseudonym for Beyoncé. OK, FINE, THAT'S NOT TRUE.

Lisa lives by the Devon seaside, stuffing cream teas in the gobs of anyone who comes to visit, and writing stuff down that she hopes is funny. Her first novel was the copyright-infringing *Sweet Valley Twins: The Twins Holiday Horror*, which she wrote in primary school and gave up on after five pages. Twenty-ish years later Lisa went on to be a *real author* and wrote the Novelicious Debut of the Year, *The Twelve Dates of Christmas*, and never looked back.

Follow Lisa online for all her book news and Beyoncé-obsessing:

www.lisadickenson.com
Twitter: @LisaWritesStuff
Facebook: /LisaWritesStuff
Instagram: lisawritesstuff

*Also by Lisa Dickenson*

The Twelve Dates of Christmas
You Had Me at Merlot
Mistletoe on 34th Street
Catch Me if You Cannes

Lisa Dickenson

# my sisters and me

sphere

SPHERE

First published in Great Britain in 2018 by Sphere

1 3 5 7 9 10 8 6 4 2

A CIP catalogue record for this book
is available from the British Library.

ISBN 978-0-7515-6311-5

Typeset in Caslon by M Rules
Printed and bound in Great Britain by
Clays Ltd, Elcograf S.p.A.

Papers used by Sphere are from well-managed forests
and other responsible sources.

Sphere
An imprint of
Little, Brown Book Group
Carmelite House
50 Victoria Embankment
London EC4Y 0DZ

An Hachette UK Company
www.hachette.co.uk

www.littlebrown.co.uk

Dedicated to the sisterhood,
my Strong Women Squad

# Prologue

Emmy shifted in her seat, the hard plastic as unforgiving as her hangover. 'Come on, Jared, you know we haven't done anything wrong.'

'This is clearly a case of Maplewood bullshittery,' Rae scoffed next to her, peeling fragmented pigments of last night's lipstick from her mouth and dropping them on the table like a pink pile of ash. 'This town ain't big enough for the three of us.'

PC Jared Jones mirrored Emmy's shuffling, uncomfortable under the gaze of the three sisters. 'How can I not bring you in for questioning? The misdemeanours are stacking up against you.'

'Please tell us exactly what we've done wrong?' prompted Noelle, who sat up straight, business-face on, the knowledge of the law behind her unwavering smile.

Emmy pushed her hair away from her face, and feeling something against her fingers, pulled a small leaf from the tangles. She met Jared's eye for a second.

He refocused on his paperwork, a blush creeping out from under his collar. 'I've had reports of theft, criminal damage, threatening language, antisocial behaviour, disturbing the peace, breaking and entering, devil worship, kidnapping—'

'*Alleged* kidnapping,' Noelle interrupted.

'It's all alleged,' sighed Emmy.

'Then help me out here, ladies,' said Jared, holding his head in his hands. 'You can't keep this silence up. Where is she? Where's the mayor?'

# Chapter 1

In Hyde Park, London, the late summer sun was already dipping, as if it knew September began tomorrow, and it wanted an early night before the task of reddening the leaves was here. Rae Lake was 'backstage' in a pop-up trailer, warming up her voice to play Musetta in a stripped-down alfresco performance of *La Bohème*, her curtain call in twenty minutes. She stood in a sumptuous red satin gown, furry slipper boots and a black hoodie while she waited to go on.

Next to her, her husband Finn was popping Tangfastics and keeping her company.

'I am so looking forward to not having to wear a pissing dress for two whole months,' she said, the corset gripping her tightly.

'Me too,' agreed Finn, and she smiled at him.

'Are you sticking around for the whole thing or do you think you'll go and get a burger?'

'I'll stick it out, it's a nice evening. Plus, you're bloody good in this part and I like being all smug-face in the audience telling people you're my wife.'

Rae grinned. 'It sucks that this has fallen on our last night together though. Bad planning on my part. As soon as the show's over, let's go and grab a bite to eat.'

'You don't want to go for cast drinks?'

'Christ, no. I want to hang out with you. I'll see them all again in what'll feel like no time at all.' Rae was a soprano for the London Operatic Society, a musical style her younger, rock-obsessed self would never have imagined becoming her life.

Finn wrapped a big bear arm around her waist and snuggled her over to him. 'Are you going to miss me, missus?'

'No, I just want to get one final bone in before I go and sow my oats in Maplewood.' Of course she would miss him. Rae had one soft spot, and it was Finn-shaped. They met when he was freelancing as a sound engineer for the Royal Variety Performance eight years ago. She came offstage so pumped from being part of a *Phantom of the Opera* medley that she felt on top of the world, and told him she wanted to take him home.

He was six-foot-seven to her five-five, large in tummy, huge in heart, and with dark-rimmed glasses and a big dark beard. He was her bear, and four years later they married near Abbey Road Studios.

'On a scale of one to ten, where are your stress levels about tomorrow?' Finn released her and went back to the Tangfastics.

'My stress levels are non-existent. Apart from the fact I haven't packed a single thing yet. I'm looking forward to some time off, hanging with my sisters, spending some time at the house again. What I *am* worried about is the other two.'

Rae, middle sister Emmy, and their youngest sister Noelle were heading south to Maplewood, Devon – their home town. Leaving tomorrow afternoon, they were embarking on a two-month sabbatical from their respective jobs around the country, plus a bit of holiday leave tagged on, to go back to the place they grew up, despite not having returned for more than fleeting visits since their school days.

Now, apparently, they all thought they were Kirstie Allsopp and at their mother, Willow's, request, the sisters were reuniting to renovate the family home. Willow had become quite the adventurer since their father passed a little over a year ago, and no longer needed a huge, crumbling house in the woods to herself. The idea was that, while Willow was away on another of her world cruises, the girls would have a clear-out, spruce the place up and whack it on Airbnb for all those months of the year that their mum was sailing up the Nile, or trekking the Himalayas, or drinking mimosas with billionaires at the Beverly Hills Wilshire (true story).

The sisters, super-close, but in an arms-distance kinda way, hadn't spent this much time together in years.

'How's Emmy doing? She nervous?' Finn asked.

'Emmy has a huge stick up her arse at the best of times, so two months in Maplewood in a crumbling house and a power struggle between three siblings is making her super-chill, as you can imagine.' Rae was half kidding. She loved her little sister, who was quiet and careful and so independent she'd forged a career working for the space programme, but she really hoped she could relax on this break. Emmy, more than any of them, had a real aversion to going back to where she grew up and reliving old memories, and their father's death the year before had only made the canyon deeper. If ever Emmy could find an excuse to transport their mother from Devon to Oxford, instead of her having to go home, she'd taken it.

'It'll be fine,' Rae continued. 'I doubt we'll even recognise the town, let alone the people, any more.'

She wished she actually knew, in her heart, that these next two months would be smooth sailing for the three of them. Growing up, Rae was always the one to protect her sisters when the bullying and the rumours got too much – or before it even reached them – but they were all adults now. The pettiness and the cruelty was behind them. Rae just didn't want to spend nine-plus weeks on edge, listening for whispers in the walls.

'Right.' She whipped off the hoodie, needing to shake out of this concern and focus on her performance. 'You fuck off and I'll see you at the end.'

Finn stood and gave her a warm kiss. 'Good luck, lady.'

'Love you, bear.'

Off he went and she composed herself into Rae the Opera Singer. She applied a last coat of lipstick and smoothed the goddamned dress. At least Noelle seemed to be looking forward to the trip, but then she was the epitome of the hippy love child their mother and father had once been, so she was generally happy about everything. Funny girl. Emmy might be a work in progress. They really had been so close growing up, even with four years' difference between the youngest, Noelle, now twenty-nine, and Rae, the oldest at thirty-three. They had to be. And man, it would be good to be back living under the same roof again.

Rae put on a huge, genuine smile, felt the tingling sensation ripple through her as the anticipation and excitement of going on stage flooded her veins. Many years ago, she got this rush from being Maplewood's wild child – from being in her rock band, drinking, sneaking out of the house and smoking with her friends at the top of the hill. Now it came from this: from belting out her voice and seeing those that used to drag her and her family down stand up and applaud her. It felt good.

She still liked a drink though. *Mmmm, gin.*

While her sister was captivating an audience from the London stage that evening, Emmy Lake was working late. She sat in her robotics lab at the European Space Agency's Science and Innovation Campus in Harwell, near Oxford, hunched over, unaware that most of her colleagues had left for the day. Quite a while ago. She was so close to finishing her new piece of machine vision technology that even one giant leap by mankind across the floor of the lab wouldn't have been able to break her concentration.

Sure, she had tomorrow as well, one final day of work before her two-month sabbatical, but she knew she wouldn't be able to sleep tonight with excitement if she left without testing her creation.

Emmy was living her dream: after graduating from university ten years ago, she'd joined the ESA as an Aerospace Engineer. After spending most of her career working on spacecraft design via her computer screen, she'd recently progressed to the exciting (and trendy!) world of robotics and automation. And she loved it. Knowing that the things she was literally holding and making with her own two hands could end up out there in space, going about their little jobs in the ways she taught them, well, that was almost like being up in space herself. It was like sending her children up into space. In a good way.

She started to softly hum the *Star Wars* theme tune to herself as she neared the end of her testing. She was going to miss this place. They say there's no place like home, but here was her home now. Here in the lab, in the Innovation Centre. She thought of Harwell as 'Space Town', and it was exactly the kind of town she used to dream of growing up in – full of like-minded people who looked up to the universe and explored it with not only their imagination, but with their brains. She was at home here.

'Enough, Emmy,' she scolded herself. She'd promised to keep an open mind. This was a good chance to reconnect with her sisters, and although it made her a bit sick with worry on what she'd miss out on, she really should take some time off work once in a while.

She sat back in her seat and beamed to herself. It worked. Her technology worked. She felt a million dollars, like the inventor George Devol, or Anthony Hopkins's character from *Westworld*. She had made a tiny robot! 'I'm your mum,' she whispered, before packing it away carefully into dust-proof casing.

Emmy looked at the clock. It was closing on nine p.m. now. She should get home and pack, since Rae was picking her up tomorrow evening almost as soon as she got home.

She contemplated taking her baby robot home with her – it wrenched her to leave it here, sleeping alone. But no. It would be okay. It had to fend for its little self while she was on leave, as did she. Which was ridiculous really, because she loved living alone and when she got to Maplewood she'd be – for the first time since university – sleeping under the same roof as other people. But there was something about Maplewood that meant no matter how surrounded she was by her sisters, her parents, the woods, she felt more alone than ever.

'*Enough*, Emmy.'

Noelle Lake had given up on packing. She'd plonked all of her things to take on the floor, but as the last two hours of August began their countdown, she sat cross-legged on her sofa in Bristol with a huge bowl of ice cream and her eyes glued to *Stranger Things*. Also scattered around her were legal briefs for court the next day, one with a huge stain from a blob of Ben & Jerry's Chocolate Fudge Brownie that had flung itself from her spoon when she jumped at one of the scenes on the TV.

For an environmental lawyer, the irony was not lost on Noelle that her own home often resembled an environmental hazard.

Noelle was intrigued about going home to Maplewood. It would be a very interesting situation, she had no doubt. She wouldn't say she was as excited as Rae seemed (though Rae was queen at putting on a front, and Noelle highly suspected she wasn't quite as mad-keen as she was making out), but she definitely wasn't as trepidatious as Emmy. It would just be interesting, to see how the town had evolved, how the three of them would cope living back in the same four walls as each other, that's if they had it in them to completely renovate the family home without cocking it all up or burning it down.

What time was it in Peru? Her brain, as usual, flittered about from one thing to another, though she always kept a handle on where each thought had been left off.

Peru was six hours behind at this time of year, which meant it was around five in the afternoon. She paused *Stranger Things*, scooped up another spoonful of ice cream, and reached for her phone.

It took eight rings before her mother, Willow, picked up, sounding out of breath and a little annoyed. 'What, darling?' she used as a greeting.

'Mum! How's Peru? How's the Inca Trail? Are you in the middle of hiking?'

'No, I'd just flaming well finished hiking for the day, taken my boots off, unleashed my poor smelly feet into the air and had settled down for a glass of toddy. Then you ring and I have to go charging off up a hill to get better reception. What's wrong? Can't you get in the house? I told you you'd forget your key.'

'No, no, we're heading there tomorrow evening. I'm still at home. I'm eating ice cream and watching TV. I forgot I'd bought a job lot of Ben & Jerry's when there was an offer in Tesco a couple of weeks ago, so I'm using it all up, in case my freezer breaks while I'm away or something.'

'That is a hardship, so comparable to my situation.' Her mother made one of those long, low exhalation noises that everyone past their mid-twenties does when they stand up or sit down. 'Just settling down on a rock. It is quite a spectacular view from up here.'

'Are you having a lovely time?'

'Oh yes, we get to Machu Picchu tomorrow. Your dad would have loved it over here, the scenery is straight out of *National Geographic*.'

'He loved a good landscape. How's the walking?'

'Fine, fine; there's life in this old girl yet.'

'Plenty.' Noelle smiled into the phone. She wanted to be her mum when she grew up: full of life. Rae got her no-nonsense attitude from her mother; Emmy had inherited her ability to dream big and think far, far beyond the confines of her own homestead; and Noelle liked to think she was the happy hippy branch of her mother. The one that smiled in the face of adversity, cared for the earth around her and allowed her heart to be open to the world and all it had to offer.

'So you're heading home tomorrow?' Willow asked.

'Yep, tomorrow evening. I'll be meeting Em and Rae at the house.'

'I should tell you something . . . '

'What?'

'I know when you girls normally come home you stay very close. Too close, sometimes, it's like you think you're quarantined in the house. But moving back for a couple of months means you'll have to get out and about.'

'I know, I'm actually looking forward to it. It feels like for ever since we went into the centre of Maplewood.'

'Yes, well. Lots will seem different, of course, since you lived here before. But you probably will see some familiar faces.'

Noelle swallowed her mouthful of ice cream. She was beginning to feel a little sick now, but whether it was the ice cream or the beginning tingles of nerves, she wasn't sure. 'Like Jenny?'

'Yes, like Jenny. I think I've mentioned before that I occasionally see her around, but I just want you to prepare yourself that you might as well.'

'Okay. Thanks, Mum.'

'I have to go, love, I'm completely famished, and your ice cream slurps aren't doing me any favours. Safe drive tomorrow, good luck with the house and I'll see you at Christmas.'

'I'll call you from Maplewood,' added Noelle.

'Not too often. Just be with your sisters.'

They hung up and Noelle looked at the mess on her floor, her mind elsewhere, already in her home town.

Noelle tried not to think about Jenny too often. Which was hard, because she thought about her all the time.

# Chapter 2

The following day, Rae was stomping around the house throwing things in and out of suitcases and ignoring her husband.

'Are you bringing anything back up with you?' he asked, wondering why he'd even opened this can of worms, already heading for the back door.

'My childhood crap is *heirlooms*, of course I'm bringing it all back with me. I'm not sending it all to the dump. How rude are you!'

'I wasn't suggesting it went to the dump, it's just that I know you're going to be having a big clear-out while you're down there. I was thinking maybe you should save some suitcase space.'

She stared daggers at him to rival Lady Macbeth, and he tried not to laugh. He knew she wasn't angry with him; she always got like this when she and her sisters went home. She was so busy thinking about how they were going to cope, she forgot how to cope herself. With that, he nodded, and backed out into the garden of their St Albans town house.

Back inside, Rae surveyed the problem. The problem was that what she really needed was battle armour, and all she had were sweatshirts and ripped jeans.

Fifteen years. Fifteen years since she'd lived in Maplewood. She'd been in such a rush to grow up and get out that it slightly blew her mind she was going back to live there again. But, also, she needed to chill the fuck out because it was only nine weeks – an extended visit really – she was hardly relocating. She needed to stop being so dramatic.

She sighed and stomped towards the back door, flinging it open. 'Just so you know,' she called to Finn. 'I'm going to leave most of my shit here. I need to save some suitcase space. And I came up with that plan all on my own. And I feel like you don't understand how much I wish you were coming with me, so stick that up your behind.' She smiled at him, and he came over from his spot on their swinging seat to bend his head to her, and enjoyed her with a long, bittersweet kiss.

'I wish I was coming too,' he said, cursing his project manager role at an audio-visual design company, which was swamping him at the moment. She nuzzled into him, and he promised, 'I'll be down to visit as soon as I can. Just don't all kill each other before then.'

'I might kill them, but I'll be fine.'

'That's the spirit.'

'All right, I need to get going soon. Will you help me load the car?'

Finn followed her inside and stopped at the fridge. 'I bought you a present – a six-pack of beers to get you through the first night.'

Rae smirked, and took them from him.

Once upon a time, Rae Lake used to disappear for a few days, sometimes a couple of weeks, when it all got too much and she just needed some space. This felt like she was doing the opposite, going back in time, returning to the lion's den. She was leaving her grown-up life and her independence and having a homecoming of sorts.

It frightened her a little. But then, a growing part of her felt a spark of true excitement. Because this sister had always kinda liked the things that frightened her a little.

Emmy closed the lid of her laptop, washed her 'I Need My Space' mug one last time, and bid farewell to her little robotic machine.

The door of her lab swung open and in trotted Alex and Mack, her co-workers, and her friends. They were carrying a gift, wrapped in spaceship wrapping paper.

'I can't believe you're going,' wailed Alex, throwing her arms around Emmy, smacking her slightly on the head with the gift.

'Who's going to be the life and soul of the party now?' Mack deadpanned, before he ducked out of the way of Alex's foot donkey-kicking at him.

'You guys,' Emmy said, touched. 'I'll be back before I'm even missed. Just don't let anyone take over my lab. Or take credit for my research! Or take my glow-in-the-dark stars.'

'We won't. Open your gift.' Alex perched on a stool.

Emmy tore open the paper and pulled out a bottle of wine and a sweatshirt which was pale cream at the front, with large lettering that said, *Remember you're a Jedi.*

'Turn it over,' prompted Alex.

The back of the sweatshirt was black, with a quote from *Star Wars*' Yoda warning to be careful about looking at the dark side because it can look back at you. 'I love this, thank you!'

Alex grinned. 'It seemed perfect for you. You have to wear it any time you feel yourself getting angry, or thinking too much about how those Maplewood baddies are getting to you. You need to remember you're strong. Also, we thought the jumper might be good as the weather gets colder, and spending that long with family can send anyone to alcohol. How are you feeling?'

Emmy needed a moment to collect her thoughts. This was such a thoughtful present, and Yoda was right. If she spent her whole time back in Devon focusing on the bad memories, she was in danger of letting them define her again. She couldn't let that happen – she'd moved on. Dammit. 'Nervous,' she replied. 'I hardly ever go back home, especially now Dad's ... gone, and Mum's off travelling all the time. I think the longest I've spent at home since I first moved away is probably three or four days. Nine weeks is going to feel like *for ever*. We'll actually have to leave the house and be part of the community!' She laughed loudly to cover her panic as she thought about who might still live there.

To say Emmy and her sisters had a tough child-hood was an understatement. The short history is that they were the weird family from the outskirts of town, and all three were bullied in different ways. Rae was judged and looked down upon for the type of personality she had, which only made her act out even more. Noelle was talked about because of who she was, ignorance being the opposite of bliss. And

Emmy was the classic target: bookish, friendless, from a family of weirdos and with no hope of fitting in, she seemed the get the brunt, although she knew even now it would have been a lot worse without Rae around to act as bodyguard.

'The nerd is coming home,' Emmy said, in a robot-voice that made even her cringe, but at least it shook her from her thoughts.

Mack gave her a final one-armed hug. 'If anyone gives you any trouble, just remind them you don't need to listen to their shit any more. You're a grown-up. With your own lab. Just tell them you're an astronaut.'

'Okay, I'll do that.'

'And you can always hop back on the train from darkest Devon and come and see us.'

'When do you set off?' asked Alex.

'Tonight. In fact, I'd better get going, Rae's picking me up on her way past.' Emmy pulled them both in for a group hug. She was going to miss this place and these people. Going home to Maplewood just felt like the opposite of going home.

She bundled up her things and held her new sweater close. *Did she have to do this?* Yes, of course she did. And it might be fun. It was still work, after all, what she and her sisters were heading south to do. Just very different work.

'See you later, alligator,' Alex said, as Emmy headed to the door.

'In a while, crocodile,' Mack added.

Emmy gave them a final wave and stepped out the door and into her sabbatical. 'See you soon, baboons.' *I am a Jedi*.

Noelle walked out of Bristol County Court with all the last of the summer sunshine in her step. Her case had wrapped up far earlier than she expected, with a positive result (the Earth was saved for now!), and she was now *free* for two whole months!

The first day of September was everything it should be: sunny skies, even as the day was coming to a close, the faintest chill in the mostly warm air, whispers of amber tickling the edges of the leaves.

Since she had thought she'd be staying late to wrap up all her paperwork, Noelle had already packed everything into her car and had it with her in the city centre. She was ready to drive down to the house, but she decided to enjoy Bristol for just a smidge more, considering how lovely an early evening it was.

Crossing the river, Noelle strolled to Starbucks, a smile dancing on her face. She'd not thought to bring

21

her reusable cup today, but even she could live on the edge just this once. Although as she reached the counter she caved and picked up one of their twelve-pound ceramic travel mugs instead.

'Pumpkin Spice Latte, please,' she asked with pride. *Hello, autumn*.

The barista's motionless face betrayed the fact he'd probably spent the whole day making these drinks. 'Sure. Name, please?'

'Noelle. Thank you!' He picked up a black marker and wrote her name on the side of the travel mug (she hoped it wasn't permanent), and she moved to the side.

'I love your bag,' she commented to a woman with a large mustard-yellow tote, as she waited for her warm drink. 'My sister Emmy could do with one of those, she has to carry these huge files to and from work.'

The woman smiled and went back to her phone.

'Where's it from?' Noelle asked. She could do with one too, actually.

'Oasis,' the woman replied.

'Great, thank you! I haven't seen my two sisters for ages, but I'm about to spend over two months with them doing up our old family home, and I can't wait—'

'Pumpkin Spice Latte for . . . Nowhere?'

'Ooops, I think that's me! Nice to talk to you,

and thanks for the bag tip.' Noelle took her drink and left the coffee shop, breathing in the cinnamon and nutmeg, and feeling all seasonal and toasty and *You've Got Mail*.

Autumn was the best season. And their family home, surrounded by trees and a haven for hedgehogs, squirrels and dormice, never looked better than it did in the last months of the year.

Ever since the mention of Jenny last night, Noelle's slight nerves had been transforming themselves into adrenaline. She was coming home.

# Chapter 3

Rae pounded the car horn with her fist outside Emmy's house, hollering '*Emmmmyyyyyyy*' out of the driver's seat window.

Emmy flung open her front door. 'Would you shush?' she cried into the dusk. It was only early evening but the autumnal sun had already dipped, and the street upon which Emmy lived was quiet and peaceful – up until the appearance of her older sister.

Rae jumped out of the car and headed round to the boot, squishing her belongings to one side. Two-plus months' worth of luggage fitted Tetris-style into her raspberry-coloured KA.

'I'll be two minutes,' Emmy called, backing away from the door and into the house. 'Do you want a coffee?'

Rae appeared at the door, grabbing Emmy and demanding a tight hug, all the while thinking how she'd missed these bony shoulders, this freckled face. Time apart from her sisters was always too long. 'Nope, we'll break up the journey with a coffee stop at a service station. Let's hit the road, arsehole. Are these all your cases? What's in the coolbox?'

'Just stuff from my fridge that needs using up.' Emmy looked back down the hall into her home. It wasn't like she'd be gone that long, and if she really needed space from her sisters, or from Maplewood, she just needed to do what Mack suggested: jump on a train and come back to Oxford for a couple of nights. Noooooo big deal.

'Sooo, how did it feel stepping away from the lab for two and a half months? Did anyone give you a leaving present? Did you feel like you were heading off to have a baby? I don't think I've ever known you to take more than a week off at one time.' Rae fired questions as she swooped around collecting up Emmy's neatly stacked bags, a coat from the coat rack, a TV guide from her living room.

'It felt fine, a little sad; they'll barely even notice I'm gone, I'm sure.'

'Jesus Christ, don't do that from now until November.'

'Do what?'

'That – *you*!' Rae looked her sister up and down.

'How was that robot bionic eye thing you were working on? Did you finish it in time?'

'Yep! I mean it's not really a bionic eye, it's a—'

Rae made a loud snoring noise. 'Hurry up and go into space, will you, I want to tell everyone my sister is an astronaut.'

Emmy was distracted, trying to remember if she'd prepared her house for its lonesome spell. Was the heating off, but not *too* off so that the pipes wouldn't freeze if winter came early? Was the compost bin empty? Were there conkers in the corner of every room, because she didn't want to come back and find a family of four thousand tarantulas had taken up residence? 'How about you? I bet your voice is looking forward to a break. You actually already look like you've been away from the opera scene for way more than one day,' she added, her sister already beginning to look more like her old, potty-mouthed, Harley-Quinn-on-a-day-off self.

Rae hesitated, midway through scraping her hair back into a scruffy high ponytail. 'Actually, about that . . . '

'What? Wait – don't tell me you haven't taken the time off. We all agreed—'

'No, I have, I totally have. I just have one performance I have to come back to London for, all the way in November, at least two months away. We'll be so close to finishing doing up the house then anyway, and I'll only be gone for the weekend.'

'Are you also going to be coming back and forth to visit Finn?' Emmy asked, finally stepping over her doorstep and into the cold night air, locking her door behind her, lingering on every clack and pop of the latches as if she was leaving a part of her safely inside.

'Nope, he's about to start a huge project at work and will be travelling loads for it anyway. He's going to come and stay, if he can, for a weekend some time midway.'

Rae felt a wash of loneliness thinking about her Finn, her big bear, her electric blanket. But she shook her head, evaporating those thoughts. She'd be fine. She and Finn were solid as a rock and a few weeks apart was a chance to bring back that closeness with her sisters. It would be fun.

She hoped. But Maplewood had a way of getting under her skin, whether she was two hundred miles away or back in her childhood home. She remembered it as gossipy, hard work – and cold. And she couldn't shake the suspicion that Maplewood might be exactly as she remembered.

Apparently, Rae's voice wasn't planning to take any kind of break, as she'd sung loudly along to every track on the eighties rock anthem playlist in the car. But two hours into the journey and Emmy was zoned out, staring at the tail lights and headlights that ribboned across the inky motorway.

'Where are you?' asked Rae, muting Aerosmith.

Emmy looked over. 'Hmm?'

'Where's your head at? You've barely sung along at all, and you're not even eating the Haribo.'

'Oh, no thanks. When my road trip buddy is a professional singer, the journey is more enjoyable for everyone if I don't join in.'

Rae picked up a jelly cola bottle and leaned over, forcing it into Emmy's mouth. 'Talk to me, Emmaline.'

Emmy took a breath. She hadn't meant to slip into a funk already – she already felt like a teenager again and she wasn't even over the Devon border. She really needed to give this the open mind it deserved. The problem was, in her field it was crucial to worry about things that hadn't happened yet. She literally had to plan for the worst. So, it was hard to shake that and be all idealist – all *Noelle* – about it. Another Haribo would help. 'Sorry. Right, how about a round of twenty questions?'

'How about you tell me what's on your mind?'

'How about that game you like, Snog, Marry or Kill?' Emmy tried.

'How about ... okay, Snog, Marry or Kill and then you have to talk to me properly. Snog, marry or kill: me, Noelle and Finn.'

Emmy laughed, 'Oh my god. Really?'

'You *have* to do it.'

'Marry Noelle—'

'Why Noelle and not me?' Rae cried.

'Because she's all earthy and makes soup and she has pretty hair so we'd have pretty-haired children.'

'Well, that's gross and incest, and you're not her type anyway.'

'Snog Finn—'

'*Bitch!* Stop snogging my husband!'

'And kill you, for making me answer this awkward question!' Emmy concluded. 'Okay, snog, marry or kill ... um ... '

'Let's talk about you now,' interrupted Rae.

'Why? I get to do a round.'

'What's going on? Is work okay? You didn't lose another beagle up there, did you?'

'Only a few,' Emmy smiled. 'It's just ... aren't you nervous?'

'About going home?'

'Yes.'

Rae considered her words, wary of fuelling the fire. 'A little, but it's not like we haven't been home at all since we moved out or anything, we were back at Easter.'

'But fleetingly. It's always fleetingly. This time it's *lastingly*.'

'What are you so worried about?'

Emmy paused, flicking her hair above her lip like a moustache while she collected her words. 'I'm worried that nothing will have changed.'

'Everything's changed. We've all changed. You haven't lived there for what . . . thirteen years? Only eleven for Noelle but it must be *fifteen* for me? I'm sure it's going to be very different.' She was so *not* sure.

'Yeah, well, you better hope that's the case, because the townsfolk of Maplewood hated you.' Emmy stuck her hand into the bag of Haribo, already ashamed of firing that shot.

Rae glanced over at her sister; Emmy was only two years her junior, but sometimes Rae felt so much older. And with feeling older came feeling responsible. She often wondered whether if she'd made more effort to fit in, calm down, be one of the crowd, life might not have been so hard on her younger sisters. Noelle, there was no helping, she had her own battles, but Emmy . . . Rae felt she'd laid such foundations that Emmy was almost set up to fail. 'Do you remember when I had that music exam and I wrote my song about female genital mutilation?'

'How could I forget it, it was so graphic? And angry.'

'Yep. I thought it was pretty good – still do, actually. But anyway, I remember Mrs Whatsherface, my music teacher, almost fainting when I started adding in the interpretive dance moves.'

'I think it was the language that nearly killed her, from what I heard.'

'I was suspended for a week for that. And I failed the exam. But look at me now,' Rae sang. 'You know, I am looking forward to reconnecting with that Rae of the past, she was hilaire. Anyway, I'm not sorry for the song, but just so you know – I'm sorry that teacher then had it in for you after you joined her class.'

Emmy sighed. 'Oh, that's okay – music would never have won me top grades anyway. Did you know people used to say Mum and Dad locked me in my room studying so I wouldn't turn out like you?'

'Okay, first of all – you wish they'd locked you in your room. I've never known a kid who liked to stay in more than you did.'

'I went outside to play. Sometimes.'

'Yeah, when your little bestie, Jared, dragged you out into the woods.'

Emmy couldn't really argue with that; she had

treated her bedroom like a sanctuary. 'Jared wasn't my little best friend, he was – well, my *only* friend. So there.'

Rolling her eyes, Rae replied, 'All right, noted. Anyway, secondly – yes, I do remember that rumour. And I also remember telling everyone it wasn't true.'

'With your fists?'

'. . . Sometimes with my fists. But they were basically saying my sister was a hermit and my parents were like, crazy people holding you captive. Honestly, it never took much to make them jump to the worst conclusions, did it?'

'My point exactly.' Emmy paused for a while. 'But thank you for defending me.'

Rae would always defend her, and she was ready again if need be. She ripped open a second bag of sweets using her teeth. 'Look, if it's that bad when we get back we'll just paint the house in reds and blacks and market it on Airbnb as a great location for group sex parties. That'll show 'em.'

With a yawn, Emmy nodded, thoughts of faces from her past dancing in her mind. 'That'll show 'em,' she agreed. She could see it now, the Lake sisters returning to their home town like a tornado, shock blanketing the faces of the bullies and the judgemental. Would that be the worst thing in the world?

# Chapter 4

Eventually, at close to ten p.m., Rae crunched the car over the rough gravel driveway, creeping through the blackness towards the front of the house. Their home was surrounded by woods; tall pine trees that stretched towards the sun during summer and cast feathery shadows upon the gnarled oaks that curled beneath them.

It sat on the very outskirts of the small market town of Maplewood, the first house you got to; the type that visitors to the area would drive past and say, 'Wait, was that a building in there? Are we here yet?' then drive on, not hitting any other sign of civilisation for several minutes, and so assume they'd imagined the house hidden in the woods.

Their home was far enough away from inner Maplewood that when the sisters did occasionally venture home they could cocoon themselves within its walls and under the shade of the trees and rarely have to go out until it was time to leave. They hadn't laid eyes on the town itself, not even driven through it, for what felt like a lifetime.

The house sat at the end of an unkempt driveway that newcomers often lost their way on, veering into the woods and having to reverse back through tight gaps between tree trunks. *Spotlights*, Rae thought to herself, imagining tiny bulbs at the foot of the trees, lighting the way for their future guests who might arrive after dark.

Of course, the girls knew the road like the back of their hands. Years of running up and down, pretending to be horses or spaceships or Olympians, and later, first kisses and stolen cigarettes, away from the eyeline of the house. Shielded from the traffic on the main road, and as loud as they liked all the way out here, this was their playground.

'Wake up, snooze-face,' coaxed Rae, and Emmy lifted her head from where it leaned against the car window. She hadn't been asleep, just lulled into a sensation of going through the motions; her body returning to Maplewood, her mind a screensaver.

Emmy squinted into the dark, trying to make out the house among the trees, until there it was, right in front of her. Tall and wide, raised a little off the mulchy ground and fronted by a vast decking area with steps leading up the centre to the door. With the moonlight slicing through the gaps in the trees and highlighting the peeling paint and broken bannisters, Emmy felt more than ever that it resembled the houses in American horror films from the seventies.

On that happy thought, she spotted a small figure sitting on the steps surrounded by paperwork, shielding her eyes from the car headlights, a grin visible on her face. Emmy's heart blossomed at the sight of her little sister, and it was as if it was thirteen years earlier, and Noelle was doing her homework out on the decking, where she always found it easier to concentrate, there among nature.

Rae shoved the car into Park before it had barely come to a halt, and leapt out to throw her arms around Noelle. Emmy too jumped from the vehicle, her legs stiff but slightly shaking, and she ran to Noelle, wrapping herself around both sisters in a three-person embrace. All right, so maybe coming home did feel a tiny bit like *home*.

'How are you here before us? I thought you had to work late tonight, otherwise I would have picked you up!' asked Rae, detangling herself and walking to the boot as she talked. She opened it and one of Emmy's suitcases tumbled out on to the dirt below.

Noelle, one tiny arm still wrapped around Emmy's waist, moved them both towards the car to help unpack. 'I know, I thought I'd be there for hours finishing things off – someone in Weston-super-Mare was claiming they owned the seabed and wanted to start work on a submarine restaurant, and ... Well, anyway, turns out they didn't and that was the end of that, so here I am. *But* I don't have any keys.'

'How long have you been waiting for?' Emmy asked, dropping her arm from Noelle to retrieve her suitcase.

'Not long. I was sat in the car for a while but it got a bit stuffy, so I moved to the porch and all the little bugaboos helped me finish up my legal briefs by the light of my phone.'

Noelle loved everything about nature, from creepy-crawlies to the way the wind blew, and she adored being outside. She suited being born in a house in the woods – from as soon as she could, she would run barefoot for what seemed like miles, playing games in her head (when her sisters grew too old for make-believe), and scrambling into dens between trees. Her hair was long and curly and sun-kissed, and her limbs small but strong. She used to think she was Mowgli. She still did, in a way. Not a day would go by without her taking a couple of hours out of her job to go climbing, or for a run in the rain, or to practise yoga in the middle of her garden in full, unashamed view of the neighbours who surrounded her terraced house.

The three of them emptied the two cars and hauled their belongings up the steps, dumping everything on the decking before the front door.

'Home, bitches,' said Rae, philosophically.

'Two whole months back in Maplewood,' murmured Emmy.

They stood awkwardly, looking up at the house, which creaked in hostile response to the wind that fluttered the weakest of the summer leaves off their branches. Homecoming was a funny thing, and none of the sisters quite knew what to expect.

'The three of us don't spend nearly enough time together,' Noelle broke the silence. She picked up the nearest bag with one hand, and Emmy's coolbox with the other, and smiled towards the door with determination, demanding her sisters get on board. 'I'm looking forward to being back in the nest with you guys.'

Rae turned the keys in the locks and pushed open the heavy wooden door, disturbing a pile of post on the carpet below that was highlighted by moonlight peeping through the curtains. She stepped over the threshold, dumped the bag she was carrying right in the way of Emmy and Noelle, and felt along the wall for the light switch.

As the hallway illuminated, Noelle stepped around her sister and plonked down her first load, removing her coat and dumping it on the stairs like she'd always done. 'It's really quiet here without Mum.'

'And without Dad,' added Emmy. She'd only been back once since the funeral, and it felt so strange to think he didn't live here any more. This old house felt alive, felt safe, with her dad in it. Many times he'd comforted her, or sat there with an interested smile while she told him excitedly in great detail about the plot of her latest Baby-Sitters Club book. He'd ask questions like, 'Which one is Kristy again?' and 'Those are some adventures those girls get into. Do you want adventures like that, Emmy?'

She moved into the hallway and looked around. She felt off-kilter, like she was in someone else's home. She grew up in these walls, but for years now she'd only thought of it as 'Mum and Dad's house', and then 'Mum's house'. 'I wonder what Mum's doing right now,' she mused aloud.

Noelle stooped behind Emmy and picked up a postcard from the floor, partially obscured by junk mail and bank statements. 'I spoke to her yesterday, she was just finishing the Inca Trail. Here, she must have sent a postcard a week or so ago. She says, "Spawn, welcome home! Thank you for undertaking the house spruce-up while I'm away. Don't let those 60 Minute Makeover people in, I don't want everything replaced with MDF."'

'Pretty sure it's mostly MDF anyway,' Rae remarked.

Noelle continued reading. '"Help yourselves to anything of course. No parties!!! PLEASE make your rooms presentable and no longer like shrines to your teenage selves. This is not an excuse to snoop through all my stuff!"'

Rae interrupted again. 'Um, excuse me; this is the *perfect* excuse to snoop through all Mum's stuff. She's right about our bedrooms though. Emmy, your shelf of Natural Collection toiletries is probably poisonous by now.'

'And finally she says, "Currently in Peru, thinking about doing the Inca Trail, not sure I can be bothered. See you (and the new improved house in the woods!) in a couple of months. Kiss kiss kiss, Mumbo."' Noelle looked at the front of the postcard, which was a close-up of a llama wearing rainbow tassels from its ears.

'I wonder how this place will look in two months,' Emmy mused, pulling in a few more bags from the porch. 'Where do we even start?'

'We start,' Rae said, dumping the last of the bags down and locking the front door behind her, 'with a drink.'

'I brought some wine,' offered Noelle, unzipping a suitcase in the middle of the hall.

'Me too, and beer,' Emmy said, carrying the coolbox towards the kitchen.

'No, no, no, I'm talking a "Mum and Dad's drinks cabinet" drink.' Rae ushered them into the living room and opened the dark mahogany corner unit. Jewel-coloured bottles containing various levels of silky clear and amber liquids sparkled at them. Aged whiskies, brandy, Vermouth, an open Baileys that should probably be chucked, gin (three types) and, bizarrely, a bottle of Sourz Apple. Rae poured the three of them brandies into chunky crystal glasses. Her mother was not the type to have things like actual brandy glasses.

The sisters took up their natural spaces in the living room, facing a fireplace that wasn't lit. The air was cold and a little musty, but they'd figure out how Willow's new boiler worked tomorrow, and open a few windows in the morning.

Noelle curled cat-like on to the rug in front of the unlit fire, propping cushions around her, and swirled her drink round her glass. Rae flopped across the length

40

of one of the sunken-seated sofas, exhaling like the weary traveller she was. And Emmy climbed into her dad's old leather armchair, her feet under her bottom, and stroked the worn arm where he used to dig his thumbnail absentmindedly into the material while he watched movies.

'It really is quiet without Mum barking and singing and hollering at Noelle to pick up her crap, isn't it?' said Rae.

Emmy nodded and sipped at her brandy, which was like foul-tasting fire in her throat. Ugh, no wonder she rarely drank, lemonade was much tastier. 'I wonder if this is how she felt after Dad died. Just ... like everything was quiet.'

'I miss Dad,' said Noelle, lying back against the cushions, her glass now balanced on her chest. 'Remember when he grew that big bushy moustache because Mum was really sad that TV show ended, with that man in from *Three Men and a Little Lady*?'

'*Magnum, P.I.* and Tom Selleck,' said Rae.

'Those are the ones. She was sad and he wanted to cheer her up, so he grew it really big but I used to pull on it so much it gave him a rash, so he shaved it off.' Noelle took a swig. 'I saved the clippings in a matchbox for years.'

'Ew.' Rae sat up. 'You freak.'

'I was only about two. It's one of my earliest memories. The box is probably still in my room somewhere.'

'Probably, your room is a shithole,' she agreed.

Noelle smiled, remembering her father for a while. Then she said, 'And I miss Mum. Do you think she's lonely, Emmy?'

Emmy's chest tightened with guilt while she searched for an answer. Why didn't she know if her mum was lonely? She considered her words, mindful of her sister's feelings. 'I'm not sure if she's lonely, or she's bored. I do think living all the way out here in the woods, in this house, which basically hasn't changed in three decades, must be a pretty quiet existence now.'

'When she goes on holiday now she always chooses group tours, or cruises.' Noelle continued to stare at the ceiling. 'She must want some company. We should make more effort with her.'

'I think she's probably okay with being on her own,' Emmy countered. 'Mum's always been very independent. But I think she does like noise and action and life.'

'It's true,' added Rae. 'Mum would hate being referred to as lonely. But she loves to people-watch, and is the nosiest cow I know. Remember that PTA meeting when we were finally all at the same school at the same time, where she spent most of it asking us to point out everyone who'd ever been mean to us out of the other kids, and then telling us snippets of gossip about their families?'

Emmy smiled. '"Don't you dare repeat this, girls, this is for information only. Knowledge is power, and nobody can ever harm you if you have power over them – and they never even have to know you have it." I remember getting that speech more than once!'

Laughter hiccuped out of Rae. 'I *always* repeated it. Mum was constantly furious at me. "Spawn of mine does not gossip!"'

'But our mother is such a gossip,' said Emmy.

Noelle sat up again, the sombre mood lifted for now. 'No, don't forget: "It's not gossip when it's within the family, it's awareness."'

'So we have less than ten weeks,' said Rae, pulling them from their reflections. 'What are we going to do with this old house?'

Noelle laughed, lightly. 'I can't believe we live here again. Sort of.'

'Let's make a plan. We should start by driving to B&Q tomorrow and buying lots of paint tester pots,' said Emmy, anxious to pull the conversation back from returning down memory lane. *Why was she finding this so much harder than her sisters seemed to be?* 'I think every room is going to need to be freshened up, don't you? I'll make a budgeting spreadsheet.'

'Definitely,' Rae agreed. 'Freshened and lightened. No more dark-purple or maroon, please. We need new carpets, the bathroom probably needs redoing, I wanted to talk to you about spotlights—' she took a yawn break '—and I guess we should think about if we want to change the structure of any of the house. Like, if we need to hire anyone to knock down walls or add en suites or anything. Whatever, let's talk about it tomorrow.' Rae stopped talking and closed her eyes.

Noelle stood up, finishing her drink and twirling her hair up into a high bun. 'Agreed. I'm going to bed. I can't wait to catch up with both of you properly, though,' she said, holding her arms out until Rae and Emmy raised themselves up and gave her a good-night hug. 'I'm so excited to have this time with you guys.'

'Me too,' agreed Rae, flicking Noelle's bun. 'Maplewood might be the armpit of the world as we know it, but we're going to have fun.'

Emmy bid good night to her sisters and they climbed the stairs, taking a handful of belongings with them, and parting ways on the landing. Their three rooms were arranged in a row, with their mum's bedroom, the master bedroom, watching over them all at the end of the landing. Noelle's room was next to Willow's, followed by Emmy and then Rae on the end, next to the bathroom. Rae's bedroom overlooked the conservatory and had always been the perfect escape route if any of them had somewhere to be – somewhere they shouldn't be.

Emmy closed the door to her bedroom and let the silence fill her ears. No, not silence. Muted noise. The type of silence you get when you live with roommates, which she hadn't done for a while, where things in the house just stir and shift and there are creaks of drawers and steps going towards the bathroom and sneezes at unexpected moments.

She walked around her room once, barefoot, making an effort not to add to those small noises beyond the walls. She wandered past her dressing table, running her hands over the old pots and bottles – the pencil pot filled with glitter pens that had long since dried up – and felt ... disconnected. This could all go in the bin. Maybe not tonight, but tomorrow. Lining the walls were posters of pop stars with frosted eyeshadow or floppy curtain hairstyles. She had so loved those boys with the floppy hairstyles. They were clean and safe and they sang to her with sweet, high voices about taking it slow and loving her for ever and never breaking her heart.

They didn't really make her heart flutter any more. Maybe a tiny bit. Maybe just that one from 5ive.

Emmy took her clothes off and left them on the floor,

standing for a moment in just her underwear, imagining what teenage her would have thought of her grown-up body. She would have pretended she didn't care about the lumps and the thread veins, the breasts that had never grown any bigger. She would have pretended she didn't care because she also pretended that she didn't care that she'd never had a boyfriend, and she pretended she didn't care that she was called a saddo and a science nerd, and that people made fun of her for living out in the woods, and made up horrible rumours about her mental health, and didn't want to be her friend, and the fact that she once said in an English class at thirteen, without realising she was supposed to have grown out of them, that her current read was a Point Horror.

The Emmy of now really didn't care whether boys paid attention to her. The Emmy of now could see very clearly that her science-nerd ways had landed her a corker of a job, and she was independent, she liked her body (as much as anyone does), she liked her book choices, she still liked Point Horror, dammit, and she liked who she was. She *didn't* like the Emmy of her past. Past Emmy was a reminder of how she'd felt embarrassed to be herself and how she'd been close to throwing it away just to try and fit in.

Emmy pulled herself from her thoughts and dragged

on a T-shirt, a musty Mickey Mouse one she found squashed into the top of her chest of drawers, and climbed into bed.

For a while she lay still, looking at the room, trying to remember what it must have felt like to be a teenager in these walls. Lonely? Confused? Desperate to change? A tear, followed by a few more, rolled down her face all of a sudden. Why didn't she feel any fondness for the place she grew up? How was that *fair*? Emmy didn't feel at home in her own home, and the realisation crushed her. How could she spend over two months back in this town, when it never wanted her here in the first place?

She hadn't meant to imply any blame on Rae's part while she was in the car. Rae and her wild-child ways were only part of what caused a general hostility towards her family. She knew there had been gossip about her parents too, even before any of them came along. And where rumours lie, people avoid. Emmy had a problem making friends, because nobody was allowed to come and play at her house. Until she found Jared, and then the story changed to how she thought she was too good for the other girls at school so hung out with a boy. She couldn't have won.

Emmy flipped off the light switch on her bedside lamp and the room went black, momentarily, before her eyes adjusted to a ceiling full of stars – hundreds of them, glowing in the dark and carefully positioned to recreate as many of the constellations as possible. Emmy laughed out loud, despite the wetness on her cheeks. She'd forgotten this ceiling. How was she ever going to go to sleep with all of this beaming down at her?

But her eyes closed soon enough, and as Emmy rolled on to her side, a small light, no bigger than one of the stars on her ceiling, opened up inside her, and Past Emmy was there, willing her back, and smiling with happiness as *NSYNC sang her a beautiful lullaby.

Even if she wasn't ready to believe it yet, Emmy was home.

# Chapter 5

Emmy woke up to a large and intimidating crack. Noise-wise. She sprang up in bed and bumped her head on the bookshelf above her. A cluster of Baby-Sitters Club books tumbled down on to her.

*Crack. Crack. Rippppppp.*

Pushing *Mary Anne Saves the Day* to the side, Emmy silenced the sound of her breath, her hearing focused on the downstairs of the big house. It was still night, or at least barely morning.

*CRACK.*

Nope. She hadn't come all the way back here, after all this time, just for someone to assault their house and smash the doors down. She felt that feeling she got sometimes, that she'd always been prone to get, of deep-seated anger trying to bubble to the surface. *Do not treat my family like this.*

Stepping from her bed was like entering an ice bar in a bad dream, where you've forgotten to wear make-up and you're not dressed properly and you don't really know why you've come here. The house was freezing, and before she could face any attackers, Emmy shoved on three jumpers and four pairs of socks.

Marching from her room she flung open Noelle's door, only to find her sister sound asleep, oblivious to everything. She lay on her bed like she was Sleeping Beauty herself, if Sleeping Beauty's hair was a tangled mess and her mouth a little dribblier.

Rae's door was wide open, the bed empty.

Thundering down the stairs and rounding the corner to the kitchen, Emmy came face-to-face with an axe that almost wedged itself into her face. 'What the heck?!'

'Good morning!' grinned Rae, retracting the heavy axe and propping it by her side. She was dressed in her pyjamas and a pair of child's pink swimming goggles. 'Did I wake you?'

Emmy looked from her sister to the wooden kitchen door, which stood, injured, as if Jack Nicolson had gone past on a rampage. Oak panels were dislocated and splintered in the centre, though the frame itself was intact. 'What on earth are you doing?'

'This place was freezing when I woke up. So I'm getting wood for the fire.'

'We live *in the woods*,' cried Emmy, throwing her arms wide. 'Why would you murder the kitchen door?'

Rae picked up the axe again, grinning. 'Because it's rotten with woodworm, so we're going to have to replace it anyway. This way, I'm solving two issues with one ... axe. And it's super-fun.' She raised the axe over her head and *crack!* brought it back down through the door, sending another shard of oak flying across the room. 'You want a go?'

Emmy shook her head; it felt far too early for chopping wood and noise and stuff. She blew into her hands.

'It's great cardio, it'll warm you up in no time. Good for stress relief too ... ' Rae waved the axe in the air like a proper psycho.

Emmy hesitated, memories of her tears from last night swimming in her head. She'd heard about 'rage rooms' where people go to smash things up and let off steam – it was apparently very therapeutic. Maybe it *could* help her start the day in less of a funk than she ended it yesterday? She grabbed the axe and swung it sideways like she was trying out for the New York Yankees. She laughed, endorphins flying.

'Whoa, mamma!' Rae stepped backwards as the rusty old doorknob shot across the room and wedged itself under the dishwasher. 'I'll put the kettle on.'

As Rae brewed a cafetière of dark-roast coffee, she watched Emmy take another few smacks at the door. 'So are you feeling more ... *present* today?'

Emmy stopped and peeled off one of her layers. She faced Rae, panting. 'Was I a big grumpy cow yesterday? Was it obvious?'

'You were just very quiet.'

'Well—' *Smack.* 'New day, new beginnings and all. In other words, we've got a lot to do and we'll be here for a number of weeks, so I guess I'd better just get used to it.'

'I like being home,' Noelle said, stepping into the room with barely more than a glance at what *was* the door. She picked her way over some wood shards, yawning. 'I think. Don't you?'

'I'm just uneasy about it,' replied Emmy.

'Uneasy about what?'

'Well, we've been back loads of times, but for a whirlwind day or two, and we've barely left the house. Now we're back for two—' she dug the axe back into the door '—flippin' – months. What if we run into people again?'

Rae poured the coffees and then stirred creamer

into them. '*That* I'm nervous about. The people of Maplewood hated me, as Emmy kindly pointed out in the car last night!'

'They hated all of us,' said Emmy. 'We were the weirdos who lived in the woods.'

'The big bad Lake sisters,' Rae cackled. 'Causing havoc, doing strange things, kissing their sons and daughters, and, well, they had a point I guess.'

Noelle poked her nose inside a cupboard. 'Well, we're not the weirdos we once were, and I'm sure the people in the town have grown up just like we have. Although, I really don't think we were ever that bad ... We need food.'

'We weren't bad, that's what was so frustrating. We were just different. Rae was a bit naughty—'

'I prefer "fun-loving".'

'Rae was the naughty one, Noelle came out as gay and I was the biggest geek in the school. Plus, we were hippies, and everyone thought our parents were doggers.'

Rae howled. 'I'd forgotten that! Or at least I'd suppressed it. Honestly, one act of passion in the back of the car, accidentally parked near the fun-run route, and suddenly you're a local sex pest. But they had to make Noelle somehow!'

Noelle gasped. 'That wasn't how I was made, was it?'

'She's joking, you were made like the rest of us, as a result of some kind of moon and mother-earth worshipping session in the back garden.'

'Oh good.' Noelle looked back in the cupboard again. 'Seriously, we need food. We're going to have to go into the town, like it or not, you two.'

Rae stopped her coffee cup midway to her mouth. 'Today?'

Emmy put the axe down. '*Today*, today? Like, go into the town itself? To the shops?'

'Yes,' said Noelle. 'I for one would like to see the old haunts again. It's been too long. Don't be such scaredy-cats.'

Rae put down her cup. 'Nobody calls me a scaredy-cat, baby-face. You're right, this could be fun.'

'Can't we just drive out to Tesco?'

'No, Emmy.' Rae pushed her sister out the kitchen 'door' and up the staircase. 'We're going to go into town, have a wonderful time, and everyone is going to say how fine and upstanding we appear now, and then we're going to shit on their front lawns.'

Rae padded about her bedroom, which in the space of twelve hours had become as chaotic as it was a decade and a half ago. Her clobber to see her through the stay was everywhere, mixed in with items that had lived, unused, in the room since her teenage years. Rae hadn't slept well, the bed had felt cold without her bear of a husband next to her, and so she'd spent a couple of hours last night unpacking and pulling things from drawers and cupboards, chuckling to herself. The hair-crimper was definitely going to be put to use again at some point. There wasn't enough hair-crimping in the opera world.

She looked at the disarray on the floor and decided upon skinny jeans, ankle boots and an oversized hoodie. She pulled her hair into a ponytail and looked in the mirror. And then she used the stubby end of an old black kohl eyeliner she'd found in a drawer and drew heavy smudges around her lids. She was bound to get some kind of eye infection from the long-expired item, but it was worth it to see a shadow of her former self grinning back at her. *There's my girl*.

Rae emerged from the bedroom to her sisters already waiting for her.

Emmy stared at her. 'Rae.'

'What?'

'You can't wear *that* hoodie into town.'

'Why not, Mother Teresa, like your Skechers are the height of sophistication?'

'Because of what it says.' Emmy waved an arm at the huge gold lettering emblazoned on the front.

'"Lady Garden"? Excuse me, this is a charity jumper to support gynaecological cancer. Or to show you *don't* support it. You know what I mean. Anyway, it's not like it says "vagina". I think it's quite pretty, and it's comfortable and it's my favourite jumper. I wear it all the time back home.'

'I don't think Maplewood is ready for you and your lady garden.'

'Maplewood is lucky to have me and my lady garden. The beauty of being a grown-up is wearing what you want and not being judged. At least, not caring when people judge you. You should try it – maybe in comfier clothing that pole would have room to just slip on out your a-hole.'

'Noelle, help me out here, can't we at least *try* and ingratiate ourselves back into the town?'

'You know what, Emmy? Because you said that . . . ' Rae stomped back into her bedroom and returned moments later, sitting on the floor and pulling on some shoes ' . . . I'm going to wear these.'

'The Dr. Martens!' cried Noelle, skipping happily around the landing.

Rae stood up, wincing internally at the feel of her feet squeezed into the old leather, the soles patchy and worn, the toes decorated with Tipp-Ex pen doodles of ying and yang. 'Perfect,' she said.

'Really?' Emmy raised an eyebrow. 'You're going out in a "lady garden" hoodie and fifteen-year-old Dr. Martens?'

'Yes, I am. And they're nearly twenty years old, actually; I got them when I was fourteen and wore them almost every day after that. And I looked just like Gwen Stefani.'

'We're really doing this?' asked Emmy, shaking her head.

'We are really doing this, *little* sister.'

Emmy, who had always felt like she was at least ten years older than her mad siblings, hated being reminded she was the middle child. She felt a bubble of rebellion expand inside her, and she marched into her bedroom. She opened a few drawers and found what she was after, exiting her bedroom triumphantly. 'I'll wear these then. Aren't they becoming?'

Rae paled. 'As if you can even still see out of those things, it must be like looking through ice cubes.'

Emmy adjusted the massive frames, vast in diameter and with iceberg-thick glass. They made her contact lenses ache, she couldn't actually wear these anywhere. 'I can see just fine.'

Rae raised an eyebrow and snaked an arm back into her room, grabbing something from her dressing table, her eyes never leaving Emmy's. Never leaving the fish tank that enclosed her eyes, at least.

In Rae's grip was a thin aerosol can, a layer of dust coating the cap, which Rae removed and lobbed back into her bedroom. She shook the can.

Noelle shrieked and legged it for the safety of her room, while Emmy stood fast, prepared for battle. 'You wouldn't dare.'

'Watch me. No ... *smell me*.' Rae opened fire and in long, deliberate strokes doused herself in Charlie Red. The sickly scent stuck to the inside of Emmy's nostrils and she retreated, flashbacks of Rae as a teen coming in thick and fast.

In her room, Emmy stripped off her woolly jumpers and dragged a box of old clothing from the back of her wardrobe. She pulled out what had once been an item of clothing so dear to her. Her favourite crop top – ribbed, turtle-necked and black with pink lettering that spelled 'Girl Power'. Not that she'd ever worn it in public; she'd have been far too self-conscious, but sometimes she'd worn it in her room and pretended she was tough like Ginger Spice. Emmy dragged it over her chest, the sleeves gripping her arms like blood pressure monitors while her humble pot belly protruded beneath. She patted it as she walked out of the room.

Rae rolled her eyes. 'I am burning that T-shirt.'

'It's my *favourite* T-shirt, actually.'

'It's still your favourite T-shirt? Can you even breathe?'

'No, thanks to your perfume.'

'Charlie Red is a classic, as are Dr. Martens.'

At that moment Noelle danced out of her room, twirling in a full-length tie-dyed dress covered in tiny plastic mirrors, rainbow fringing and hessian straps. 'Guys, look what I found, I loved this dress! I'm going to wear this.'

Emmy and Rae looked at each other, and as Emmy pulled off the crop top Rae kicked off the boots. 'Thanks for ruining the fun, Noelle,' said Rae.

'That dress is never coming outside ever again,' added Emmy, with a smile. 'What a hippy.'

Holding scraps of coloured paper against the wall as makeshift paint charts, Emmy and Noelle waited in the kitchen for Rae, who'd had to shower off the over-whelming scent of Charlie Red. When she appeared, her wet hair was pulled back and the Dr. Martens had been swapped for plimsolls. The Lady Garden sweatshirt was still there, and now smelling of ancient body spray, but Rae shut up her sister with a 'It's a *charity* hoodie.'

As they stepped out of the house, they saw in the light of day just how much work was needed to the outside. They remembered the house as having peeling paint and cobwebs that clung to the woodwork, but it was looking worse than ever.

'This looks like it belongs to a witch,' said Noelle. 'You know, more than it used to.'

'I guess Mum's away so much she just doesn't get around to taking care of it,' Emmy said, running her hands over a faded rocking chair. 'We have a lot of work ahead of us.'

Rae moved in between them and down the steps, heading for the driveway. 'First, we eat. Come on.'

The ground was mulchy beneath them, wet with dew and the first of the autumn's fallen leaves. It was overcast, the air grey and cool, but not cold yet as such. It was a thirty-minute walk to the centre of the town, and the sisters strolled with their eyes wide open, peeping at houses and into passing car windows, for signs of familiarity.

'That was Jared's house!' Emmy pointed at a bungalow halfway around a cul-de-sac just as the scenery got more residential.

'I *loved* Jared, he was such an adorable little dork, just like you Emmy,' said Rae, fondly. 'Do you know what he's doing now?'

'I don't know, actually … I never really go on Facebook. I wonder if his parents still live there.'

Rae peered at her from the corner of her eye, and acted super-casual. 'Jared was good for you. He always made you feel safe. Maybe you should pop in and say hi to them, just in case, ask how their son is?'

Emmy would fly to the moon if she could, but to walk up that pathway this soon after getting back? That seemed too giant a step. At this point, she didn't want to remember the good things any more than the bad, she just wanted to Move On.

Rae sensed her sister's mood. 'Maybe not today, then. Do you remember when we had that sleepover with Jared and we made him watch the *Friday the 13th* movies with us, and he nearly cried?'

'He did not cry,' Emmy defended him in a shot. 'He was just a bit freaked out. His mum, probably rightly so, never let him watch horror movies.'

Jared and Emmy had clicked from the start in a purely platonic way. He'd befriended the sisters when he and his parents had moved to Maplewood at the start of the summer of 1998. He was twelve, just like Emmy, and he spent the summer holidays going back and forth between his house and theirs, happy to have new friends who lived in a cool old house in a whole wood that he could play in. He hadn't realised they were the unpopular kids at school, and that their 'creepy' secluded lifestyle was one of the reasons others were put off by them. To his credit, come the start of the school year, when the kids were all too happy to fill him in with stories about feral children and cults and witchcraft in the woods, he wasn't fazed one bit. In a way, he had sacrificed his own potential popularity to remain friends with the girls. Being a boy who was a 'raging nerd' (i.e. smart) wasn't as much of a stigma as it was for a girl, so he had other friends too, but he was always loyal to the Lake sisters – and to Emmy in particular.

'Did you ever kiss Jared?' Noelle asked, all of a sudden.

'Me?' Emmy pointed at herself. 'No, it was never like that.'

'I did.'

'*What?*' cried Rae, coming to a stop. 'Why would he kiss you and refuse to kiss me?'

'Why was he even contemplating kissing either of you?!'

'It was only a little kiss, on the first summer he was here. I was ten, and he was twelve, and I don't think he'd kissed anyone before. So he kissed me. I liked to tease him sometimes, when we were all a little older, that he turned me gay, but I didn't really have a clue at the time why I thought kissing a boy was gross.' Noelle laughed at the memory. Maybe she had a bit of a clue. She'd definitely practised kissing on a picture of this new pop star from one of Emmy's magazines, called Britney Spears. 'It was only a peck from Jared, though, and I think it was practice because he wanted to kiss you, Emmy.'

'No, he didn't . . .'

'No, Noelle's right,' said Rae. 'I tried to kiss him one night when I came home drunk and he was heading home down the driveway. You two had been studying for your GCSEs or something. I remember throwing my arms around him and kissing him all over his soft little cheeks, but he wouldn't let me kiss his lips, and I always thought it was because he was saving them for you. Also, I'd recently puked, so that might have been a factor too.'

Emmy smiled, thinking of Jared, whose shy and nervous disposition was partly what had drawn them so close. He was her confidant, her shoulder to cry on, her source of laughter and the person who had made her snap out of it when she almost lost herself to the bullies. She'd thought about him a lot when she first left; they'd tried to stay in touch after school but drifted apart the further they moved through university. But the less she visited home the less he'd popped into her mind, and the bonds that had once held them together had melted away naturally. Now he was a fond memory, one of few, from a time of her life that was all but closed.

'I wonder what's changed,' Noelle was saying in her usual full-of-wonder voice. 'I wonder if Annette's Newsagent's is still there with all the 1p sweets.'

'Well, I don't mean to sound morbid,' said Rae. 'But Annette herself must be long gone. She was about a hundred and three when we were kids. And a total bitch.'

'Rae, don't speak ill of the dead!'

'Actually, Noey, she really wasn't that nice,' added Emmy. 'She always made us spill out our sweets bags on to the counter so she could count them and make sure we weren't shoplifting. Nobody else had to do that.'

Rae nodded. 'If we were ever even a penny or two out she'd act like she knew it all along. "Is that how they raise you out in the woods?" she'd say.'

Noelle's face fell. 'I never realised. I thought she was just disapproving of me, but I forgave her, it was a generational thing.'

'She disapproved of all of us.'

'Look!' Emmy pointed to the end of the road, where the houses started merging into the beginnings of town. 'The cinema's still there!' She was determined not to slip back into her bad mood so easily.

'Oh, it looks so nice,' said Noelle. 'Different,

smarter – but look at the original features they've kept. It's beautiful.'

'I puked on those steps.'

'Of course you did, Rae,' Emmy laughed. 'And there – the gardening shop is now a New Look. This feels so weird.'

'It's like going back in time,' agreed Noelle. 'It's kind of magical.'

Rae was running her hand along a wall, kicking absentmindedly at the leaves, and Emmy felt like she was seeing a mirror image of the teenage Rae once again, who'd probably made the same gestures a hundred times. Rae stopped, all of a sudden, and looked down. 'Look! This gap in the wall right here, where the stone is missing. I used to hide cigarettes in there!'

Noelle laughed. 'You did? I used to hide notes for Jenny.'

Rae saw Noelle's smile begin to drift away and she came to the rescue with a little distraction. 'Shall we get some breakfast? If it's still there, I know exactly where we should go.'

Her sisters' faces lit up, and they all whooped in unison, 'The Wooden Café!'

They threw a left at the next road as if they'd walked this route only yesterday, their mouths already hungry for buttery bacon baps, stacks of hash browns, all-you-can-eat Coco Pops. Even Noelle, who'd been vegetarian all her life, vegan as a teenager, couldn't resist this one little treat on the side.

'It's here.' Emmy sighed with genuine happiness when it came into view. 'And it looks exactly the same.'

Rae smiled. 'Remembered something you liked about Maplewood?'

'Maybe just one thing.' *One more thing*, she corrected herself, thinking of Jared.

They pushed open the door of the café. Inside, it resembled a log cabin, and the fire was burning like it always seemed to be, no matter the season. The décor was a little different – where there used to be a milk-shake machine to the left of the counter was now a shining stainless-steel coffee contraption, puffing out plumes of steam as the already-busy baristas banged scoops of nutty-smelling grounds on the sides. What used to be mismatched dining chairs and round tables were now tartan armchairs and low coffee tables. A basket of blankets sat by the door and Rae grabbed three, even though it was pretty toasty inside anyway.

The three of them snuggled down in their chairs and gazed at the surroundings. Emmy did a sweep and didn't see a single face she recognised, and let out a long exhale, her body relaxing. 'I always liked this place.'

Rae smiled and then ordered a whopping amount of

breakfast for all of them, including juice, hot chocolates and many bacon products.

'So I must say, this is better than being at work,' said Noelle, accepting a hot chocolate mounded with trembling whipped cream. 'Two and a half months of no court cases, no legal jargon, no long hours at the office—'

'Just long hours of manual labour,' Rae jumped in.

'That's true. It'll be nice though, to do something physical. I can't wait to paint the outside of the house, clear up the garden ... Well, anything that means I can just spend long days outside.'

Rae and Emmy exchanged a look. 'Consider the exterior all yours,' said Emmy. 'We should make a bit of a plan over the next few days and then go shopping.'

'We do need a plan,' Rae agreed. 'Do we need some kind of theme?'

'Theme? Like making the house resemble Hogwarts?' asked Emmy.

'A theme – like nautical, country B&B, modern.'

'How about traditional Devon?' Noelle said, sticking her nose into her hot choc. 'It's a little cliché, but we're trying to attract tourists to the house. If I was going to Hollywood, I'd want modern. Or by the sea, I'd want nautical. If I was coming down to stay at a house in the woods, in a beautiful small market town in the heart of Devonshire, I'd want ... what's traditionally Devon?'

Rae thought about it. 'Cider? Cream teas? Custard?'

'Okay, that's the kitchen cupboards sorted. But for the décor ... Emmy, what images do you conjure up when you think of Devon?'

Emmy sat back in her armchair and held her hot chocolate close, the aroma wafting upwards, the spices filling her senses. 'Apart from mud, and being pushed into it as part of a daily ritual?'

'Oh my god, you're such a downer,' said Rae, but not without kindness. 'Apart from that.'

Emmy closed her eyes. 'You know, I really hated that they did that just to make my glasses muddy. Like I chose to wear them *because* I was a nerd. You wore glasses, Noelle, and no one made fun of you for it.'

'I was a lesbian, I'd already handed them ammo on a plate.'

'You were so good at brushing it off though,' said Emmy.

'It bothered me sometimes. First I was the grubby hippy kid, then I came out and I was the horrible kid that turned poor angelic Jenny gay. Rae, do you remember flipping out at Mum and Dad one time when you came home after you'd moved away? You said that everyone thought our family was effed-up, with one sister accused of being suicidal, one sister who was gay, and hippy parents.'

'I said that? And you heard?'

'Yeah, you wanted them to do more to protect us. But it was good for me to hear it. I've always had a bit of a habit, even now, of scrubbing my memories clean so everything is idyllic, but that taught me that you can't always pretend things aren't happening, you just have to learn to not listen to it instead.' The three were silent for a moment, until Noelle added, 'Now, Emmy, describe to me your image of Devon.'

Emmy inhaled, letting thoughts of her past pass, and thought about rolling hills and rocky tors and pebble beaches. 'I see Dartmoor, lots of greens from trees, moss, grass, and brown from scrubby patches of earth where people have trekked up and down the tors, and on fuzzy Dartmoor ponies. I see ... ice-cream vans under blue skies but also sitting there in torrential rain and wind. I see sheep grazing, lambs hopping about, stony walls, old churches, purple heather, blackberries hanging off brambles and lovely sharp sunsets.'

Emmy opened her eyes to see her sisters staring at her, eyebrows raised. She laughed. 'What?'

'Nothing,' Noelle said, and smiled up at a waitress who was buckling under the weight of all the plates of bacon.

'What?' Emmy asked again. Her sisters were so annoying.

'Nothing,' Rae echoed, and grinned as she bit into a hash brown. 'Nothing at all.'

# Chapter 6

An hour later the girls walked out of The Wooden Café, stomachs full, faces pink from the heat of the fireplace, and full of motivation for starting the house renovations.

'I was just thinking we could open out that whole space – let the living room merge into the kitchen and the hallway,' Rae was saying.

'It's good to have energy flow through the house,' added Noelle with a nod.

Emmy, however, was shaking her head. 'You're just saying that because you've chopped the door down and don't want to put another one up. It's freezing in that house; I think we need doorways.'

'That's not it *at all*,' Rae protested, though that totally was it. 'We could install one of those middle-of-the-room electric flame-y fireplace things that they always have on *Grand Designs*.'

'We do not have a *Grand Designs* budget though, and I'm not getting out a loan just so a few holidaymakers can dry their socks off a bit quicker. Besides, we said we weren't going to go with a modern theme.'

'Fine, make it a campfire instead then—'

'Wahey, look who it is! It's the wicked witches of Maplewood!' came a shout from outside the pub garden the girls were walking past. Emmy turned to look, cursing herself for doing so.

There before them were two people who were ... Well, 'shadows of their former selves' is the polite phrasing. Men who, at school, were good-looking and popular and arrogant AF, but were now bald and fat, and Rae for one thought that if no good came from the rest of this entire two months, the knowledge that Tom Bradleigh was now less Freddie Prinze Jr and more Fred Flintstone was quite satisfying.

Rae stepped forward a little, a natural instinct, so that she was between them and her sisters. On one side of her, she could see that Emmy was freezing up. On the other, Noelle looked like she was trying to place the men.

Kelvin Somethingorother – the one who'd yelled out – stayed seated, stuffing the last of his chips in his gob, while Tom wandered over to the fence with his pint.

'Bloody hell, all right, girls?' he said, looking them up and down with an amused expression as if they were three show ponies trotting past for his inspection.

Back at the table, the veins on Kelvin's once-a-rugby-player neck bulged with the urge to guffaw some other clever line about witches if only he could get those chips down a bit quicker.

'Hello Tom, Kelvin,' said Rae through tight lips.

'Rae Lake,' declared Kelvin finally, striding over and wiping ketchupy fingers on his jeans. 'Last time I saw you was that sixth-form party where you were offering BJs to everyone!'

Tom threw his head back and laughed.

'You *wish*.' Rae seethed. These were the boys at school that always got the laughs – even from the ones they were making fun of, because it was easier to laugh along than show how it was cutting you to pieces inside. Rae had never once laughed at their jokes, though, and she wasn't about to start now. These guys were nothing.

Tom slurped his lager. 'Smile, love, it was a long time ago. Just having a laugh. What brings you lot back?'

Noelle spoke up before Rae could jump the fence and punch him in the face, which would not be unheard of behaviour. 'We're taking short breaks from our busy, important careers to fix up our old house—'

'About time,' Kelvin interjected.

'What are *you* doing here? Don't tell us you never left,' Emmy cut in, feeling the rage build inside her, and ashamed that her voice came out sounding weak. Tom and Kelvin were hardly her worst enemies, but for a while at the age of fifteen she'd had a crush on Tom, lord knows why, and one time he'd caught her staring and he and all his friends had guffawed at her for a week, telling anyone that would listen that Rae Lake's little sister was caught trying to put a love spell on him.

Luckily, Emmy was wise enough for the crush to evaporate instantly.

Tom turned and waved at the table. 'Maplewood's our town. We're dads now, me and Kelv.'

'Together?' asked Noelle.

'No, we're not *gay*,' laughed Kelvin, though when all three sisters' eyes turned to daggers, even he had the decency to look a little abashed. 'Oh, that's right, you had a thing with that blonde girl, I heard about that after we left school. If only you two had been a bit older you could've been pretty popular at our parties.' Kelvin looked dopey and pleased with himself, and Noelle stung. She wasn't stupid, she knew society was far from where it needed to be, but it made her feel a little sick to think of her relationship with Jenny being reduced to frat boy entertainment. But she put a hand on Rae's arm – she didn't want this conversation to escalate; it wasn't worth it.

Kelvin rambled on. 'Tom's wife is Maisie, do you remember her from our year, Rae? That's their kid, Donovan. My girlfriend's not someone you'd know, and my kid is that one – Alfie.' He pointed at the small boy in the high chair who was staring into the distance, half a chip dangling from his mouth.

'You two. Have offspring. What a wonderful world,' said Rae, her voice quiet and measured.

'Yep, we're doing the girls a favour; thought we'd give them a break and bring the little lads to the pub with us this afternoon.' Tom beamed with pride. Pride for himself and Kelvin.

'But they are your kids?' asked Rae.

'Yep,' he nodded.

'So you're not really doing your partners a favour?'

'Yeah, we are, they're off shopping or something.'

Rae and her sisters exchanged looks, exasperated. 'Well, bravo then. Lucky girls. They must be so grateful to you for mucking in and looking after the kids that you're fifty per cent responsible for.'

Kelvin was about to sit back down, bored of reminiscing with some girls he barely even remembered;

Tom was sipping his pint, thinking over Rae's words. Suddenly Kelvin fixed Emmy with a once-over. 'You were a massive swot in school, weren't you? Do you remember that, Tom, that Rae Lake's little sister was this total nerd back at school?' He turned back to her, nodding with appreciation. 'You're definitely more passable now.'

Emmy was slipping. She wanted to be able to ignore them, safe in the knowledge that she was a better person than they'd ever be. Or even better, she wanted to shoot Kelvin down with something clever and feminist, and give him a real whopping chunk of her mind. But the teenage Emmy inside her dragged at her sleeves and begged her to run away. She made her forget her words and struggle to collect her thoughts because annoyance and frustration were flooding over the top of them.

'Let's go,' said Rae with a big-sister abruptness. 'Gentlemen, it's been ... something.' She turned and walked away, Emmy and Noelle close by. Behind them, they heard the unmistakeable sniggering of Tom and Kelvin.

'So that was fun,' Rae said through gritted teeth as they marched away. 'What a treat to come back and see how grown-up everyone here has become and how we've all moved on from the past …' *March, march, march.*

'They're just silly boys, they always will be,' said Noelle, squeezing Emmy's hand, who was still silent.

Emmy huffed through her nostrils and came to a stop. She might have even stamped her foot a little. 'I just. I just. *Passable.*'

Her sisters stopped and looked at her. Emmy continued, 'Now I'm *passable*. I don't want to be passable!'

'You still want Tom Bradleigh to fancy you?'

'No!' Emmy actually gagged. 'Not at all – I'm not angry that he *only* thinks I'm passable, I'm angry that he even thinks I'd want to be on his radar! How dare he call a woman passable as if she's met his criteria! I'm so – flippin' – angry.'

'You should tell him next time,' Rae coaxed. 'You're a grown-up now. Tell him what a massive bellend he is and then whack him in the nuts with a blunt object.'

'But I'm angry at me too!' Emmy burst out. She clenched her fist. 'I am *so okay* in my real life. I'm confident at work, with myself; I'm happy, but this place just makes me retreat backwards. It sucks the life out of me and I become the same tongue-tied dweeb I always used to be and it's infuriating!'

'You were never a dweeb, or a nerd or any of that,' said Noelle. 'Rae's right – you were just shy and young.'

'But I'm not young now, I'm old. Sort of. I just need the little kid version of Emmy to back off and be gone for good. I'm better without her.'

'I'm not,' Rae said with uncharacteristic softness. 'I like all the Emmys in my life. I need them all.'

'No, you don't.'

'I do. If eight-year-old Emmy hadn't read a book about poisonous berries and run off to find Mum to take me to hospital after I scoffed my way through that lily-of-the-valley bush in the woods I might not be here. If teenage Emmy had told my friends that time she caught me dancing to her S Club 7 CD my life would have been over. And you would have had every right to – I ribbed you for loving them.'

Noelle joined in. 'I always liked how my big sister Emmy confided in me about her shyness, and how hearing her stories actually helped me begin to accept who I was.'

'One of my favourite Emmys,' continued Rae, 'was the Emmy that ran into my bedroom when she was about nine years old to tell me how earth is just this tiny planet in the very corner of a galaxy, in a universe where there are billions of galaxies. Because she knew that any pain and heartache that happens in a small town is shit, really shit, but it can be put into perspective.'

'Actually, my favourite Emmy was the one that defied them all and did her best and smashed it, and got out, and now has her dream career,' Noelle added. 'And she's paving the way for girls, because she's part of the ten per cent of women engineers in the UK.'

Emmy chewed her hair a little, wide-eyed. 'How do you know that fact?'

'I'm really proud of you. But I'm also a lawyer and I like to have my facts straight when I boast about you to people.'

Eventually, Emmy spoke up again, warmed to the heart by their remarks but still on edge. 'Thank you. I just don't want to feel how I used to feel about myself. I get worried if I think I'm slipping back.' She spat out her hair and sought something to distract her, spotting a familiar sight across the street. 'Hey, does anyone want some penny sweets?'

Annette's Newsagent's was like stepping into a time warp. The outside was the same, the inside was the same, the smell was the same and, lo and behold, the old lady behind the counter was the very same. Annette was still going strong. Ish.

The shop bell dingled as they walked inside, and

Annette looked up from her magazine. She stared hard at the three girls, lost in thought and sucking on her dentures despite them all mumbling a greeting.

They peered around the shop, though the one-penny sweets were sadly no more – replaced with jars that were instead kept safely behind the counter.

A bark of recognition leapt from Annette's mouth, just as the sisters were checking the sell-by dates on some packets of Space Invaders. The three of them looked up.

'Mah!' Annette barked again, a crooked finger pointing at them. 'You put those down.'

'We were just looking at them,' replied Noelle. She lowered the bag and stepped away. She didn't mind – they were indeed rather out of date.

'I know you three, you can't come in here and fool me just because you're out of your school uniforms.' Annette shuffled around the counter towards them, the bones in her hands clacking noisily against the wooden top as she helped herself around.

'We're not school kids,' Rae said. 'But thank you?'

'You're those Lake girls, from out there in the woods! I'm old but I'm not blind yet. I see you, and I see where those hands are.'

Emmy pulled her hands from her pockets and looked at them. 'What about our hands?'

'Always thieving in my shop, you are.' Annette was circling them, herding them towards the door like she was a sheepdog and they were confused lambs.

'We haven't been in here for years,' Emmy stuttered.

'Please could you tell us exactly what you're accusing us of?' Noelle asked, smiling sweetly.

'Of thieving! Pinching! Dirty little hands from that dirty great house. I won't have you in here, I've got a business to run.'

'Okay, lady, calm down, we never stole anything from you,' protested Rae, pushing to the back of her mind the time she sneaked a Solero out of the shop by stuffing it up her sleeve. She'd been so nervous about eating it within sight that it melted by the time she got far enough away. The wrapper had burst and mango-coloured ice cream had stained the entire right-hand sleeve of her school shirt. Her mum was maaaaaaaaaaad . . .

'Mah!' Annette barked again in response, wafting her arms towards the doorway.

And with that the Lake sisters were bundled out through the door like three drunks at a Western saloon. Behind them, Annette shut the door, locked it and switched all the lights out, despite it only being midday.

On the pavement, Emmy swallowed and kicked at

the ground. She wanted to go home. No, not to the house in the woods, to Oxford. She was ready to get the hell out of Maplewood, and she'd been here less than twenty-four hours.

'Let's just go back to the house, I've had enough of this place for today.' Emmy turned away from her sisters and walked down the road, her shoulders hunched and her gaze low. Pursing her lips like a drawstring was all that kept her from yelling out in frustration.

She stomped along for a couple of minutes, completely enveloped in her own thoughts, before she began to sense her sisters weren't following. She spun around, looking for them, just as a taxi rolled up beside her, her sisters in the back. Rae leaned over from the middle seat and opened the door. 'Get in. I'm treating us to a cab home.'

'It's less than thirty minutes' walk!'

'Thirty minutes of my life I'm not wasting wandering about Maplewank. No offence,' she added to the taxi driver. 'We used to live here too so we're allowed to say it.'

Emmy conceded to the logic and climbed into the cab, buckling up and staring out the window. Rae stared straight ahead. Noelle stared out of the window on the other side.

'You're a happy bunch,' commented the taxi driver.

'We are, usually,' replied Rae. 'This town sucks the life out of us.'

'Oh. Sorry about that.' The taxi driver focused on the road, and the girls focused on the silence.

From her spot in the taxi, Noelle watched the trees and the pavements rush by. The houses this close to town were large and pretty; smart-looking with no peeling paint and no spiders, and therefore, in her eyes, no character.

*Maplewood, you're not making this easy.*

She was trying to be positive, she was trying so hard. She wanted to love her home again like she'd done when she was little, before things had got complicated. And she really did need these two months to recuperate. She'd gone into environmental law with the hope of changing the world for the better. She had succeeded for the most part, but sometimes it felt like all she wanted to do was grab people by the shoulders and plead into their faces: *I'm doing this for you. You can't just wreck the world you live in and then expect me to try and convince you not to do it. Just STOP IT.*

It was exhausting. It was overwhelming. But she could do it; she was just very ready for a bit of time out with her family. She wasn't sure she had the energy to spend the next two months trying to get the others on board, especially when she wasn't sure she was all that on board herself any more.

And why did those Space Invaders have to be out of date? She just wanted a packet of Space Invaders, no strings attached.

Up ahead at the side of the road were two people stood chatting, a dog in between them, and Noelle watched them as the taxi drew closer.

She sat up, her breath catching and her hand slapping against the window as they whooshed past the figures. She whipped her head back, watching through the back window as the people retreated into the distance.

The world muffled around her and became slow motion and disorienting. She felt under water. She couldn't breathe, she couldn't think, she could only stare into the distance through strands of hair that stuck to her face.

*Jenny.*

Was that really Jenny? Was she really still in Maplewood? And had she seen Noelle, had she looked up and then followed the taxi with her eyes as it drove further away?

'Are you okay? Noelle?'

Noelle dragged her eyes from the window long

enough to glance at her sisters, who were looking at her, concerned. She ignored Rae's question and went back to looking out the window.

'Did you see her?'

'Who?'

'Did you see Jenny? Outside? Was it her?'

Emmy and Rae contorted themselves to look out of the back window too, but the car had curved around the corner, leaving the centre of town and the houses and the person who might have been Jenny far behind.

'Jenny still lives in Maplewood?' Emmy asked. 'You haven't spoken to her in a long time, right?'

Noelle wanted to sink back under the water and lose herself. 'Not since the day I left her on her own.'

Jenny. Noelle still remembered everything about the first time she kissed Jenny. They were both nervous kids, afraid of growing up, and afraid of how much growing up they'd have to do if kissing each other meant what they thought it meant. They'd met at secondary school, with Jenny fitting in, oh, only a scrape more than Noelle did, and by the age of thirteen they'd found each other. Noelle finally had a friend – a hard thing to achieve thanks to the stigma attached to her family, to her sisters – and she loved how Jenny seemed into the same things. Not occupied with making boys notice her or being popular. She liked animals and the outdoors, and when Jenny came over to play Noelle felt herself light up. As the two of them lay in the meadows talking and laughing, it was like the sunbeams were soaking into her skin, and then collecting inside her soul.

At fourteen, Noelle knew. She'd always been so aware of herself and the world around her – she'd known all along, if she'd only let herself admit it to herself. The way she felt about Jenny was no longer just friendship.

Rae was getting ready to leave home and the life Noelle knew was changing, so she took the plunge. 'Help me,' she'd said to her older sisters, through salted, tear-stained cheeks, while Emmy was helping Rae pack up her bags to take to London.

They'd both dropped what they were holding to rush over, and they listened and soothed as Noelle opened up about who she was. 'Well,' Rae had said, 'no shit, Sherlock,' but stopped herself from saying any more.

'What do I do?' Noelle asked them. 'What if she doesn't want to be friends any more?'

'What if she's been waiting for you to say it first all along?' Emmy had replied, sitting her sister down on the bed.

When Noelle had told Jenny how she felt they'd both cried, and Jenny had torn down a poster of Justin Timberlake that hung on Noelle's walls and called her a liar. Noelle had sobbed that she *was* a liar and tore up another poster, this time of Daniel Radcliffe as a young Harry Potter. Underneath, was a hidden picture of Mandy Moore and Jenny had started laughing. Not cruelly, but because she was happy and confused and delighted and scared that Noelle was the same as her.

They'd talked – deep, heart-achingly teenage conversations that Noelle couldn't recollect the wording of now, about whether they *should* be girlfriend and girlfriend or whether they only thought they wanted that because they were friends, and they didn't know anybody else who was gay. But again, Noelle knew. She was drawn to Jenny for her kindness, her laugh, the way her blonde hair glinted almost white in the sunlight, and she wanted to be more than friends.

At fifteen they kissed, and it was the start of ... everything.

# Chapter 7

After a brief stop for supplies at Spar – Rae's demand – the taxi pulled up at the end of the driveway. 'You three live down there?' the driver asked, turning to look back at the three sisters. 'I've never seen you before.'

'Strange but true,' said Rae, pushing her sisters out the doors and climbing out as fast as possible. She handed the driver a twenty and marched off before he could give her any change.

Rae unlocked the door. 'In,' she commanded, and once her younger sisters were inside, with the shopping bags dumped on the kitchen counter, Rae faced them. Before her, Noelle was fiddling with one of the plastic bags and staring into the distance in thought. She looked like she'd seen the Ghost of Christmas Past. Emmy was glum, retreating into herself. And, sure,

Emmy was never exactly one bottle of Grey Goose away from a party, but she was usually happy in a practical kind of way.

Rae sighed, missing Finn. If anyone could put a smile on a group of miserable cows' faces it was him. 'So Maplewood still sucks, and half the town still live here, including Jenny, which I think might be causing Noelle to have a nervous breakdown. To hell with them. We're staying in. We have some food now and a *lot* of drink, and I'll bash the shit out of anyone else that dares to come over here and make either of you sad.'

'But what if it *was* Jenny?' asked Noelle. 'Shouldn't I go back out and look for her? No, I shouldn't do that. Well, maybe I should. No, she won't want to see me.'

Emmy gently pulled the bag away from her. 'I think you need a bit of time to digest this, Noey. Do a bit of online stalking first; see if she still lives here. It might not have even been her.'

Noelle nodded, but she was sure it had been Jenny. That white glint of hair was something she'd never forget, and had never seen in quite the same way on anyone else.

Rae was already glugging large quantities of wine into glasses. 'Hunker down, kids. Grab those *House Beautiful* magazines, Noelle. Take the crisps, Emmy.

We're going to drink, and do up this house, and then get the chuff outta here. Agreed?'

Emmy picked up a glass and raised it to her sister. 'Agreed.' They looked at Noelle.

For a moment, Noelle fiddled with her hair like she always had, casting her eyes towards the front door. Finally, she grabbed a wine glass. 'Okay, agreed.'

Later that afternoon, the girls were teetering about sloshed and surrounded by ripped-out pages from interior design magazines. The CD player in the corner of the living room was blasting *Megahits 96* (from Emmy's personal collection) and the three of them were screeching along to '2 Become 1' as if they were the three Spice Girls members that never made it past the first audition.

Noelle sniffled when the song ended, and got up to pause the music.

'Cock off!' cried Rae at the silence.

Noelle hovered by the stereo. 'That song is so real. It's so, like, I think *I* might need some love like ... like ... '

'Like a Spices Girl – a Spice Girl,' Emmy nodded, hiccuping. Woo, it didn't take much wine to go to her head.

'Like Emma Bunton.' Noelle pouted. 'When she wore platforms she looked a bit like Emma Bunton, you know.'

'I know,' nodded Emmy. 'She was lucky to have you.'

Rae topped up the wine, her lips stained deep purple. 'What are you two on about? Is this about Jenny? Should we call Jenny?'

'No! Be sensible,' said Emmy.

'Yes!' said Noelle. 'I want to know if she, I don't know . . . '

Rae climbed up off her spot on the floor, still clasping her wine glass. 'Don't call Jenny now. I don't think drunk calling is a good idea. See, Emmy, suck on that – I'm being sensible as shit. We can call Finn if you like, and practise on him?'

Emmy tried to perch on the arm of the sofa and listen intently to her older sister. Only one butt cheek made contact but she just went with it and hovered in a squat position. 'Practise what?'

'Practise what she'd say to Jenny.'

'I don't know what I'd say to Jenny.'

'She doesn't know what she'd say to Jenny,' pointed out Emmy.

'I want to call Finn. Let's call Finn.' Rae was already getting her phone out. She placed it in the middle of the carpet and lay down in front of it, encouraging her sisters to do the same. It rang, on speakerphone.

'Hello, sweetheart!' boomed Finn's voice, which always sounded smiley. 'How are you?'

'Finnnnnnnn, we miss you, you're on speaker-phone, say hello to Miss Emmy and Miss Noelle.'

'Hello, ladies,' Finn chuckled. 'Been on the vino already, have you?'

'How does he know?' whispered Emmy, extremely loudly.

Noelle banged her fist on the carpet. 'HA.'

'Finn? Finn? Finn?' Emmy commanded attention.

'He's listening, you moron,' said Rae. 'Emmy's had, like, one glass of wine, babe.'

'Uh-oh!'

'Finn. Did you ever play Dream Phone?' asked Emmy.

'Can't say I did, Emmy,' he replied.

'I did!' Noelle stuck her hand in the air and then found the crisps on the way back down.

Emmy stuffed a few crisps in as well, while she spoke to Rae's husband. 'Finn, Dream Phone was this game we used to have. It was Rae's, actually, because she was the one with the boys—'

'NOT *WITH* THE BOYS,' Noelle interrupted, and gave her big sister a thumbs up. 'Just older and knew *things*.'

Emmy continued. 'Dream Phone was a game where you had this phone and you put the phone in the middle, just like this!'

'Except the phone was pink,' added Noelle, spraying crumbs on to Rae's iPhone.

Emmy nodded. 'But the phone was *pink*. *Yes*. And the phone played voices, like of boys, and you had to guess who fancied you, and it was a really good game, and actually boys didn't really call us on the phone ever, so my make-believe boyfriend for years was called Bruce.'

There was silence while Finn waited to see if that was the end of the story. The girls stared at the phone. Eventually, Emmy spoke again. 'And this is like Dream Phone because you're on the phone and you're a boy and you fancy Rae and we're all here ...' She stopped and took a drink and thought about her old flame Bruce. She wondered if he was still up in the attic, waiting to take her out for pizza.

'Okay then,' said Finn. 'Dream Phone sounds like a good game, I'll have to look into that one. So how are you doing?'

Rae took over before Emmy could start babbling again. 'This town is shit, Finn, and it's full of shit. Everyone is just as much of an arsehole as we remembered, so we're not going out any more. Send food!'

'Do you guys want to come home? I can come and get you all? We could torch the house and claim on the insurance, then just buy your mum a new place?'

'Nope,' said Rae. 'Thank you, though, you're a good husband. We're going to stick it out; we're just not going to bother trying to make friends while we're here.'

Emmy scrambled back down to the phone and interrupted her big sister. 'You know what Steve Irwin once said? He said, "Crocodiles are easy. They try to kill and eat you. People are harder. Sometimes they pretend to be your friend first."'

'Thanks, Emmaline, that's really relevant,' snorted Rae.

'I love Steve Irwin.' Emmy sat back. She thought that quote was actually extremely relevant.

Rae continued down the phone to Finn. 'We have found one potential friend though, we might have found Noelle's first girlfriend.'

'Her name is Jenny,' shouted Noelle at the phone, as by this point she was slumped backwards holding two bags of crisps against her chest.

'That's good,' said Finn. 'Did things end amicably?'

'Noooooope,' Noelle replied, sitting back upright and pushing the crisps to the side. 'Shall I call her, Finn?'

'Right now?'

'Yep.'

'Do you have her number?'

'I have the number she had at school, but she shared her mobile with her mum at the time.'

'I think you should wait a bit.' Finn's voice was soothing and decisive. But ... he was biased, because he knew she'd been drinking wine all afternoon. You know who wasn't biased? Her Magic 8-Ball.

'Be right back.' Noelle hopped up and scuttled out the room.

Rae picked up the phone and took it off speaker, while Emmy retreated back to their dad's armchair. 'Thanks for listening, bear,' she said to her husband.

'Of course! Are you okay? Really?'

Rae looked at Emmy, who was lost in thought, then looked at Noelle, who was edging back into the room shaking the Magic 8-Ball and checking its answer several times over. She took a deep breath. 'We will be.'

Rae awoke early the following day, her throat scratchy from dehydration rather than from singing, for a change. Although, there had been quite a lot of singing, thinking about it, hadn't there?

She crept down the stairs and, once in the kitchen,

opened the blind and let the dawn light fill the space. Wood shards from the half-chopped door, wine stains and crisp packets were strewn around the room. And a saucepan filled with cold sticky pasta sat on the draining board from when they'd decided they were hungry and twenty minutes later decided maybe they weren't. Pulling her phone from her pocket, she called Finn again.

He answered on the second ring, sounding sleepy. 'Hello, missus, how's that head of yours?'

'It's fine, thank you,' she rasped, filling a mug with water with her spare hand. 'Did I wake you?'

'It's not a problem at all – I like hearing your voice. So, did she call her? Did Noelle call Jenny?'

'No,' Rae said. 'We didn't even know if we had her current number, so on reflection it would never have happened anyway. I've told you about Jenny, right?'

'I know the name, and Noelle's mentioned her before in a passing, ex-girlfriend, coming-out-story kinda way. Why didn't it end well?'

Rae peeped up towards the stairs to check her sister wasn't listening. 'You know how we joke that Noelle is like a permanent nineteen-year-old? A bit dreamy and idealist, grown-up enough to let the bad thoughts flow off her, young enough to not be disillusioned?'

'Yep.'

'Well, even when she was younger she was like that too. Like, early teenage Noelle, I mean after she came to terms with who she was, was always very wise and adult-like. She got it into her head that she and Jenny needed time apart to be free spirits or something, so she kinda jumped ship without saying goodbye. I think she meant well – I think Jenny hadn't wanted to split up but Noey thought she knew what would be best for both of them. Obviously now she realises it was a bit of a dick move.'

Finn whistled down the phone. 'Jenny's going to scratch her eyes out if they cross paths!'

'Yeah, that's what I'm afraid of. And Emmy is being exactly as I thought she'd be, all introverted and afraid, which is both sad and infuriating. But she was funny as fuck after a couple of drinks last night. It was nice to see her let her hair down. A little. Like, a few strands. But she's struggling a bit, and I feel like I might have to be her mum again while we're here, and I was never a very good fake mum.'

'Is she asking you to do that?'

'Not yet, but I don't want her wandering around like a sad-sack. We have a lot of work to do here. How are you, though? I miss you.' God, she missed him. She had only been away two nights and already she felt a world apart from her whole world.

'I miss you too,' he answered, his voice sooth-ing. 'I'm starfishing all over the bed but it's lonely without you.'

'Same. Two months, bear, are we going to be able to do this?'

'It's only going to be, what, four or five weeks until we see each other, and you know that if you need me I'll be down in a shot. And how are *you*?' her hus-band asked.

'I'm okay.' Rae gazed around the room. 'It *is* weird being back. The house feels so different, but still the same ... you know? Fifteen years have gone past, though, since I used to walk through this door every day. Come down these stairs each morning. Sneak out of my window. Watch old Westerns with Dad and annoy him by cheering for the baddies. I don't know if we're going to be able to drag it into the here and now, with so many memories clawing us back. And I don't know if I have it in me to be the driving force the whole time, if these two are distracted.'

'Don't take off though, stick it out.' He knew her so well. She'd told him everything, and he knew that growing up she'd sometimes got to the point that she needed a time out, and would vanish for a few days. She couldn't let that happen this time. 'You three are going to do a great job,' he continued. 'The amount of

*Location, Location, Location* you watch, you're going to nail it. Sometimes literally!' he laughed. 'What's the plan for today?'

'First, coffee and a trip to the recycling centre to get rid of all these wine bottles.' She prodded at the pasta, a spark of renewed energy igniting inside her. Finn could always lift her spirits. 'Then I think we need to make a really good *list*.'

Emmy woke up with a hangover and a determination. She wore the hangover like a war medal: she was a grown-up now, and she could enjoy a drink now and then, and she could not be dragged back to the frightened girl she once was. She had to not let that happen, because at less than forty-eight hours in, even she was finding herself a bit unbearable.

'Fake it till you make it,' she repeated to herself in the mirror, as best she could see without her contacts in yet. If she didn't believe in her soul that she was at peace with this place, then she would try her hardest to front it.

In the room next door, Noelle was in a slightly different mood. She lay in bed thinking of all the imaginary conversations she would have with Jenny in the imaginary scenario she'd created where they reunited. She was thinking about the ways she would apologise, the way she would explain herself; at one point, she thought of pointing out all the good things in Jenny's life since Noelle left her, as a way of showing it was a good move, except Noelle had very much kept her distance and so didn't really know anything about Jenny's life since she'd gone.

She was basically working on an opening argument.

The thing about making a to-do list is that it can be a really effective form of procrastination, especially when the to-do list gets so long it has to be divided into sections for every room. It was getting to the stage the sisters needed to stop fannying around with lists and start making some actual decisions. The result was that chaos had descended on the house.

'We don't have an endless pot of money,' Emmy was saying, her hands in the air. 'I'm not paying out for a brand-new toilet when ours is fine, just so strangers can poop in it!'

'The bathroom *so* needs doing,' Rae countered. 'It's grotty AF. And Mum left us a pretty decent budget for this. In fact, I think it's about time we install a second bathroom and stop living like a commune. I'm on Team Poop.'

'But we can't do everything! You're already on Team New Kitchen, Team Fireplace in the Middle of the Room, Team Landscape the Garden. You're not the project manager.'

'Why don't we just write down everything – *everything* – that we would like to do and scale back from there?' said Noelle, who was half listening and half scrolling through Facebook on her laptop for clues on Jenny.

'Because she's stubborn and annoying and she won't scale back,' Emmy cried.

'I'M STUBBORN?! You do know we're down here to make over the house, right? Not just preserve it as it was while at the same time complain about how much we hate everything about it?'

Emmy was taken aback. Her sister had a point. Why did she always have to have a point? 'I'm not ... I just ... we need to be realistic and you're just being, like, a fairy, like, money princess.'

'Good one. You're being a knob.'

'Oh hush, both of you,' said Noelle, looking up from

her laptop. 'You're both silly-billies. Here, use my Magic 8-Ball.'

Emmy took it from Noelle. 'Why?'

'Use that to decide how we kick things off, if you really need to.'

Rae snatched the ball from Emmy and spoke at it. 'Is Emmy a knob . . . Ha! "Signs point to yes"! I think we should use this for all our decisions.'

Noelle snapped the laptop shut. She couldn't concentrate on cyberstalking with all this racket. And jokes aside, she really did want to give Jenny, the possibility of Jenny, her full concentration, otherwise she'd have sleepless nights thinking about 'what ifs' for weeks. She needed to know if she was going to run into her again during these two-and-a-bit months. And, more importantly for her heart, if she was going to always be looking out for someone who wasn't really there. 'Come on,' she said, grabbing her legal pad and marching the other two up the stairs. They stopped outside their mum's room.

'Here's what we're going to do,' she said, snapping into her cheerfully persuasive lawyer voice, like Mary Poppins on a mission to clean the nursery. 'We're going to start with a quick tour of the whole house and note down the structural changes and cosmetic changes needed for each room. I don't want to hear about colour schemes or budgets or any of that detail, please and thank you – this is all about the basics.'

Rae shook the Magic 8-Ball. 'Is Noelle right? . . . "Signs point to yes" again, it's clearly broken, but let's go with your little plan anyway.' She caught Emmy's eye and they shared a sheepish smile, the knob-calling forgiven.

Noelle continued, 'After that, well, we'll probably stop for food. Then after *that* I think we should start with the clear-out.'

'Noooooooooo,' Rae wailed, at the same time Emmy whooped.

'Our rooms are full of old crap, we *need* this clear-out,' said Emmy.

'We'll start with your room, then, I'm having fun rediscovering the girl I was. Actually, we should start with Noey's room, that'll take at least a month.'

'I'm no hoarder!' said Noelle.

'Aren't you?' Rae replied. 'Who can tell under all the mountains of crap that cover every surface within minutes of you arriving anywhere?'

'That's true, but I was thinking we should start with the loft.'

Emmy looked up at the loft hatch, thinking of the spider settlement that was bound to have created a city up there. 'Why? Nobody who rents the place is going to go up there.'

'Because it needs to happen, and we might want to store other things up there that Mum, or us, will want to keep but we don't want left out. It's not a big attic, so we have to clear it out first.'

Rae sighed. 'You're so logical and lawyer-y. Fine. Where shall we begin the tour?'

Noelle opened the door in front of them. 'Mum's room.'

'Mum and Dad's room,' Emmy corrected her, without really thinking. She hadn't meant it in a pedantic way, it's just that this room still felt very *his*. She'd never stopped to think before about the fact that he didn't share that bed any more. That he didn't sit with his skinny, hairy legs dangling over the side, drinking a cup of tea and watching the sun come up through the trees through their big bedroom window. She wondered if her mum still slept on 'her' side of the bed. She wondered if the bedside table on his side still contained his reading glasses and his leather bookmark, and a drawer full of letters and cards and notes his daughters had written him over the years.

She looked away from the bedside table and cleared her throat a little. 'I don't know if Mum wanted this room to be rented out. This is still hers. Should it be off limits?'

'I don't know, I didn't think to ask her,' replied

Noelle. 'I know she doesn't want us to rifle through all her things, but I expect she'd like a fresh coat of paint on the walls, and maybe a new carpet down.'

Emmy nodded, forcing herself to get on board. 'Those windows need replacing for sure, the glass is all discoloured. They – she – has a gorgeous view from in here. Regardless of whether it's for her or for tourists it would be good to get that back.'

'Maybe we could add a stained-glass panel at the top?'

'She'd like that.'

Noelle made some notes. 'We could always have a lock added to the door, and then it's her decision.'

'What about a new bed?' Rae asked.

'No,' both sisters said with firmness.

'No, it's her bed, she should make that decision when she's back,' Emmy elaborated. 'Same with the furniture in here. I don't think we should change it at all.'

'So just a little cosmetic, plus the windows,' said Noelle, heading out of the room with Rae.

Emmy hung back, just for a moment. When she heard the gasp of Rae entering Noelle's room she took the second of alone time to scamper to her father's side of the bed, where she sat facing the window. She closed her eyes and let her feet dangle.

Once, Emmy had fallen from the roof. She was fourteen, and she'd climbed up so she could stargaze. She knew it was silly and dangerous, but she'd had a tough day and she just wanted to remind herself that there was more out there than this, that she just needed to hang on a little longer.

But she'd slipped, and fallen. Thankfully, due to the house's long sloping roof, the worst that happened was that she broke her leg. When she came back from the hospital her dad carried her straight into this room, which he'd decked out temporarily with her favourite bed cover, her soft toys, and a stack of her books – books about space, books about adventures and interesting places, books about strong young women making it on their own. Emmy's best friends were inside the pages of these books. 'This is the best room to see the stars from,' her dad had said, knowing she didn't need a lecture to know not to climb up on the roof again. Her parents slept in her room for two weeks.

Soon enough, the sound of her sisters bickering next door brought her back and she left her mum and dad's room, closing the door quietly behind her. Inside Noelle's bedroom, as expected, it was like one of those museum installations to show you how an apartment feels and looks after an earthquake.

'So we're just going to torch Noey's room,' Rae filled her in. 'It's the only way.'

Noelle was taking the berating good-naturedly, like

she always did, and she laughed as she used her foot to sweep a pile of clothes under the bed. 'Pish. There, sorted. My room needs nothing doing.'

It actually didn't need much. A huge clear-out, a coat of paint and a new slick of varnish on the wooden floor, and this room would be back to sparkling. Because despite her mess, Noelle had a way of keeping everything that lay underneath pristine. Even the bed was in good condition, but they would replace all the mattresses anyway.

On to Emmy's room. Emmy stepped in first. 'Pretty much everything can be chucked,' she said, and immediately had a flash image of younger Emmy looking up from the bed after devouring one the Baby-Sitters Club books.

'Well … we'll get to that,' said Noelle. 'For now, I think we tone down the yellow walls, new curtains, this zig-zag carpet should go, if that's okay, perhaps replace the hot air balloon lampshade, and scrubbing the stickers off the wardrobe doors are on you.'

'Fine.'

It was finally Rae's turn, and she waltzed into her room, her arms wide and proud as she showed off the shrine to her teenage self. As the oldest, she had the biggest room. The walls were a deep mauve and the skirting boards silver. A semi-deflated blow-up chair sat in the corner, and there was a whole shelving unit filled with candles, candlesticks, incense sticks and other knick-knacks from her nineties pagan phase. A huge *My So-Called Life* poster hung on the wall, along with a lot of smaller magazine pull-outs of grunge bands, pierced boys and Gwen Stefani. 'I think my room should just stay as is.'

'Your room belongs in a museum,' commented Emmy. She pointed at a box on a shelf. 'Why did you have so many Walkmans?'

'Don't you remember?' Noelle wandered over to Rae's cabinet full of cassettes and CDs. 'She used to listen to music *all the time*. I had to schedule in time to make my big sister play with me, because she was always plugged in, warbling to some band.'

'I thought I was going to grow up to be in No Doubt,' confirmed Rae. 'I wanted to be in a grungy rock band so much. I thought – *if I can just get out of Maplewood and meet some like-minded people, we'll be on* CD:UK *in no time*. Where did it all go wrong? How did I find myself singing opera at the crappy Royal Albert Hall?' She laughed.

'All right, mosh-pit-head, back to business.' Noelle turned back to her legal pad. 'These walls are going to need several coats, and the skirting boards will need a proper sanding down. But I wondered if this room, as it's so big, could be marketed as a potential kids' room? We could get twin beds, make it quite bright and fun – anyway, I don't know, I'm getting ahead of myself. New windows are needed in here, though; those ones are permanently damaged with shoe marks from when you climbed in and out.'

Rae inspected the window frame, proud of all those momentous escapes that were preserved in time with scuff marks and stiletto-heel holes. 'Excuse me, where we *all* climbed in and out.'

'Yes, but you were escaping to go drinking with that gaggle of other Goth kids, I was only ever escaping to go and sit in the garden.' Emmy joined her sister by the window and they looked out across the roof of the conservatory, towards the little den in between the trees. 'I really might as well have used the front door.'

Noelle appeared behind them and stage-whispered in Emmy's ear, 'But sometimes, you'd be escaping to go and sit in the garden *with Jared*.'

Emmy moved away from the window, a trickle of nostalgia warming her face. Whatever happened to Jared?

# Chapter 8

The sisters bored fairly quickly with repeating that the rest of the house needed carpets and paint and the odd new window. The main structural changes seemed to be confined to building a window seat in the living room; changing out the glass in some of the other windows in the house; doing something with the heating and something with the doors but nobody could decide what yet; some landscaping around the front of the house and the driveway; redoing the decking on the porch; putting in some spotlights; and *getting quotes* for the bathroom to be redone.

Following a lunch of toast and cheese and some cheese on toast (they really needed to do a proper shop), they found themselves back on the landing staring up at the loft hatch.

'How do we get up there?' asked Emmy.

They stared a bit more.

'You're an astronautical engineer, isn't figuring out ways to go upwards your thing?' Rae asked.

'Mm, not quite. Does it have one of those ladders that flop down when you pull the rope?' Emmy pondered. But there was no rope.

'I think I remember Dad using a stepladder when he went up there.' Noelle looked around her. 'So if we could just find that stepladder.'

'The garage?' Emmy suggested, and stared at Noelle. She did *not* want to go in the garage.

Noelle reached into her bedroom to grab her trainers. 'I'll go. Though how you managed to spend days and sometimes nights out in that den considering how scared you are of spiders getting *inside* the house never fails to amaze me.'

'It's because I'm ... a complex woman.'

'It's because you're a massive knob,' Rae joked.

Finally, Noelle staggered back up the stairs with a paint-splattered chrome stepladder. 'You guys, the garage is a gold mine. There's paint and furniture and tools. We are going to be so amazing at this whole house renovation thing.' She plonked down the stepladder. 'Wish me luck.'

Up Noelle climbed, pushing the hatch out of the way

and fumbling about the dusty beams and fuzzy loft insulation to find a light switch. She found one, and a very seventies amber light bulb ignited. 'Oh wow,' she breathed, looking around her.

'What's up there?' Emmy called up at Noelle's headless body. 'Can you see Dream Phone?'

'Come up and see. What's up here is ... us ... preserved in time.'

'Do you see spiders?'

'Nope.' Noelle gripped the sides of the hatch and pulled herself up and into the attic, closely followed by Rae, and not so closely followed by Emmy.

The attic probably looked like every other attic in every other home, but at the same time was so intrinsically linked to them. A rocking horse wearing a green foil wig and a cape stood by the hatch – a toy that had been Rae's, then Emmy's, then Noelle's, and had been loved dearly by each one of them. There were boxes marked 'Emmy's Sylvanians' and 'Crap of Rae's' and 'Dressing Up Clothes'. There were trunks that looked like props from movies about finding mysterious trunks in the attic. There was a set of six dining chairs crammed on top of each other, several lamps, a huge box TV, plastic crates full of more recently stored items that looked modern next to the musty cardboard. Boxes of school work, university prospectuses, a doll's house of Rae's labelled the 'Haunted Badger Mansion', a chest of drawers covered in stickers (Emmy's – as evidenced throughout her bedroom, stickers played a prominent part in her childhood interior design) and mountains of books that belonged to Noelle, on top of which was a box labelled 'Noelle's Furby + Furby home and garden, please don't touch and don't talk too loudly'.

'Where do we start?' asked Emmy.

'We start, of course,' Rae said, making herself comfortable on the floor and crossing her legs, 'with the mystery trunk.'

She lifted the lid of the trunk, after a little fiddling with the rusty clasp, and heaved it wide open. It was lined with paper-thin material and filled to the brim with *stuff*. 'What's this?' she pulled out a wad of material and unravelled it. 'Oh. It's just a coat or cloak of some kind. Something from the sixties, I expect.' She dug her hands into the trunk, pushing around papers and trinkets. 'So this must be a load of Mum and Dad's stuff.'

'Hey, Mum did say she didn't want us snooping,' said Emmy, feeling like a saddo even as she said it.

'We're not snooping, we're helping her have a clear-out.'

'I don't know, Rae ...'

'Come onnnnnnn, aren't you curious what they were like before we came along? What even brought them

113

to Maplewood anyway, I never asked. They didn't grow up here.'

Emmy looked at Noelle.

'Don't look at me, I want to know all the secrets.' Noelle settled in front of the trunk next to Rae, and a moment later, Emmy crossed her legs and sank down next to them.

The three sisters were rifling through the trunk some time later, singing loudly to the Sugababes on Emmy's boombox that they'd plugged in in the hallway beneath them, when Rae pulled out a yellowed newspaper page. 'Oh my god.'

So far, the trunk had taught them that their dad was a very ugly baby but had some awesome memorabilia from the flower power era, and that their mum, Willow, had passports stamped from all over the world in the sixties and seventies.

But this was something else. Rae unfolded the newspaper page fully and reread the article headline. 'Oh my *god*.'

'What?' Noelle put down the photo album she was flicking through of her mum as a teenager – all floppy hats and big shades and stick-thin legs.

114

'Did you know Mum and Dad were, like, Wiccans?'

'You mean they did witchcraft?' Noelle's eyes lit up.

Rae kept reading. 'I don't know, but Maplewood certainly thought they did. When's this from?' Rae turned the paper over. '1979, five years before I was born. It says, well, a whole bunch of bullshit about Wiccans which sounds pretty sensationalised to me, and how the town was peaceful until "the arrival of the mysterious Mr and Mrs Lake".'

Noelle looked thoughtful. 'What did Mum and Dad do to make the newspaper write this stuff?'

Emmy reached over, taking the paper from Rae. 'Let me see that. "Although there was nothing out of the ordinary to report on that particular night, Willow Lake, 26, has twice been cautioned for public indecency in the woods, which was suspected to be part of neo-pagan worship." In the woods? So Mum was naked in her own garden and some weirdo reported it to the police, or the newspaper.'

Noelle cut in. 'Wait, go back to the beginning, what night? What's the story about?'

Taking the paper back off Emmy, Rae started the article again, from the top this time, rather than skipping around. 'Okay, it says that last night – so May the eighteenth in 1979 – a bunch of people came here, to this house, in the middle of the night to try and prove our parents were practising Satanism.' Rae put down the paper. 'This bloody place Salem Witch Trialled Mum and Dad!' She thought back to Tom and Kelvin calling them witches on their first day back in town and felt herself begin to fume. She stood up, bumped her head on an eave and sat back down. 'This town! They've always had it in for us – before we were born it was our parents.'

Emmy was in shock, and said sadly, 'They came to the house in the night – imagine how Mum and Dad must have felt?'

'They never mentioned it to any of us, maybe that means they weren't that bothered?' Noelle suggested.

'Wait a minute, wait a minute, I can tell you how they felt,' said Rae, her mood lifting a little as she pulled a photo out of the trunk that had been tucked under the newspaper cutting, the same date scribbled on the back. She held it up. In the photo was their mum and dad in their twenties, their mum looking so like Noelle, and their dad with big floppy hair like Mick Jagger at a hippy convention. Both absolutely stark naked. Both clutching a handful of daisies and holding their middle fingers up to the camera. Willow had a pointed, garish witch's hat on her head and looked like she was mid-laughter.

Noelle took the photo, screamed, and threw it at

Emmy. 'NO!' cried Emmy, throwing the photo in turn back at Rae, who had started laughing. 'Naked parents!'

'This makes me *so* happy,' said Rae. How could she have thought for a second that a bunch of bastards would have got her mother down? 'Knowing Mum, she probably posted a copy of this photo to everyone in town.'

'They *were* Wiccans though, you know,' said Noelle, reaching into the box and pulling out a book. 'Look at all this stuff. It makes sense now you've said it.'

'What about this makes sense?' asked Emmy.

'I saw them once, naked, doing a dance out in the meadow. It was really, really early in the morning before any of us were usually up. I just assumed they'd ... you know ... and were celebrating. But, actually, I think they might have been communing with nature as part of their spirituality.'

'Ew, you saw them naked?' Rae gagged.

'They've seen me naked, it's not that unfair,' smiled Noelle. 'Plus, they were far away. It was quite beautiful, actually; I remember they looked so happy and free. Have either of you ever thought about being a nudist?'

'I like being naked in the bath, or with the lights out, but that's it,' said Emmy. She picked up the photo of her parents (but covered their rude parts). She smiled at their laughing faces. 'It must just not have bothered them at all. Do you think?'

'I never saw anything bother Mum,' Noelle stated, happier again despite the burn of injustice she felt in her heart for her family.

Rae didn't answer. Instead she went back to the trunk to see what other treasures could be found. Perhaps it was because she was older. Perhaps it was because her veins oozed with the same protective blood Willow had for the two younger girls. But while a bully would never get their mum down, Rae knew that other things could. Herself, for one thing.

'Did I ever tell you that Mum and I fell out for several years?' Rae asked without looking up.

'When?' asked Noelle.

'When I was a teenager. Late teenager. I mean, it was on and off, but I was really, really angry with her for a lot of reasons. It's partly why I kept going off on my time outs.'

'She was pretty angry at you for a lot of reasons too, from what I remember, but I didn't realise you'd properly fallen out,' Emmy added.

'The fact that she was angry at me was one of the reasons I was angry at her – it was like a never-ending cycle.'

Noelle had never liked anyone saying bad things about her mum, so asked her next question carefully. 'But why were you so angry?'

'Mainly because I felt like I had to raise my two little sisters. Sorry, but that's just how I felt at the time.'

'You didn't have to raise us,' said Emmy. 'Mum and Dad did that, they were always around.'

'They were around, but Mum always wanted us to figure out how to solve our problems on our own. She was a lioness around her cubs when she needed to be, but I felt like all too often she was hands-off, and when you two – no, when we *all* – were being bullied it was me who had to keep stepping in. Like, Emmy, after you fell off the roof and everyone thought you'd tried to commit suicide.'

'I remember.'

'Mum thought the other kids might be more sympathetic if they believed that you had tried, and she also thought nobody had the right to question another person's mental health. So she let it lie. I didn't want those arseholes at school to think they'd had that much of an effect on you, and anyway you were stronger than all of them put together, so I stood up for you. As always. I felt like I had this tough bitch reputation because I had to.'

'But ... you did love all that grungy stuff and your bands and drinking. It's not that Mum made you that way,' Noelle said. At four years Rae's junior, she felt like she'd been sheltered from this feud, somehow.

'I remember you going away sometimes, but Mum and Dad never seemed worried, so I didn't know I had to be.'

'You didn't have to be,' said Rae. 'I was okay. I only did it when I was over sixteen, and I never went very far, really. Emmy, you always had some idea of where I was going, and it helped me to clear my head and have a couple of days out.'

Emmy nodded. 'I hated it when you disappeared. I always thought you were going to get raped or murdered. But in my heart, I knew that you talked a big talk but you wouldn't put yourself in danger.'

'So where did you go?' asked Noelle.

Rae thought about it. 'Anywhere. We didn't really have mobiles back then, not to any large extent, so I'd just go to places where I wasn't very reachable. Often, I went to youth hostels, and pretended I was a couple of years older. I liked to hang with gorgeous Aussie backpackers and feel really grown-up. I always came back, so Mum and Dad really didn't have any need to worry.' She wished they had worried though, just a little bit more. 'The drinking and the rock music was my everyday release though, and I liked it, so it made me so mad when Mum would tell me off and try and contain me. I was like, "*Mum, I just need to cut loose*." I was being a bratty cow, looking back, but that's just how I felt at the time.'

Emmy and Noelle glanced at each other, unsure what to say. Eventually, Emmy spoke up. 'I had no idea you felt like that.'

'Yeah, well. I was mad about a lot of things really, and taking it out on and blaming parents is just a rite of passage, I suppose.'

'What else were you mad about?' Noelle asked.

'I was very, very mad that nobody would be in a band with me. And I was also fuming that my soprano singing voice was more suited to opera, which I fashionably hated but also secretly loved. All of that combined was Mum's fault, in my eyes, at the time. Stupid witch.' Rae shrugged, the moment passed. One of the best things about being a grown-up was the ability to let it go.

'Look at this photo of Mum and Dad on their wedding day,' Noelle said, changing the subject to happier things. 'Don't worry, they aren't naked.'

She held the album out for her sisters to see, and they smiled.

'They were such hippies, even then,' Emmy said, noting her mum's flower garland in lieu of a veil.

'I wonder if they were Wiccans before they met?' said Rae.

'I don't know,' Noelle answered. 'It seems like the kind of thing you get into as a couple. Like ballroom dancing.'

Rae nodded. 'Ballroom naked dancing.'

Noelle snapped the photo album shut. 'Okay, I'm going to bring this downstairs with me to look through when we've all got the image of Mum and Dad in the buff a little further out of our minds.'

Emmy hauled a box towards the hatch, marked 'photo albums'. 'Let's take these down too. I hope the one of Rae dressed as a bumblebee in primary school is in here.'

'I hope the one of you crying on your potty is in there,' she retorted.

*I hope there are a lot of happy memories in there*, thought Noelle.

Emmy was pretty happy. She wasn't going to commit to that fully, but being holed up here with her sisters was kind of nice, she was willing to admit that much.

It was later that night and she sat alone in the soon-to-be kids' room, Rae's bedroom, while her sisters were downstairs watching TV. She was cutting out really cool – and accurate – stencils she'd made of planets and spacecraft to go on the ceiling. Noelle had limited her to the ceiling because she said space wasn't very 'Devon' so the walls needed to be reserved for stencils of squirrels and sheep.

What Rae had said earlier was playing on her mind. As much as she felt some of her burden came as a result of who Rae had been, she also saw that Rae too carried a weight she had never asked for – and that was Emmy's safety, and later Noelle's. Emmy had never asked too many questions when Rae went walkabout – even between sisters everyone still needed something that was just theirs – but it helped to be more in the know all these years later.

If she just kept treating it like a big summer camp, like they were hunkering down and working towards a goal and spending quality time together, bonding and growing closer, this time at home would fly by. Maybe Emmy should suggest some activities to keep them stimulated in between the decorating? They could go out at night and look for constellations? Not on the rooftop, though.

Here in the bedroom, she had her *Star Wars* sweatshirt on, and her headphones in as she listened to pop songs. She could pleasantly ignore both the outside world and all the little reminders of Past Emmy, and focus on having a bit of time out for Now Emmy. Because Now Emmy was *cool*.

Yes, Emmy was fine. Emmy was going to stay right where she was.

# Chapter 9

'Do we have anything for breakfast?' Noelle asked Rae with a yawn a few mornings later. She hadn't slept well these past three nights, instead waking frequently from repetitive dreams of kissing Jenny and then kissing Mandy Moore, and then both women turning on her right when she needed them, because she had to pack a whole houseful of things into a suitcase before the Prime Minister arrived.

And so here she was, rubbing her eyes and looking at her big sister to make her some food because she couldn't remember where the bowls were and she was feeling a bit sleepy and pathetic.

Rae was wearing an ancient *Buffy the Vampire Slayer* sweatshirt with the sleeves rolled up, and was already covered in paint speckles. On the kitchen wall behind her were about fourteen splotches of paint in various shades of moorland green. Over the past two days, the sisters had spent a fortune on tester pots during their many trips back and forth to B&Q for DIY supplies.

'Just cornflakes again, or there's the crust of the bread if you want toast. I'll pop over to the big Tesco again later on and get some more nosh.'

'Actually, what I'd really like would be a bacon sandwich.'

'Okay, I'll pick up what we need.'

'A really buttery bacon sandwich …' Noelle eyed her sister as she sat down on the counter. 'Maybe by a fireplace …'

'You want to go back to The Wooden Café?' Rae asked with surprise.

'I've got cabin fever.'

'We've been out every day!'

'But just to hardware shops and supermarkets. I want to go for a walk.'

'How about we drive over to the coast and have a walk on the beach? You like beaches and all that shit.' The thought of hanging out near more judgemental Maplewood arseholes màde even Rae appreciate the thought of a coastal ramble.

'She wants to go Jenny-spotting,' Emmy said, wandering into the kitchen while scraping her hair up in a bun. She sat next to Noelle at the counter and squeezed at a spot on her chin.

'I do not, I just want to ... well, yes, go Jenny-spotting. My online investigations – Google, Facebook, Instagram, etc. – show nothing definitive but I think she's still down here. If not in Maplewood, I think she's in Devon.'

Rae put her hands on her hips. 'Don't you remember what happened the last time we went into the centre? Don't you remember how pissed off we got? And then how *pissed* we got? We said we were going to just stay away and do our own thing from now on.'

Emmy, who had been very keen on her summer-camp way of thinking of the whole trip, was about to agree with Rae when a thought occurred to her. 'I think we should go back,' she said.

Rae turned to her. '*You* think we should go back? Your attitude changes daily, I can't keep up.'

'It does not. Well, yes it does. But I realised that I don't want to regress back to "old" Emmy who was too afraid to leave the house. We're grown-ups now. We will not be bullied. I doubt Mum and Dad lived in solitary confinement out here in the woods for the past eleven years since Noelle flew the nest, so I'm damned if we're going to.' She was sounding braver than she really was, but she'd been listening to her Jennifer Lopez back catalogue since six a.m. so she was feeling pretty empowered right now.

'Come onnnnnn, Rae,' whined Noelle. 'I'm bored of talking about paint rollers and clearing things up.'

'We've barely made a dent in the place!'

'But we have two months. Let's be brave and go back into town. This time we'll be prepared.'

'I'm going to argue back if anyone says anything mean,' declared Emmy.

'All right, She-Ra,' sighed Rae. 'Let's go. But when we get back I need a decision on some of these paint swatches. The house looks like some kind of patchwork, tie-dyed sheet from Noey's closet.' Ugh. Getting serious about paint was not in her job description. Emmy might be wanting to keep a distance from the girl she was, but Rae felt like maybe it was time she lost a little of the boring adult and brought back a little of the party girl.

The women walked stiffly and with caution. They moved like they were practising walking in a super-casual manner, as they made their way into town for the second time. Noelle's eyes flicked back and forth looking for any clue, any sign, of her first love. Emmy held her head high and strode with purpose, but it was clearly very unnatural. And Rae was kicking at leaves and banging sticks on walls like she was daring the residents to issue her with an ASBO.

It was another sunny autumnal day and the leaves were falling rapidly from the trees, creating long orange walkways beside the roads. They'd just reached the first of the shops, and Rae was midway through kicking a huge sweeping ball of leaves up into the sunshine, when she saw something up ahead that caused her to stop dead. There, on the other side of the street, and looking very intently at a bench, was . . .

'Gabbi!' Rae hollered across the road at her old friend. The woman turned, surprised, and it took her a moment before recognition swept over her face.

'Rae Lake, well I haven't seen you in a long time!' she smiled, reserved, as Rae dodged the traffic to cross the street to her.

'Gabbi Reynold, what are you still doing in this shithole?'

The man next to Gabbi, a scrawny chap in his early twenties wearing a Tesco Everyday Value suit, gulped. Gabbi stuttered, 'Oh, I'm really settled in Maplewood; there's no place like home, right?'

'Urm . . .' Rae remembered many nights with her

group of girlfriends, all of whom she'd lost touch with now, where they'd sit and smoke at the top of the cliff that looked down over the town, planning their futures – all of which involved getting out ASAP.

'What are you up to now?' Gabbi asked in a polite voice.

'I live up in London – well, near London. I'm an opera singer.'

'You always had a set of lungs on you.'

'What about you, what's with the suit, Hillary Clinton? I think the only time I've seen you in a suit was when we all had to go to cou—'

Gabbi laughed loudly, cutting Rae off. 'How long are you around for Rae? I had better get on, I'm actually working at the moment, but it would be good to have a proper catch-up?'

'I'm around for a couple of months, actually.'

Gabbi hesitated, eyes wide. 'Okay, here's my address.' She scribbled on a piece of paper the scrawny chap handed her. 'Come over this afternoon for a coffee?'

'Sounds good,' said Rae, clearly sensing she was being dismissed.

'Excuse me,' said the scrawny chap, turning back to Gabbi. 'Mayor Reynold, as I was saying—'

'*Mayor* Reynold? Mayor of *Maplewood*?'

Gabbi edged away, taking the scrawny chap by the

sleeve and pulling him with her. 'See you this afternoon, Rae.'

'You sure will ... ' Rae walked back to her sisters, who were emerging from the sweetshop with an enormous bag of swag. A new sweetshop, not Annette's ancient old cobweb shop.

Emmy handed her a sherbet dip. 'Was that your old friend Gabbi?'

Rae nodded, too shocked to talk.

Emmy chewed on her Chewits. 'She looks well. I always imagined your friends to grow up looking sixty when they were only thirty, the amount you all smoked.'

'Hey! I look all right, don't I?'

'Of course. I mean, Noelle is the beautiful glowing angel of the family, and you look like you were her tribute in *The Hunger Games*. Similar, but a little more weathered. These are compliments.'

'God, no wonder you don't have a boyfriend. Anyway, Gabbi is motherflippin' Mayor of Maplewood now! I can't believe Mum never mentioned it.'

'How well did Mum know your friends though? There was quite a gaggle of your band of misfits, and it's not like they came over to the house to play a lot.' Emmy answered.

'She's the mayor?' Noelle stepped into the

130

conversation, having finished her gobstopper. 'Good for her, this country needs more women in power.'

'Just when you think this town hasn't changed at all, you find out the girl that used to throw up around the back of the council offices after a big night of drinking Hooch now runs them.'

'Maybe she still throws up behind them, then,' said Noelle. 'You know, after the office Christmas party or whatever.'

A siren blooped next to them and a police car pulled up to the kerb, the fluorescent yellow reflecting the sunlight back into the girls' faces. Emmy felt her guard go up, and Rae clenched her teeth. 'What the . . . ?'

'Excuse me, ladies. Please put down the strawberry bonbons and put your hands where I can see them,' an officer said, stepping out of the car and swaggering around to face them, his aviator shades blocking half his face.

'Are you kidding me?' said Rae. 'What the hell are we supposed to have done? Do you want to check our receipts for this one pound fifty's worth of sweets? This is bullsh—'

'JARED!' Noelle suddenly squealed, and the policeman took off his glasses, grinning.

'JARED!' the three of them screamed, and jumped on him, wrapping their arms around him. Emmy's mind raced and her mouth beamed as she lost her sight and sound by being pulled in and squished into his chest. She also lost all her words. Jared was *here*.

'Who do you think you are, some FBI agent?' Rae swatted him on the arm. 'I was about ready to assault a police officer!'

'Your face though!' Jared grinned broadly, his arm still slung around Emmy's shoulders. He was taller now – they both were – but while they'd been similar heights growing up, he'd grown more and was now a good five inches above her.

'Jared,' Emmy breathed, and she wriggled an arm free to reach up and touch his face. *Yep, really, really here.*

'Hey, Emmy.' He smiled down at her and it was like it was a million years ago and she'd just, actually, finally, got home.

She made herself find her voice. 'So you're a police-man now?' She couldn't stop looking up at him. And looking him up and down. 'You bulked up.'

'I had a second growth spurt at uni, and I looked more like an awkward beanpole than when you knew me. So I hit the gym and came back to save this town from the likes of you dastardly women. What are you guys doing back?' He directed this at Emmy, his face so familiar it lit sparkles inside her.

'We're doing up Mum's house, it's going to become

a holiday let because she's always away on holiday,' she answered. Wow, it was good to see him. She wished she could find something more meaningful to say so he knew that.

'Noooo, don't change a thing about that house, it's the coolest house in Maplewood.'

'You are literally the only person that thinks that,' said Rae.

'I think it too,' Noelle piped up, before sticking another bonbon in.

Jared let his arm drop from Emmy's shoulders and instead he rested a hand on her back, his other hand on Rae. 'Sorry about your dad passing. I moved back here just over a year ago, and I meant to drop you an email then actually, to get back in touch and let you know the craziness that was me coming back to live in Maplewood. But right around then was when your dad died. It didn't seem the right time to have a reunion, and then I just kept meaning to get in touch, but I'm rubbish. I was meant to be at the funeral but I got called to a car accident over on the A30. I drove over to your house the next day but your mum said you'd all gone back already.'

'Yeah, we didn't stay long,' Emmy mumbled, a thread of worry forming in her stomach. Should she have stayed longer? 'Thank you, and thank you for the flowers you sent. And sorry for never saying thank you for the flowers. Did Mum seem okay afterwards?'

'Oh yeah, your mum was pretty convinced his ghost was still there getting annoyed with her because she'd whacked the heating up since he'd died. She actually seemed excited about getting a new boiler.'

The girls laughed; typical Willow.

'Jared, you remember Jenny, right?' asked Noelle.

'Of course, she still lives here.'

'Okay, that answers my next question.' Noelle disappeared into herself.

'Does everyone we used to know still live here? Did we leave and you all decided it was finally worth living in Maplewood?' Rae asked.

Jared laughed. 'No, there are a few people from school, a few that came home to start families or whatever. I think you'll see a lot of familiar faces, but there are so many people I haven't come across in years.'

'Will you come over?' Emmy asked, and all of a sudden she was aware how different that sounded adult-to-adult than all the times she'd asked him over when they were kids. 'I mean to catch up, with us all, properly? It would be good to see you back in your rightful place – making us cocktails from Mum's drinks cabinet.'

'Using only tiny amounts from each bottle so we didn't get caught.'

Noelle was snapped back to reality. 'Maybe I could even have some this time around!'

'Maybe Emmy could too,' Rae smirked.

'Hey, I used to try it,' Emmy protested. 'It's not my fault you always took gulps and didn't leave much for anyone else.'

'I'd love to come over, when do you want me?'

'Today, today, today!' the three women chanted.

'I'm just finishing my shift and I need to return the car and get changed; I could be there in an hour?'

'Give us two hours, we're actually on our way to breakfast,' said Emmy.

'The Wooden Café?'

'Where else?'

With that, Jared climbed back in the police car, stuck his sunglasses back on his face, and with a friendly grin and a siren bloop he drove away. Emmy stood waving on the kerb.

'*Goodbye Jared, I've loved you since before I even had my first period*,' Rae whispered in her ear.

'Shut up, I do not love him.'

'He looks good though, doesn't he?' said Noelle.

'Come on,' Emmy said, putting her sweets into her handbag. 'If Jared's coming over, even though *I don't love him*, I still think we should finish breakfast and get back in time to move our bras and other crap out of the living room. And for Noelle to maybe finally move that suitcase away from the bottom of the stairs.'

Over the years, all three sisters had been distant from their home town but never from their parents. They'd all seen each other over the months, but often at the houses of the three sisters, and the number of times the girls had come back to Maplewood had reduced to maybe a few a year. It occurred to Emmy now that her mother and father hadn't really spoken much about the town, or who was doing what, or who of their friends still lived nearby. Had they been sheltering their kids, mindful of how much it hurt to think about home? *Jared* though – why wouldn't her mum have told her Jared was back? And told Noelle that Jenny actually lived there?

They walked on to The Wooden Café, Noelle and Rae chatting about their memories of Jared always being at their house. Emmy smiled, listening to them. Jared had always made her feel safe, and now he was a big strapping policeman. She wondered if he'd still be up for sleepovers in the woods? And then she got all flushed and tripped over the pavement, because Emmy Lake was not one to have inappropriate thoughts about a friend.

A police officer, though . . .

# Chapter 10

'I'm going to ask him all about Jenny,' Noelle declared, after the girls had done a sweep of the house and moved their discarded underwear, their teenage diaries and the amassed crisp packets out of the way.

'Are you sure you want to do that?' asked Emmy, hugging a bottle of red wine in an attempt to warm it up. They were putting together a simple lunch of antipasti, but as it was the end of a shift for Jared, Emmy wasn't sure if he'd fancy a drink with his meal or not. 'What if what he says about Jenny isn't stuff you want to hear?'

'What wouldn't I want to hear?'

'I don't know . . . that she's happily in a relationship.'

'I hope she is happy – I don't expect her to have waited for me. I just want to know what she's been up to, what she's like now, if she ever mentions me, or if she's ever, I don't know, said anything about how she's never loved anyone like she's loved me and having me back in her life is her greatest ever wish.'

'Is that how you feel?'

'Yes, probably. She was my most serious relationship.'

'You dated Sarah for a couple of years?'

'On and off, but it was never serious, it was more companionship, and long-distance at that. Jenny *knew* me.'

'She knew you *then*,' commented Rae, wandering into the room and taking the bottle from Emmy, and pouring them all a glass (one ready for Jared as well). Then Rae remembered she was driving over to Gabbi's later, so reluctantly swapped hers for a fizzy water.

'Even so, she was my first love, and as such I now want to know everything about her.'

Rae swirled her water. 'But what if seeing her again shatters the dream? What if she's boring as fuck, or doesn't care about the environment? What if she, like, takes milk bottles and chucks them into rivers?'

'No, no, that's not going to happen.'

'What if she works at one of those places where they put down stray animals, or chops down trees to build houses, but not even for people that need houses, people who just want second homes. What if she uses an aerosol deodorant?'

The doorbell rang. 'Let's find out, shall we?' Noelle said.

The three sisters raced to the door without putting down their drinks, and cheered as Jared made his way into their home for the first time in years.

'Whoa, this place is exactly as I remember it!' he exclaimed. 'Except for that big door into the kitchen, where did that go – oh, there's some of it.'

Emmy handed him his wine and he kicked off his shoes – she was pleased to see how comfortably he fitted back into the house, like he'd last been here yesterday. Their front door had always been open for Jared. 'Let's give you the tour. The re-tour. So you can see what we're planning to do.'

She led him into the living room, trailed by Rae and Noelle. 'This is surreal,' he said, looking only at her.

'I know,' Emmy agreed. 'You. Here. Anyway, the idea is to make this open plan with the kitchen, hence Rae smashing the shit out of the door. We're going to brighten up the whole room, maybe go pale green so it still fits in with our Devon woodland theme, rip up the carpet, and we have new sofas coming in about six weeks.'

'What are you going to do with the old sofas?'

'Just chuck them, they're pretty saggy now. Apart from Dad's chair, we'll keep that of course.'

'We will?' asked Rae.

Emmy looked at her sister, surprised. 'Of course, we can't get rid of Dad's chair.'

'I don't think Mum would mind ...' Rae said with care.

No, this didn't feel right. Emmy touched the worn arm. She supposed she didn't want strangers sitting in it. 'We could move it to Mum's room.'

There was a silence in the room for a moment, before Jared piped up with 'I taught you all breakdancing in this room.'

'*Excuse me,*' interrupted Rae. 'Emmy taught you, and *then* you taught us.'

'How did you know that?' cried Emmy.

'Because my room is next to yours and the entire day before I kept hearing banging and thudding and cries of "Ouch!" and "You're not doing it right, Jared!" – I thought you'd just discovered the joy of sex, until the next morning Jared returned with a cap on backwards, thinking he was fresh out of a Run-DMC video.'

Emmy and Jared shared the smallest of glances. It was never like that ...

'Why didn't you just teach us all, Emmy?' Noelle asked.

'Because you would have laughed at me so much! Let's not forget my World's Biggest Dork status.'

'We didn't think you were a dork! Wait, yes we did,'

Rae corrected herself. 'But I thought it was cool that you knew how to breakdance.'

'It was only made-up stuff, but thank you.'

'Do you remember the routine?' asked Jared.

'No, do you?' Emmy started to blush.

'I might do, but let's save that for another visit.'

Emmy led the tour of the house quickly, succinctly, and then they sat down to a lunch of probing questions about the people who still lived in the town. Primarily who were linked to or might know about Jenny.

'Why don't you get in touch with her?' Jared asked, polishing off the last of the Parma ham. 'She's still really nice, I doubt she'd be mad at you about anything.'

Noelle replied, 'I think I should wait and see if she comes to me?'

'But does she know you're back?'

'Fair point . . . ' Noelle had always prided herself on knowing exactly who she was since she came out. She was unafraid, and unashamed. But there had been times, especially as she grew up and university was creeping closer, when her big strong walls began to wobble under the weight of pressure. Pressure because she and Jenny had been through so much, and Noelle felt responsible for Jenny's happiness. She'd begun to think that Jenny would be better off being free, rather than stuck with her just because they were both gay. It made her cringe to even remember that, because it wasn't true, it was her cowardly way of wishing that she too were free. Gay or not, she was too young to have been in such an intense relationship. She wanted to fly away, and she didn't know if there would be a welcome migration home.

After a moment, she shook herself out of it. She was a lawyer, dammit, and a very good one. This indecisiveness was not part of her nature. 'I need to do something myself about this rather than obsessing over the unknowns.'

'Amen, sister,' Rae cried, and starting clearing up the plates. She checked her watch. 'Okay kids, Mummy has to go and scrub up then head to see the mayor now. Good to see you, Jared, come over again really soon?' She leant over to give him a peck on the cheek and saw Emmy sit up taller. 'Relax, Em, I'm not trying to snog him again. Remember that Jared?' She cackled and left the kitchen.

'I'm going to go and start scrubbing the outside walls and obsess over Jenny some more,' Noelle smiled, leaving Emmy and Jared alone.

There was a break in the conversation and Emmy racked her brain for something to say. It used to feel so easy with Jared – he was her best friend, pretty much her only friend if we're being honest – and she would tell him everything. He'd even been the one who'd told her she was having her first period, when she suddenly starting bleeding and freaking out, and he laughed (kindly) and told her what it was, and that maybe she'd better go and find her sisters or her mum, and he'd see her again in a few days.

But as adults the distance between their lives seemed huge – too big to know where to start, or how they'd get back to a place of discussing her period pains.

'Do you want some more wine?' she asked him, because when adulting, wine is usually a safe topic.

'Sure, thanks,' he said. He sounded relaxed, but then he always had seemed relaxed, and she remembered him confessing to her that it was practice and often he was just hiding his nerves.

'This is a good grape, apparently, it's usually a ten-pound bottle. We only paid five. It was on an offer. Um. South America.'

'Oh.'

'Yep.' Something occurred to her. 'Unless you'd prefer a Coke float?'

'A Coke float! I haven't had one of those for so long!'

'You haven't? But they were always your favourite.' Emmy smiled at the memory. 'Although we don't actually have any ice cream. Or Coke.'

'Wine is good.'

Emmy poured a fresh glass for them both and looked

at the window. 'It's lovely outside – you can't beat this time of year. Blue skies, air cooling down, caramel leaves. Do you want to take the wines outside for a walk around the woods?'

'That sounds perfect. It's good to be back at your house, it's been too long.' They put on their shoes and Jared looked up at her. 'It's good to see you again.'

'I'm sorry I went AWOL after school,' Emmy said as they stepped out the front door, waving at Noelle who was on her knees studying a bug, a bowl of soapy water beside her. They went down the steps and turned left, circling the side of the house and then walking the familiar path through the garden and in among the trees. 'Life away from here was just easier. I could be myself around, well, everyone, not just you and my family. I just stopped trying to fit in here ... I just stopped, but I didn't mean to lose you in the process.'

'You didn't go AWOL, you just grew up. Did you think I was annoyed?' Jared asked her.

'I don't know, because you're being so nice, but I felt bad for losing touch with you. It was my fault that during uni we drifted apart.'

'You don't have anything to feel bad about.'

Emmy took a slurp of her red wine, which was chilling below ideal in the cold air and under the shade of the trees. She felt happy, though, which was nice. 'So,

I want to know everything. How are you? How did you become a police officer? What's your life like now?'

'Life is good,' Jared declared. Then he thought about it some more. 'Wait … is it? I think it's okay. I like my job and my house and I'm watching some good TV at the moment, but I think you're about to say you've spent your twenties fronting NASA and I'm about to realise my life sucks.'

Emmy laughed. 'I definitely haven't been doing that. So what happened to Scotland, you lived there for a few years, right?'

'Yeah, when I finished my law degree I tried a few different jobs around the country but ended up realising law enforcement was the thing for me. Who knew?'

'If fourteen-year-old Jared had said he was going to be fighting crime out on the rough streets when he grew up I would never have believed it. No offence – you were just always the more bookish, paperwork type. Less "put your hands up", more "put your tax code on this form for me". I'm sorry, I am sounding like such a cow.'

'Not at all.' Jared shook his head. 'It's all true. I always thought the police officers were the cool guys, the brave ones. Now I know that, well, that's totally true because I'm really cool and brave.'

'But why Maplewood? I don't mean to be horrible

about your home it's just that we used to complain about this place all the time.' She crunched on over the leaves, anxious to hear his answer, unsure why it mattered whether he felt the same as her or not.

'We did,' he agreed. 'I'll always remember what you used to tell me about your ambitions.'

Emmy smiled. 'Space is bigger than Maplewood,' she said, a mantra she used to tell herself all the time; a motivation to work hard and get out.

Jared continued, 'But you know I moved around a lot when I was little? This was the first place that not only did we stay in, but that felt like home to me.'

'But . . .'

'I know we used to hate some of the kids at school. I know how awful a lot of people were to you and your family. But I was one of the lucky ones because, to me, you guys *were* my extended family. I grew up alongside the best family in town, and all those other kids had no idea what they were missing out on. So, for me, Maplewood actually holds a huge place in my heart. The people . . . some of them I'd have happily thrown in a prison cell overnight given the opportunity. But the place drew me back. Home sweet home.'

Emmy exhaled, staring ahead, and only realised she'd come to a stop when her feet began to sink into the mulch beneath her. 'But without me you could have been so much more popular. I always thought your childhood was a little bit worse because of me. I was selfish with you, Jared.' She turned to him, her glass now empty, and wished she hadn't drunk her wine so quickly.

'We were friends, you weren't selfish. When did you become so hard on yourself?' He faced her too. It was still odd him looking down towards her rather than them being on the same level.

'I'm just older and wiser now I guess. Thankfully nothing like the girl I was.' Jared looked ready to protest when a burst of rock music rang out from the direction of Rae's room where she was getting ready. 'Some of us, however, seem to be regressing quite well.' She fake-drank from her empty glass and started walking again. 'Where do you live now?'

Jared crunched along beside her again. 'A little closer into town, but not too far from Mum and Dad's place. Dad's getting a little forgetful these days. That was actually the catalyst to come back.'

'I'm so sorry,' Emmy said, linking an arm in with Jared's without even really thinking about it.

'Thanks.'

'How did I not know this? I should have come back and been with you.'

'No, you shouldn't have.'

'Do you think your dad copes better with you around?'

'I think so. Sometimes he doesn't remember who I am, but other times he does, and for those times it's worth it.' They walked in silence for a little bit before Jared spoke up again. 'Your mum's doing fine, you know. Don't be worrying about her.'

A thread she'd been trying not to pick loosened itself a little more inside her. 'I should have come home more.'

'Where do you live now, by the way? I know you're in aerospace but I don't know exactly what you do for a living!' Jared bolstered the conversation up a beat.

'I live up near Oxford, a village called Harwell. I work for the European Space Agency, in the robotics department.'

'Oh my god, that is so cool. You did it, Em. And are you happy?'

She chuckled. 'That's a loaded question.'

'Okay, on the surface. Are you happy?'

Emmy nodded. 'I am. I really like my job. I don't know if it's my dream job but it's pretty much exactly what I wanted to do.'

'How long have you worked there?'

'Since uni, actually, pretty much. I get to do a little bit of travelling – not global road trips, but a couple of trips a year to the US or other sites in Europe. I really like building things that are going to go up into space.

It feels ... womanly?' She laughed as she said it, wondering how she could express in words what she meant.

Jared coaxed her to go on.

'Some people like creating people and putting them out there into the world. I create things. It takes time and patience and it's hard but I can do it, I know I can do it, and I wish more women were in this field because it feels really amazing.'

They reached the den, and Emmy bent down to peer inside. The blankets and glued-on pictures were long gone, but their look-out hole and campfire stone circle were still intact. She grinned at Jared. 'Remember this?'

'Of course. I'm not sure why we ever camped out in here when you had a nice big warm house right there, but I do remember it well.' He looked back at the house and then turned to Emmy with a mild frown. 'Your parents had a lot of faith in me, a teenage boy, letting me and you have sleepovers in the woods.'

'I think that was more because they knew I was as good-looking as a scarecrow and highly unlikely to attract any kind of suitor.'

'That's not true – I thought you were cute. I had a huge crush on you for years.'

'No, you didn't!' Emmy shrieked, and the little dork inside her high-fived herself. *Emmy Lake, you little firecracker!*

'Of course I did! Wait, you didn't know?' Jared blushed. 'I thought you knew. I thought you knew and didn't like me back, so we just ignored it.'

'You saw me period!' she shrieked some more. *Ah, so that's how we rewind thirteen years of distance and find ourselves discussing how the surf is on my crimson wave.*

'My crush did admittedly die down for a week or so around that time. But it came back, always did after you did something gross.'

Emmy sat down in front of the den, even though it made her bottom soggier than a shamed *Great British Bake Off* pie. 'But we were friends. Didn't you want to just be my friend?' Hold on. Did this mean she grew up without any friends at all? This revelation was causing her emotions to slosh about like waves in a harbour. She'd been fanciable. She'd been fancied. But she'd never wanted that, she'd wanted friendship, a confidant, someone who liked her with no agenda.

Jared sat down next to her. 'Are you mad at me?'

'I don't know. Was our, um, bond real? Were you my friend?'

'Of course! I was your friend before anything else. The other stuff was a one-sided teenage crush because you were cool and funny and clever. You made me happy, simple as that; there was nothing fake about anything. I just always held a little hope that one time,

out here, in front of our fire pit, maybe we'd have a kiss.'
He shrugged, smiling at her.

She smiled back. Here they were, side by side after
so many years, and despite her worry it didn't feel all
that weird. They took up a lot more room in the den
than they once had, him especially with his broader
shoulders and how he had to stoop his head down lower.
But it was still Jared and Emmy. It was his eyes and eye-
lashes that looked at her, his smile, albeit surrounded
with a little stubble from recently finishing a long shift.

'Do you remember the night you got drunk?' he asked.

'Not really,' she replied. Her first year of sixth form
had been pretty rough. This was after the whole 'did
she try and commit suicide' rumour, but it was the
isolation that was really getting to her. Other people
seemed to be growing up now they were sixteen,
moving on, acting like they knew everything in the
world, and the harassment died down. It became something else: complete avoidance. It was like she was an
invisible shadow. Nobody wanted to talk to her, but
nobody cared to talk about her. And Emmy was left
confused because wasn't that what she'd wanted all
along? She began to lose her way a little, be a little less
clever, be a little less her, to try and fit in. Just a little.
One night she got steaming drunk, which she'd never
done before, and it was Jared that shook her out of it

and told her she needed to stay strong, get the grades and then she could get out.

'You tried to kiss me that night, you know.'

Emmy gasped. Surely she would have remembered that? Was she a horrible drunken sex pest, like her big sister? 'No, I didn't.'

'You did. It was tempting. But instead I went all Future Jared on you and acted like a policeman. I escorted you home, gave you a stern talking-to, threatened to call Rae and tell her, and then came over every evening for the next four weeks to supervise your studying until you got back on track.'

MAYBE they should kiss, she thought. Right now. If this was a movie the music would swell and they'd lean in and have that kiss. But this wasn't a movie, so instead she broke the spell by saying, 'You kissed my sisters. Pervert.'

'I kissed your mum too. Just kidding. I only kissed one sister, and I'm very sorry about that. The other mad one kissed *me*, or at least tried to.'

'Come on,' she helped him up. 'My bum is soggy, and don't use that as an excuse to look at my bum, now I know what a massive pervert you are.'

Jared laughed, avoiding looking her way. 'So what is your dream job?'

'Hmm?' she asked, still busy thinking about the surprise revelation.

'You said your current job is close, but not your dream job. What would you love to do?'

'Um. Astronaut, I guess,' she replied. 'I always fancied going up there with my babies. Aliens are much better than people, after all.'

'So why don't you do that? You'd be great!'

'No, I wouldn't. I'm much happier in the background.'

'Not happier, safer.'

Huh.

At that point, Emmy heard a call from up at the house. 'Emmy?' Noelle shouted out into the woods.

They emerged from the trees and Jared laid a hand on her upper arm. 'I'd better let you get back to your DIY, and I need to go home for some sleep. Thank you for the lunch and the wine and the catch-up.'

'You'll come back again soon, won't you?'

'Absolutely!' he grinned. 'Two months back with the Lake sisters? Anyone who'd say no to that is clearly an idiot. I'll see you soon.'

Jared rounded the house and set off walking down the long driveway, knowing exactly where he was going. Emmy watched him leave, deep in thought.

Eventually, she called back out to her sister. 'Noey?'

'Emmy?' Noelle replied, and then trotted around the side of the house holding an unexpected bundle. 'I found us a chicken. Meet Vicky!'

# Chapter 11

Rae signalled left and turned up a long, curving drive-way towards the house that stood proudly at the top of the hill. Columns and gravel and a fancy doorknob greeted her.

Gabbi lived *here*? This girl meant business. Rae was impressed.

She walked to the front door, feeling self-conscious in a way she hardly ever felt, wishing she'd properly scrubbed up and changed out of the *Buffy* sweater and hadn't put so much eyeliner on. She hardly ever wore eyeliner any more. Why did she have to experiment today?

As predicted, the doorbell did a musical twinkle rather than a shrill ring, and Rae waited on the steps thinking that if her family had left granite lions outside the front of their house they would have been nicked in no time as part of the ritualistic pranking of the Lakes.

'Rae,' smiled Gabbi, opening the door. She looked a little more like the old her now, dressed in jeans and with her hair, though bobbed now rather than long and straggly, pinned up into a tiny ponytail.

'When you gave me your address I never put two and two together that you were living in Maplewood's answer to the White House.' Rae whistled as Gabbi ushered her in through the grand doorway. 'Shit, Gabbi, you have it made.'

'It's only while I'm in office. You know, I pretty much go by Gabrielle now.'

'Yeah, okay,' Rae scoffed. 'I'll call you Gabrielle if we're out in public, but I can't say it without thinking of your mother screaming at you using that name every time we took your dad's car. When it's me and you, can I stick to Gabbi?'

'That's fine,' Gabbi said, relaxing a little.

'Well, Gabrielle, dreams can come true,' she muttered, looking around her. Rae stopped gazing about the hallway and turned to her friend. 'I wish I wasn't driving, because we need to catch up on a lot of things, and I could do with some alcohol. Right now, it's like an episode of *Round the Twist*.'

'Would a coffee be okay?' They entered the kitchen,

which was massive and bright and very befitting of a mayor.

Rae nodded and took a seat at the kitchen island. 'Start from the beginning.'

'What do you want to know?'

*Why have you changed? Why has Maplewood not changed if you're in charge? Why didn't you leave like you said you would? Why have they forgiven your behaviour when clearly they haven't forgiven me?* 'You went away to university, didn't you? Reading, right?'

'I did. You remember how surprised I was to get in, so I couldn't turn it down. But it was good for me. I did political science and when I finished I knew that was the route I wanted to take.'

'But why come back here? I remember you as one of the most confident, opinionated girls in the school – you could have been Prime Minister!'

Gabbi laughed. 'I still could be, I'm only thirty-four! I have big plans.'

'Don't get me wrong,' said Rae, accepting her coffee and three Jammie Dodgers. 'I'm blown away that you're mayor of a town at your age – it's really, really impressive. I just don't get why ... *here?*'

'Because I grew up here.'

'But you weren't happy growing up here. At least, that's what you used to say.'

'But that's the point. I wanted my first position to mean something, and to be in the place I thought could do with some help. Imagine a mayor who grew up in a town, who went to the best school and had a great childhood and rich parents and got everything handed on a plate. When that kid becomes mayor, what would she or he change? Probably not a lot, because her view of the town is that it's great and has ample opportunity. But what about all the other kids in the town – such as you and me – who saw a different side? Who *knew* what improvements needed to be made, who *knew* what was missing? I wanted to be mayor of Maplewood because I know what can make it better.'

Rae chewed this over. Making a change. That seemed like a much easier concept now than when she had been constantly in the thick of things, growing up in Maplewood, but perhaps she was too quick to go to war rather than make peace?

'You make a lot of sense, lady,' Rae nodded. 'And do you feel you are?'

'Making it better? Slowly. There's a lot of resistance to change here, but we've made some good things happen.' Gabbi munched on her own Jammie Dodger, lost in thought for a moment. 'And at the end of the day, I'm the mayor so I can do whatever the fuck I want.'

Rae laughed. 'There's my foul-mouthed buddy! Is

157

anyone else still around? Of our friends, I mean? I've already come across a few blasts from the past, but not in a pleasant way.'

'You've run into Kelvin and Tom, I take it?'

'Yep.'

'No, not really from our group of friends, I lost touch with them. Sad, really, we were a close bunch for a while. We were the pre-mobile phone generation, you and I, and my Facebook usage nowadays is almost entirely a professional networking thing. I'm pretty boring, really. It's good to see you, though. What brings you back here?'

'My sisters and I are doing up Mum and Dad's house – Mum is a bit of a professional holiday-taker now, so we're going to list the house on Airbnb while she's away, but it needs sprucing up. As you might remember.'

'I heard about your dad last year; I'm so sorry.'

'Thanks, it was tough on Mum, and I don't think she likes being cooped up in that big house on her own for too long if she can help it.'

'It must have been tough on you guys as well.'

'It was, but Emmy took it the hardest. She's been funny about coming back here for this, for various reasons, but Dad is one of them, I can tell.' Rae stopped for a moment and thought about Emmy. She'd be all right ... Rae was sure she would.

'What are the other reasons?'

'Well, you know, the fact that we were pretty universally the most disliked family in Maplewood.'

'No, that's not true ... Well, I guess it was, but not any more.'

'I don't think we've been replaced, just forgotten. I have a horrible feeling us being back is going to just pick the scab and reopen the wound.'

'So what if it does? You're grown-ups now. And you're successful – an opera singer, did you say?'

'I did!' Rae felt a swell of pride. She'd done okay.

'That's amazing! I must say, I would have put you fronting a rock band, I never would have dreamed of you being an opera singer.'

'As unlikely as you becoming Mayor of Maplewank?'

'Ha ha, point taken!'

'I can't believe Mum didn't tell me you were mayor!'

'I mean, back when we were at school I met your mum maybe three times. That was fifteen, maybe sixteen years ago. I was MUCH skinnier back then, my hair was dyed jet black, I never looked anyone in the eye and I definitely never let anyone – apart from my mum – call me Gabrielle. I've basically completely changed, so she probably hasn't even clicked who I am. Who I *was*.'

'Same thing.'

Gabbi stood up to fetch more coffee, and more biscuits. 'You think?'

'I don't know, actually.' Rae accepted another biscuit. 'I think I'm quite different from who I was, but who I was shaped who I am, so therefore does that make me the same?'

'Maybe. And remember that who you *were* isn't the same thing as who everyone else *thought* you were.'

'Now that's true.'

'This is fun, Rae,' grinned Gabbi. 'This is the type of philosophical stuff we used to talk about over cigarettes at the top of the cliff. You don't seem that different to me, you know, and I knew you pretty well.'

Rae smiled. 'I'm still on the fence about you.'

At that moment, in walked a small girl, no older than six or seven, wearing a sun hat and a feather boa, and carrying a small suitcase. 'Hello,' she said, sitting down at the table and reaching for the Jammie Dodgers.

Rae raised her eyebrows at Gabbi, who laughed. 'This is my niece, Lily. She's staying with me for a couple of weeks while my brother's gone on holiday with his wife.'

'Hello,' the child said again. 'My mummy and daddy have gone on holiday, so I'm going to go on holiday too.'

'You are?' asked Gabbi.

'Yep, I'm all packed.' She opened her suitcase on the table and inside was a T-shirt and a deck of cards, and a lipstick that was presumably Gabbi's.

'Are you going to Las Vegas?' asked Rae.

Lily blinked at her. 'What's Lost Fingers?'

'A good time, amirite?' Rae sniggered to Gabbi under her breath. Gabbi choked on her coffee a little bit.

'Las Vegas is in America,' Gabbi told Lily.

'Like *K.C. Undercover*!'

'Exactly. Lily, this is my friend Rae, we went to school together.'

'Is she a mayor too?'

'Actually, she's an opera singer, do you know what that is?'

Lily nodded, her eyes wide. 'I saw an opera in London. Do you wear dresses?'

'On stage I do. Do you?'

'No. I like dungarees.'

'Good choice.'

Lily stood up, and looked at a watch she'd drawn in biro on her wrist. 'Listen, ladies, I have to go or I'm going to miss my boat. Nice to meet you, Rae.' The little girl picked up her suitcase and wandered into the living room, and Rae and Gabbi heard her chatting away to nobody about what a fine ship they were on and how she hoped they didn't hit an iceberg.

'My mum likes to cruise too. Perhaps they'll meet on deck some day.'

'She's a funny kid. Thank god she has a big imagination and plays on her own because I can't wrap my head around her make-believe games. Do you have kids?'

'Nope. Maybe one day, but I'm really happy at the moment. I'm married though, and my husband couldn't take the time off work for this trip, so I miss him.'

'What's his name?'

'Finn. He's really nice. You'd like him.'

'Is he an *A+ dude*?' she asked, quoting back to Rae what their friendship group used to call the hot guys back in the late nineties.

'Ha – he sure is, and he makes a great spag bol.' Rae paused. 'Gabbi, can I ask you about my mum?'

'What about her?'

'It didn't occur to me until I was back that this ... resentment ... of my family would still be trickling through this town. Is my mum treated well?'

'Absolutely! She's liked. Well, feared is perhaps more accurate.'

Rae laughed. 'Better to be feared than judged, I guess.'

'Seriously though, in the nicest possible way, I don't think people think about you guys much. Your mum doesn't particularly join in with the community, so she's just ... '

'Forgotten about?'

'No, no, that's not what I mean. The reputation of your family, that's what's been forgotten about.'

'Until now.'

Gabbi laughed. 'I guess we'll see!'

Rae stood up. 'Okay, I'd better get home, my sisters are mad at me because I demolished a door and haven't done anything to put it back together yet. You should come over sometime! You like painting walls, right?'

Gabbi rose also, and walked Rae to the door. 'Absolutely, I'd like that. It would be good to see Em and Noelle too.'

'Noelle's still gay, in case you were wondering. It wasn't a phase like Mr Richter from P.E. claimed it was.'

'Mr Richter was asked to take early retirement after someone put in a complaint about him bullying the kids.' Gabbi raised her eyebrows.

Rae gasped. 'Who?'

'Someone who remembered what a massive ball-sack he was.'

'Was it you? He was savage to you when you said you didn't want to change into your P.E. kit because your period had leaked everywhere.'

'It was an anonymous complaint, so I couldn't possibly say. But I did send him a thank-you-for-your-service gift following retirement.'

'You did? What did you send?'

'A box of tampons. So let me know when you need a hand with painting. I'm pretty busy during the daytime, usually, but maybe early evening at some point would be good, before the evenings get too dark?'

Rae felt uplifted leaving Mayor Reynold's house, even if being in the mayor's house in the first place had made her feel a little like she was cheating on her past self. God, it felt good to see something in this town that brought back happy memories – Gabbi looked really well. A little serious, a little in need of a bit of fun, judging by a couple of her comments, but well. Perhaps for old times' sake Rae could have just a little excitement while she was back in Maplewood . . .

# Chapter 12

'Noelle, where did you get the chicken from?'

Noelle tried to hand Vicky the chicken to Emmy, but she just dangled mid-air, like Noelle was Rafiki at the beginning of *The Lion King* and this fat hen was Simba. 'She was living here, in the woods.'

'Chickens don't live in the woods.'

'This one does. Isn't she lovely?' Vicky was the colour of a vanilla latte and big-bottomed like a matron in bloomers. She tilted her head at Emmy. 'She's our pet chicken now. Can you check her to make sure she's okay?'

'I'm not a vet . . .' Emmy replied. 'We can't keep a chicken, we're only here for two months.'

'She'll be eaten by foxes if she lives out here.'

Emmy blinked. What was happening? 'Just put her down and let her go.'

'No way, Vicky's one of us now. I'll find her a proper home while we're here, but for now we'll keep her and she can provide us with eggs. You like eggs, don't-you, Em? Poached eggs on warm, buttery toast . . . The yolk all yellow and runny . . . ' Noelle knew full well that poached eggs were one of Emmy's favourites.

'I'm also pretty fond of chicken drumsticks,' Emmy said, but she was smiling, and she took Vicky off Noelle to check her over the best she could, based on her limited knowledge of biology.

'I'm a good person,' Noelle said, all of a sudden, when Vicky was safely in Emmy's arms.

Emmy looked up. 'I know. Vicky can stay, we'll find her a home.'

'Yes, but, that's not what I meant.' Noelle fiddled with her hair, facing the low afternoon sunshine. 'I'm a good person, and I try and be kind to everyone, and I try and do everything I can for the planet and to make the world a safe place for everyone to enjoy. And I know I'm a lawyer, and not everyone likes lawyers, but I really try and be a good person.'

'Noey, what's wrong?' Emmy lowered Vicky the chicken on to the porch, and she clucked about by their feet, clearly very at home there.

'I'm worried about Jenny. I hurt her and she didn't ever deserve that.'

'Hey, you were just kids, she'll forgive you.'

'I wouldn't forgive me. We went through something big together, and then I just left her alone. She was alone. And it was my fault.' Noelle's insides squeezed so hard that she wanted to cry but it felt too abstract, too out of reach. She wrung her fingers round and round each other, her breathing shallow. The guilt had always been there but she'd always pushed it aside. Now it was all she could think about and it was so horrible.

Emmy led her inside where she made two steaming mugs of tea, because ... tea. 'I swear I'm not trying to trivialise anything about how you're feeling, but you're loading an awful lot of emotions on an assumption about someone else's heart. You need to see Jenny. This isn't healthy, and isn't like you.'

'But I'm scared.'

'No, you're not; you're excited.'

Noelle stopped as she was bringing the mug to her lips. 'No, I'm scared.'

'Rollercoasters are scary, but also exciting, because of the unknown, and the thrill of wanting whatever's happening to happen. So tell yourself you're not scared, but excited, and leap on board.'

Noelle pondered this. 'That sort of makes sense, but I'm not going to be asking you to write my closing arguments anytime soon. Uggghhhh, I'm just not used to spending days and nights thinking about my love life. It feels very silly. I have other stuff going on, you know.'

'I know. So talk to Jenny and then you can get back to your real life.'

Nodding, Noelle reached for her phone and found Jenny's Facebook page. 'I'm going to do it. I'll message her. I don't know if she'll see it or she'll want to talk to me, but it's worth a try.'

'Yes, queen.'

'Just do it, as Nike would say.'

'Atta girl.'

'Let's go.'

'Eye of the tiger.' Emmy was running out of motivational phrases.

'What do I say?' asked Noelle, her fingers trembling.

'Invite her over. Say you're back in town, you hate how you left things and that you want to apologise.'

'Okay. I'm going to say I'll be at the house for two months so if and when she feels she wants to talk she can come over anytime. Sound good?'

'Perfect.'

Noelle's fingers typed with lawyer-speed; she hit SEND and she sat back with her tea. Thirty seconds later, she checked the messenger app to see if Jenny had read the message yet. Thirty seconds after that, she checked again.

This ritual continued throughout the afternoon, and deep into the evening.

By the following morning, Jenny had read the message, Noelle could see that. But she hadn't responded.

On Noelle's command, the sisters threw themselves into housework. Noelle worked tirelessly on the outside, while Emmy and Rae tackled paintwork in the kitchen/living room and the hallway. Their first week back in Maplewood rolled into their second, third and then fourth, the days getting a fraction shorter and the nights a degree colder, and still Jenny hadn't responded.

The three sisters were on the porch one morning admiring the way their arm muscles were starting to pop, already sweating from putting in a couple of hours of manual labour. Emmy and Rae felt permanently covered in paint flecks, while Noelle's freckles had popped out and her skin was faintly tanned under her wildly messy top bun.

'So, I think before I do any more, we're going to need to go and buy the wood and replace this decking,' Noelle was saying. 'But it's going to take all three of us to do that job.'

This was not a job that appealed to Rae or Emmy,

who crinkled their noses, simultaneously plotting about asking Jared and Gabbi if they'd fancy coming over for a please-rebuild-our-porch party.

Then Rae spotted someone coming up the drive. 'ERM, BYE,' she said, retreating into the house and pulling Emmy with her.

Noelle turned and squinted into the sunshine. There she was. It *had* been her at the side of the road, still with the same walk and the same hair.

It had been a long time since Jenny had come around. The women met eyes and watched each other as they moved closer. Neither could prevent a small smile forming on their lips. *There you are*, Noelle thought. There was sweetness in the sadness – so much time had passed, but these two sets of eyes were now seeing each other again.

'Jenny,' she breathed.

'Hi,' Jenny said, after what felt like a decade. Actually, it really had been a decade.

She looked the same. Better, actually. Noelle felt self-conscious, and tried to smooth down the frizz and wipe the sweat from her brow.

'Thanks for coming,' Noelle said, her voice shaking.

'Thank you for inviting me. I saw you were back in town when you drove past me, and I wondered if we'd cross paths.'

There was a distance between them that Noelle hadn't expected. She'd thought Jenny would be angry, that she'd shout and cry and that then they'd never see each other again. She'd *hoped* it would be like time had never passed, but that Jenny was happy in her life and excited about rekindling a bond, if nothing more. She hadn't expected this gap. It took everything not to leap forward and take Jenny's face in her hands and kiss her again.

'Can I get you a drink?' Noelle asked, signalling towards the door.

'I'll have a tea, please,' said Jenny, remaining on the spot, her hands folded in front of her. 'Out here, if you don't mind.'

'You don't want to come in?' There was a sorrow in Noelle's voice she couldn't keep out.

'Not this time.' Jenny's reserve softened a little. 'I will, I'm sure – if you're around for a while. But not quite yet.'

Noelle nodded and went to go inside, then realised she didn't know adult Jenny at all. 'How do you take your tea?' she asked.

'Milk, no sugar, thanks.'

When Noelle reached the kitchen, her sisters jumped up from where they too had been having a tea break.

'Is she still here?' Rae asked.

'What's happening, is everything okay?' Emmy jumped in.

'What did she say to you? What did you say to her?'

Noelle pushed past them. 'I'm making her tea, we'll go from there.' As the tea was brewing, Noelle turned back to her sisters. 'She's really mad. I don't like it.'

'But she's here,' Emmy reminded her. 'And you did mess up, you're not supposed to like it – but she's willing to see you. The olive branch is out there. It might not be perfect, not everything gets to be perfect, but it's going to be okay.'

Noelle nodded, and armed with the mugs of tea she returned outside, where Jenny was sat on the porch.

'I'm sorry if you fall through the porch or anything,' Noelle said softly, as she sat down next to her. 'The wood's pretty rotten; we're going to be replacing it soon.'

Jenny raised an eyebrow. '*That's* what you're sorry for?' But there was kindness in the eyes that looked back at Noelle over the tea mug.

Noelle remembered back to that day. It was the middle of the summer before she and Jenny were due to go their separate ways to different universities. They'd been arguing more than usual – silly, bickery arguments on the surface about whether to stay together long-distance and who loved whom more. But it ran deeper. Noelle knew logically they should break up. She didn't want the friendship to end, but she felt like she had to let Jenny off the chain she'd kept her on since their early teens. Her own sexuality was something that had caused gossip, and had created a barrier between her and the other kids at school. She had Jenny so she didn't care ... but sometimes, just sometimes, she *did* care. It would bother her, and then she felt responsible for Jenny's happiness (or unhappiness) as well. She was in awe of Jenny, and she wanted her to be free and fly and maybe they'd come back to each other, but she didn't want Jenny to resent her in the future because she was all she'd known.

And in a tiny selfish corner of her heart that she tried to ignore, Noelle wanted the same thing – to be free to fly.

But Jenny thought they should give long-distance a go. She was worried that if they lost their relationship they'd lose each other as friends, even though Noelle swore it wouldn't happen.

Noelle did what she did because she was afraid of the goodbyes. She was a coward under the guise of a free spirit, and on a hot August day, she left. She moved away to university early, leaving Jenny with a love note and a million well wishes, and a promise that this was an exciting time and if it was meant to be then they'd be together again soon. 'I'll see you in the Christmas holidays!' she'd promised, with a smiley face. But when the Christmas holidays came around, Jenny didn't – and Noelle was afraid again, but this time of a hello.

'I'm sorry for being the worst type of person,' Noelle said, looking into Jenny's eyes and putting down her mug.

'You weren't the worst type of person, you were young. We were so young.'

'I was old enough to know what would hurt. I stuck my fingers in my ears and told myself I didn't know, but it's weighed on me ever since, so it's pretty safe to say I knew.'

Jenny was silent for a while, before saying, 'Do you remember why you did it?'

'Because I thought I was right and that eventually you'd thank me for it,' she winced. 'I was so wrong to just leave. I really am sorry.'

'Can I tell you about that day?'

'Of course.' Noelle didn't want to hear it, but she had to woman-up and stop running away from the truth.

Jenny swept her white-blonde hair back from her face and stared down the Lakes' driveway. 'I rode my bike over here really quickly, because I'd bought us a peace offering of a box of Feast ice creams as it was so hot. We'd fought the day before – again. They were in my rucksack and I was convinced they were going to melt and the chocolate would leak out everywhere, so I zoomed up your driveway. Your parents' car was gone, which wasn't unusual but I just remember it. I knocked on the door just as Rae was coming out – she was home for a day or two with her then-boyfriend. I remember her looking surprised to see me. "You just missed her," she said. Then she grabbed something from the hall-way – it was a letter – and she said she had to dash but that you'd left me this.'

Noelle shook her head. What had she done?

'Then Rae winked, and said she hoped we'd given each other a good send-off, and off she went,' Jenny continued. 'Even your sister thought you'd said good-bye to me. I didn't even know what she was talking about. Until I sat right here, on my own, and read your letter.'

'I'm so sorry,' Noelle whispered. How wrong and silly she had been, making decisions for other people, thinking she knew their hearts better than themselves.

'You left without me. I know we were just kids at the time, really, but there was something about you – about us – that made sense and then suddenly it didn't. I didn't just lose my girlfriend, I lost my friend, my favourite person, the one person who got me.' Jenny took a deep breath and smiled into the sunshine. 'I for-give you, you don't have to keep apologising, but it was

nice to hear it once. You owe me a backpack though –
those Feasts did melt everywhere.'

'Consider it done … Thank you.'

Standing up, Jenny left her mug of half-drunk tea on
the porch. 'I'm going to go for now. It was good to see
you again, Noelle.'

Noelle stood also, wanting to keep her here for just
a little longer. 'Do you want to stay a while? I want
to find out about you, what you've been up to, what
you do now.'

'Another time,' she said, firmly but fairly.

'Okay,' Noelle nodded, respecting her wishes. As
Jenny retreated down the driveway with a wave, Noelle
breathed in the September air, and a small feeling of
lightness akin to the leaves that drifted about her.

Tomorrow, October started. And tomorrow felt like
it would be a brand-new day.

# Chapter 13

'It's got to be done. This week.' Emmy stared at her sisters, waiting for one of them to volunteer. They were stood on the landing; all three bedroom doors wide open.

'Can't we leave it a little longer?' asked Noelle, gazing with nostalgia into her sanctuary.

'We can't.' Emmy shook her head. 'It's going to take us ages to clear everything out anyway, plus they'll probably need an industrial-strength clean, and only then can we start getting the first coats on the wall. We're already into month two.'

'The carpets arrive on November the third. We do need all the painting done by then, really.' Noelle succumbed.

'What shall we do for Halloween?' Rae changed the subject.

'Don't change the subject,' said Emmy.

'It's a good point, though,' she replied. 'Let's park that and come back to it. So, are we doing this separately or all hitting a room together?'

'Separately,' Emmy said, at the same time that Noelle said, 'Together.'

Rae and Emmy walked into their respective rooms, and Rae called out to Noelle, 'You only want to do this together because your room's a shithole.'

Inside her bedroom, Emmy pushed aside the furniture ready for three piles: Keep, Charity Shop, Chuck. The Keep pile would be pretty small, she had no doubt.

Plugging in her boombox, she lifted her big box of cassettes off the shelf for the last time. She selected one to listen to now – the *Steptacular* album – before dumping the rest of the box on to the chuck pile. Apparently, charity shops rarely even take cassettes nowadays, and it wasn't like she had a tape player up in Oxford to listen to any of these.

Except … she opened the box back up. Better to have a quick check, just to make sure she had any favourites digitised on her iTunes. Wow, the hours she must have put in, making these mix tapes by recording songs off the radio.

But they had to go. There was no point in hanging

on to things from her past, when all it would do would remind her of it.

Emmy wandered around the room collecting up things to put in the piles, and by track three ('Love's Got a Hold on My Heart'), as predicted, the Keep pile consisted of just the 'Girl Power' crop top, one Baby-Sitters Club book and a maths revision guide. It was a cool revision guide – full colour – you never know when a bad boy like that might come in handy in the future. Same with the Baby-Sitters Club book. The other piles were overflowing.

Rae wandered into the bedroom holding some cigarettes. 'Check this out, how high do you think I'd get if I smoked these? They're probably poison now, they must be at least fifteen years old, if not more! Woah – tell me that isn't a mountain of stuff you're getting rid of?'

'Yep, that pile can all go to charity, and that lot can all go to the tip.'

Rae sat down on the floor, uninvited, and began rifling through the piles. 'Noooo, you can't get rid of your Mr Blobby puppet! You loved Mr Blobby! Check out your Magic Eye book, Noelle could never do these . . .'

'Hello,' Noelle said, coming in the room, her hair inexplicably crimped and bejewelled with butterfly clips. She sat next to Rae. 'Are we doing Emmy's room first? Goodie. Oh, look at these Backstreet Boys dolls.'

'That's Westlife,' Emmy corrected her. There was no getting rid of her nosy sisters now.

'You're really giving all this stuff to charity?' asked Rae. 'Don't you want to keep some?'

'Why?'

'Because they're memories.'

'No, they're not. Memories are in my head. This is just stuff, and I clearly don't need any of it because I'd have taken it away with me before.'

'But—'

'*Rae*.' There was a reason Emmy had wanted to do this in peace, and that reason was shaped like sisters. If Emmy wanted to have closure on a tough time in her life, she needed to purge herself of all the stuff that kept bringing it back. Who knows, maybe after all this she'd start to enjoy coming home again? 'You stick to your journey down memory lane, and let me stick to mine.'

But Rae wasn't giving up. 'You're demolishing your memory lane. You're pretending it never existed.'

'I've just grown up – maybe you need to do the same, and stop parading about in black eyeliner like you think it's 1998 again.'

Rae was loving this eyeliner, and loving getting

reacquainted with herself, so her sister could just shut up right now. 'I'm not afraid of who I was, and neither should you be. Don't you think it would kill the fourteen-year-old Emmy to know that grown-up Emmy was siding with her bullies? Thinking she was pathetic and a loser and weak. Don't you like who you've become at all?'

'Yes, I do like who I've become, that's the point. I worked hard to move away from who I used to be.'

'But who you used to be shaped who you are today. Of course you're not exactly the same, everything changes, apart from Noelle perhaps. But stop bashing the girl who showed you the stars and shared her story books with you and cried with you at night, because she's already got nobody on her side – you *have* to stand by her. Let her in. *Like her.*'

Noelle wanted to point out that *she* had changed a little. She no longer felt the need to make decisions for other people. Also, she was a lawyer now, which she wasn't when she was little. But this wasn't about her at the moment.

Emmy let Rae's words sink in. She had no comeback. Was she really siding with the bullies by not being on Team Emmy? She fiddled with the corners of her Baby-Sitters Club book, which was tattered and faded through love.

The doorbell rang, interrupting their thoughts with its deep and eerie jangle. 'We should change that bell,' said Rae, hauling herself up. 'I'll get it, it's probably Gabbi, she said she'd drop over her pressure washer later today. I can't believe I'm even saying "Gabbi" and "pressure washer" in the same sentence. Maybe I should give her one of these cigarettes.'

Rae swung open the front door, but rather than being faced with Gabbi, she was faced with a large hamper. From behind the hamper out popped a teenage girl with dyed black hair, piercings up her ear, and the type of dry, crooked grin you'd see on your favourite comedienne.

'Surprise! You are the recipient of a gift hamper from The Wooden Café,' she smirked, holding out the basket.

Rae took it, peering inside at the paper-wrapped powdery pancake mix, the bottle of maple syrup, two vacuum-packed bags of bacon and various other treats. 'Thanks – who sent this?'

'I did,' the teenager answered, gazing up at the house. 'It's from me. Your house is lit.'

'Thank you . . . ? Who are you?'

'I'm Bonnie. Big fan.' She stuck her hand out.

Emmy called down from upstairs. 'Rae, who is it?'

'I don't really know,' she called back up. 'Big fan of who?'

'You guys. "The Lake sisters". You're talk of the town, you know. Everyone's all "*whaaaat, the sisters are baaaack?*"'

Noelle and Emmy appeared at the door behind Rae. 'You work at The Wooden Café,' Emmy said, then clocked the gift basket. 'You're a waitress there, right?'

'Gotta earn the cash in between the classes. So you're doing up your house, huh? Did you uncover anything weird yet?' She peered past them into the house. 'I heard it's like that old *Blair Witch* movie out the back of your house.'

Rae spoke to her sisters. 'She brought us a gift basket. She says we're the talk of the town.'

Bonnie nodded. 'You're like, famous. At least your home is. There's a whole Facebook page about it and about all the spooky shit that's happened here over the years. Can I get a snapchat with you?'

'A what?' said Emmy.

'A snapchat,' snapped Rae. 'Come on, saddo. It's that app where people add filters, like, dog tongues and things to their face.'

'. . . They what?'

Rae turned back to Bonnie. 'Do you want to come in?'

'Yeah, I do!' Bonnie bounded in like a puppy who'd just been let off the leash. 'Cool chicken,' she remarked as Vicky crossed her path.

Emmy was hissing at Rae, 'I don't think we should let teenage strangers into our home. What if she lets off a firework? What if she claims we assaulted her? This could all be part of a prank.'

Rae ignored Emmy and led Bonnie and the other two into the kitchen, where she flicked the kettle on. 'Drink?' she asked the room.

'Tea, please,' sang Noelle.

'Gin, please,' deadpanned Emmy.

'Ooo, can I have a gin?' Bonnie asked. 'No? Okay, have you got coffee?'

'We have coffee,' Rae answered.

Bonnie settled on to one of the bar stools at the breakfast island. 'I heard you guys used to have to fend for yourselves a lot because your parents would go out into the woods for days performing rituals. Is that why you always turned up at school in dirty clothes? Is that why you put a curse on your teacher?'

Rae snorted. 'We turned up at school in dirty clothes because our mum couldn't get us from the front door to the end of the drive without us having some kind of scrap or play fight, or climbing a tree. We were always clean when we left the house, though. Where are you getting this from? The Facebook page?'

'Some of it, but ever since you guys came back into town I'm hearing a lot of gossip in the café. Oh my god.

When your mum's around nobody dares to say a thing – you'll find that on the Facebook page – but the things they say about you . . . ' She whistled, and accepted her coffee gratefully.

'I hope I'm not being rude,' Bonnie continued. 'My mum's always telling me off for that. I don't believe any of it, it's just well funny. I actually think you all seem really nice, and you tip well; bonus. People are always judging me too. It's like, if you look a certain way or live a certain way, or your parents are a certain way, there must be something wrong with you because you're different. But different is good, it's well interesting. Don't you think? Cool living room.' She took a quick break from talking to peer around Noelle into the next room. 'Have you got any biscuits? I put some in the hamper, in case you want to open any.'

Noelle got the hamper and pulled out some local ginger biscuits, handing them straight to Bonnie who offered them around and then took two herself, which she set aside for a future break in her monologue.

'Have you got a laptop?' Bonnie asked. 'I'll show you that Facebook page. Oh my god, it was *so funny*. You know Annette, right? You must do, because she's literally eight hundred years old and I think she's owned the newsagent's for seven hundred of those years.'

'Oh, we know Annette,' replied Emmy.

'So you went in her shop the other week didn't you? I'm not stalking or nothing – that's just what I heard.'

'We did, yes,' Rae answered. She was both irked and intrigued as to why people were discussing them so much. She was sure people didn't care to discuss them to this extent when they actually used to live here.

'She literally put a sign up in her window saying "No Lake children allowed".'

Rae was taken aback and the sisters gasped at each other. 'That stupid old—'

'*Rae*,' Emmy warned, tilting her head at the teenager.

'Don't worry, I've heard much worse,' said Bonnie with pride. 'Well, she's been telling everyone that'll listen that you're shoplifters, but then do you know that hot policeman, PC Jones?'

Emmy, despite her impending annoyance, smiled at his name. 'Jared? Yeah, I mean he's not hot, I don't think, whatever.'

'He IS hot. Anyway, he told her to take it down and said if she had a formal complaint she had to report it to the police, otherwise this was violating your human rights. He also told her you all earn a shitload of money so are really unlikely to shoplift a bag of Frazzles.'

'How do you know all this was said?' Emmy asked. Jared was ace.

'Because one of my friends was trying to shoplift at

the time and had to look super-casual like he was just browsing for a good ten minutes while they argued. It was his first time shoplifting – I told him it was a dumb thing to do – now I think he's scared off it for ever. Nobody wants a life in a jail cell do they? Can I have another coffee please?'

Emmy gave in and sat next to Bonnie, handing her the laptop. 'Bonnie, you surely don't remember us at all – you must have been a tiny kid when we lived here?'

'Nope, you have a clean slate with me.' She tap-tap-tapped at lightning speed. 'I'm just super into creepy stuff so I've been following this page for a while. I'm kind of aware it's bullshit, but bullshit can still be fun, can't it? Check it out.' She slid the laptop back to Emmy, and Rae and Noelle huddled over her shoulder.

'"*The Maplewood House in the Woods*",' Emmy read. 'Bloody hell, it's got 186 likes. There's a map, photos, comments; this is not okay.'

'Don't worry too much about it, it's a historical landmark is all, sort of. People are interested. And it's all photos from the Internet, it's not like people have been sneaking into the grounds and taking photos of the outside.'

'How do you know that?' asked Rae.

Bonnie gulped. 'Because I'm the moderator.'

'You what?'

She held her hands up. 'I didn't start the rumours or anything – I told you, I don't start gossip. There's been a lot of stuff written about this house over the years – in the papers and online, I mean; it's Maplewood history. This is a tribute page, if anything. Anyway, it means I can remove any posts that I don't think should be on there, and I've got morals and ethics and things, and I wouldn't let anything stay up that looked like it had been taken without consent.'

'Is that why you're here?' Emmy snapped. 'To get some exclusive photos of the freak-show house?'

'Not at all!' Bonnie cried. 'I really wanted to meet you and say hello. And I wondered if, maybe … You see, I want to be a journalist one day, and I thought if I could write a really good article it would help me with my uni application. And I wanted to write about you. Or your house, if you don't want to be in it. And not gossip, I promise, about the history of it.'

Emmy glanced at her sisters. 'Let us think about it.'

'Sure.' Bonnie hopped off the stool and stuffed the biscuits in her pocket. 'Let me know what you decide, whenever. And let me know if you want me to be your eyes and ears in the town. I love a bit of undercover work.' She wandered towards the door, looking around her. 'By the way, I also babysit for the Bradleighs' kid, and he and his missus had some friends round the other day and they were all talking about you ladies. I know because I was hired to keep the kids entertained in the next room and to bring out the plates of scampi and chips when they'd heated up. But don't worry, everyone knows they're a bunch of dipshits. 'Kay, bye!'

Bonnie left the house with one final, appreciative look, and then trotted off down the driveway.

'She was like a tornado!' Noelle exhaled as they all shuffled back into the kitchen. 'I don't think I even said one word to her. She'd make a great barrister.'

'That was certainly pretty interesting.' Rae laughed. 'Did you see this hamper? ALL the bacon!'

Emmy was back in front of the laptop. 'Are you two bothered about what she was saying though? That everyone's been talking about us?'

Rae shrugged. 'Let them talk. I'm tired of caring.' She thought for a moment. 'Am I? I think I am. Either way, you can't stop people talking.'

'You can if you stop them from having anything to talk about,' said Noelle. 'If they got to know us they'd see we're very nice. And that our clothes aren't dirty and our home isn't full of shoplifted items from a newsagent's.'

'Nor is it full of voodoo dolls and sacrificed animals,' Emmy huffed, reading comments on the page.

'Just one healthy chicken.' Noelle waved out the window at Vicky, who was moonwalking in the back garden.

Emmy shook her head and stood up. 'I don't believe in having to convince people to like you. This is life, not an audition. Now if you excuse me, I'm going back upstairs to finish my clear-out. I need to say goodbye to what I now realise is a far-too-large collection of cargo-pants for one person who wasn't even in All Saints. Turns out I don't know where it's at.'

# Chapter 14

'I heard on the grapevine that you've been defending our honour?' Emmy said to Jared over the noise of the hammering rain. They were huddled in a bus shelter waiting for the latest downpour to subside. The October sky was grey, stripped of its September blues, and there was a definite feeling that winter was battering at the doors of Devon.

Jared was on duty, but it was a slow day so when Emmy had called him to see if he wanted to meet for coffee he'd suggested takeaway, and that she joined him on his walking route. Looking at her soaked hair and wet feet gave him a mini case of the guilts, but selfish as it was, the hot coffee in his hand, courtesy of her, was worth it.

'Are you talking about Annette's?' he laughed.

'"No Lake sisters allowed" is what I heard, until you came along.'

'Don't pay any attention to it, some people are never going to change.'

'That's exactly what *they* all think about *us*,' she mused.

'No, that's different. You haven't changed, but what they think about you was never right.'

'You're sweet.' She nudged him, and sipped her coffee.

'Does it bother you?'

'Of course,' she smiled. 'Wouldn't it bother you?'

'Yeah.'

'Did she come to the station in the end?'

He paused. 'Annette? ... No.'

'Why did you pause? Did someone else?'

Jared shuffled and wished the rain was louder so it could muffle his awkwardness. 'No, nobody came to the station about you. Someone else did make a comment. Something about a disturbance outside the pub, that argument between you three and Tom Bradleigh and his mate last month. There were kids there and someone thought it was inappropriate.'

Emmy groaned and stepped out of the bus shelter, not caring about the fact she now stood in full force of the rain that carried in the wind. A woman walked past that Emmy recognised from school. Emmy smiled, but the woman looked away as if she hadn't seen her. She turned back to Jared with a sigh. 'They were the ones being inappropriate! We did nothing wrong.'

'Hey, I don't doubt you. As if my painfully shy pal Emmy would ever be shouting at anyone outside a pub. And as I told this person, if one of the actual party mentioned wants to make a complaint they can, otherwise I don't want to hear about it. Although I didn't actually say those words, because I'm not supposed to discourage people from coming forward.'

Emmy was about to groan again, but she was getting sick of hearing herself groan. Was it all worth it? 'Hey, do you know a girl called Bonnie? I'd say mid-teens, works in The Wooden Café?'

'Yeah, I know her, kind of. Talks a hell of a lot and wants to be a reporter or something – she's always skipping out of the café or school when she's not supposed to and badgering me with questions if I get called to a crime scene. I think she wishes we lived in Broadchurch. Good kid, actually, though you wouldn't think so from looking at her.'

Emmy raised her eyebrows at him and he smacked a palm over his eyes.

'That was really pigeon-holing wasn't it? I didn't

mean anything by it, I guess I'm guilty of judging books by their covers too.'

'Luckily, though, history has proven that you're a goodie, not a baddie,' Emmy replied, and took his hand to pull him up. 'Come on, the rain's died down a little. Let's keep walking, someone might be getting murdered around the corner and you don't want Bonnie finding the body before you do.'

Emmy let his hand drop but not before their fingers had brushed together and they'd totally *shared a moment*. It was like *High School Musical*, if her life had been anything like that film and she wasn't ten million years older than those kids.

It was a tiny, flirty move, but how alive her heart felt to have that with someone! She wasn't falling for Jared or anything, but her everlasting fondness for him, her lack of male interaction back in her real life and the fact he was, frankly, a bit yum nowadays really had her wings uncurling. Here in Maplewood, all these years later, and even after everything that happened, he made her feel, well, not only safe – but brave. Brave to be herself.

'Do you remember,' she started, 'do you remember that time it was your birthday and we went to The Wooden Café and I made you order all of the things you wanted on the menu?'

He laughed. 'I was sooo fat by the time we left there.'

Emmy pointed at a road up ahead that curved up the hill. She knew that shortly after it went out of sight it turned from tarmac to a dirt track, and ended in a viewpoint across the town. It was where the kids always used to go to snog each other after nightfall. Emmy remembered a time she went with Jared. 'We went up there, it was early afternoon—'

'You *took* me up there. I was so excited and so nervous, because I thought you were taking me up there to give me a birthday kiss. The whole way up I was wiping my mouth in case it tasted of ketchup, and by the time we got to the top my lips were so dry and chapped.'

'You thought that's what we were doing?' Emmy was warmed by how sweet he'd been, and how clueless she had been. Was it possible she didn't always hit the mark with what people thought of her? 'But you knew me; surely you knew I'd never pluck up the courage to do something so forward.'

'Well, surely you knew that Westlife guy would never marry you, but it didn't stop you holding up a "Marry Me, Dave!" sign at their concert. People dream, when they're in loooove.'

'There was no Dave in Westlife,' she chuckled quietly. 'I really liked that afternoon, though. I didn't know you had other plans, but I remember just lying up there in the grass with you, staring at the sky. It was one of those blue-sky days where you can still see the moon. We laughed and dozed and we were the only ones up there for hours. It was like, just for that afternoon, we owned the town. We were free, like everyone else, and could enjoy it. It was a really good afternoon.'

'Do you want to go up there now?' Jared asked, checking his watch. 'I have time. No murders, yet.'

'I don't know; now I know what you're really after, I'm not sure I should lead you up there.' *Listen to you, Emmy, you Flirty Gerty!*

'Oh dammit,' said Jared, as a call suddenly came in through his radio. 'Could we rain check?'

'Sure,' she agreed, mentally calming herself down.

'Looking forward to it.' PC Jared Jones squeezed her hand, and was off. Emmy turned and looked up the hill, then decided to take a trek up on her own. She didn't need Jared there holding her hand any more; she knew that, deep down in her heart.

It was a nice added extra, though.

Back at the house later on, Emmy found Rae directing an electrician around the living room, pointing out where he should place the spotlights, and Noelle talking to the floor.

She shook out her hair and hung her jacket by the front door. Waving at Rae, she walked over to Noelle and crouched next to her. 'Whatcha doing?'

Noelle looked up and moved to the side. 'Meet our new lodger, Big Daddy!'

Emmy screamed and fell backwards, shuffling away on her bum like the next victim in a horror movie.

The electrician looked over lazily, but Rae waved her hand and commanded his attention back to the ceiling.

'Don't be afraid,' Noelle said, smiling at the absolutely huge spider on the skirting board. 'He only has seven legs and he doesn't like the rain. He won't hurt you.'

'Because I'll die instantly from his bite?'

'He won't bite you.'

'Please can you just put him outside?'

'He doesn't really get on with Vicky . . .'

'He doesn't get on with your own flesh and blood either. Please, Noey? Vicky can come and stay inside while it's raining instead.'

Noelle hopped up and scooped her hands around Big Daddy. 'Deal.'

Emmy gave her a wide berth and went upstairs to change into some drier clothes. She was midway through pulling on her sweatpants when the bedroom door swung open.

'Nice cat knickers,' Rae hooted after getting an eyeful. She came in and sat on Emmy's bed and watched her finish dressing.

In walked Noelle, holding Vicky, and the two of them sat on the bed also. 'I can't leave her downstairs while the electrician's here, I don't think she likes boys.'

'Like mother, like daughter,' Rae smirked.

'Nice cat socks, Em.'

'I miss living alone,' Emmy sighed.

Rae clapped her hands, causing Vicky to flutter her wings and jump down off Noelle's lap. 'So, I've had an idea.'

'No,' said Emmy and Noelle in unison.

'Hey!'

Emmy shook her head. 'A Rae Lake idea is never a good idea.'

'That is not true! Name one bad idea.'

Noelle piped up first. 'Fun! Okay, how about the time you tried to build one of those bedsheets-rope things to climb out of your bedroom window with, and made me go first and I fell?'

'You only fell on to the conservatory roof, you hardly had an Emmy situation, and thanks to that we then knew it was solid enough for us to walk on.'

Emmy joined in. 'What about your idea for us to sell bunches of wildflowers at the end of the road to passing cars and someone reported "gypsy kids" to the police?'

'I was just trying to make you some pocket money, Jesus.'

'How about—'

'All right, all right,' Rae cried. 'This one is a good idea, trust me.'

*Trust me, she says!* Emmy rolled her eyes at Vicky Chicken who was pecking at the eyeballs of a discarded My Little Pony.

'What month is it?' Rae asked, setting the scene.

Noelle knew this one. 'October.'

'And what happens in October?'

'*The Walking Dead* starts up again?' guessed Emmy.

'Christmas TV adverts start?'

'*Halloween*, for god's sake,' said Rae. 'So I was thinking … We're going to have a party!'

'What?' said Emmy.

'When?' asked Noelle.

'Halloween. We're going to throw Maplewood a Halloween party.'

Emmy was completely bemused. 'Who would come to a party at our house? Jared, Gabbi, Jenny, and … ? Did you forget that everyone here hates us?'

'We'd invite everyone – especially the people that hate us. Don't you want them to see another side to us, finally?'

'By having them snoop around our house? No! I don't care if they never see any side of us, in a few more weeks we'll be done with this place.'

'Emmy, you're never "done" with this place, don't you realise that?'

Emmy blinked at Rae. 'What does that mean?'

'You carry around your childhood growing up here like it's a sack full of stones. Like it defines everything about you even though you refuse to look at it.'

'I do not.'

'Actually, you do, Rae and I talk about it all the time,' Noelle added.

'You do not! Do you?'

Rae continued, 'You're so broken about how living here made you feel about yourself, but I want you to literally face your demons by partying with them. Don't you think the teenage Emmy would have loved to have hosted a party?'

'Absolutely not! It would have terrified her and probably made her miss *Doctor Who*. And what's all this "you need to get over it, you're so broken" stuff – you've been stomping around since you got back, wanting to pick a fight with anyone that gives you a turned-up nose.' Of all people, it stung to have her sister be so flippant about her feelings.

'You're right,' Rae shrugged, and Emmy was taken aback. 'I need to get over it too. When I'm angry and stomping around it's only hurting me, not anyone else. I'm pretty chill when I'm at home. And a lot of that is Finn, but a lot of it is because a group of small-minded people from a small market town don't even cross my mind. Look, it's not fair and it's not right that we would be the ones holding out the olive branch, but let's just do it. Let's show them all they're wrong and then get on with our lives.'

Emmy was quiet for a long time, watching Vicky and making snorty little huffs through her nose while she thought. Rae and Noelle stayed silent, letting her work through the shooting stars of emotions.

Eventually, she said, 'Isn't it more waving the white flag than offering the olive branch?'

'Surrendering?' Noelle clarified. 'No, I don't think so. I think what Rae's suggesting isn't giving in. Giving in would be leaving, running away or going back to hiding ourselves away from the town centre any time we come and visit Mum. This is just growing up, I guess.'

Rae nodded, watching Emmy closely. A few more snorts, but she was relenting. 'The carpets won't be down until afterwards, so we wouldn't need to worry about spillage,' Rae coaxed.

'So we'd be telling people it was a proper Halloween party? With decorations?'

'Oooooooo!' With that, Noelle was on board.

'All the decorations you want,' agreed Rae.

'And costumes? Would people dress up?'

'We can certainly put it on the invite.'

'Would we dress up?'

Uh-oh, Rae saw where this was going. She internally struggled for a few seconds before relenting. Rae had never given in to this request in the past, but if this was what it was going to take. 'Yes, we can dress up as the three Sanderson sisters from *Hocus Pocus*.'

'You can't come? Oh balls.'

Rae was on the phone to Finn later that night, talking quietly so she didn't disturb her sisters. She leaned against her bedroom window watching the silhouettes of the trees swaying in the gusty wind.

'I'm so sorry,' Finn said, his voice sad. He sounded genuinely gutted. 'I really wanted to make it down next weekend but this project is overrunning like nobody's business. Believe me, I would much rather be with you. I miss being with you.'

'I miss it too.' She too was gutted. She missed her

husband and had been counting down the days to seeing him at the midway point. 'Don't forget me up there, will you?'

'As if I ever would. I'll be down as soon as I can.'

'Do you think you'll make it here for the Halloween party?'

'I hope so. That's what, two and a half weeks away? Hopefully I can come down for that, stay a couple of days, then bring you back with me for your show.'

'Then I'll just have to come back here for about one more week, and it should all be over!' Looking around her room it was hard to believe that would be possible. The purple and silver were still there, though the window was new. Her belongings had depleted, but not disappeared. But they would get there.

She left the window and snuggled under her duvet. She needed some non-Maplewood conversation for a while. She loved her sisters, she liked reconnecting with Gabbi, but she missed her home – the home where her heart was, with Finn. 'Tell me about work,' she said, and closed her eyes, ready to hear his soft, melodic voice. 'Tell me about everything you've been doing, and make sure it sounds dull so I know you've missed me.'

# Chapter 15

'Does anyone mind if I take the morning off?' Noelle asked over breakfast the next day. 'I want to go and meet Jenny for a coffee.'

'You go, girl,' Emmy nodded through a mouthful of cereal. 'That's not cool from my lips. You go for it. You won't be able to do much to the outside of the house in this weather, and I think we're running to pretty good time inside.' The rain had finally stopped, though the decking and grounds squelched underfoot, and a low mist hung over the woods, enveloping their house.

'Actually, I was going to chuff off for a couple of hours too, if you don't mind,' Rae said. 'Gabbi's working at home this morning so asked if I fancied coming over for more of a catch-up now her niece has gone home.'

'Fine, fine, leave me to do all the hard work,' Emmy

joked. But once they were out the door, Emmy found herself unmotivated. She wandered from room to room, looking at what needed to be done and then sauntering away again. During her third trip back to the living room, she realised what the problem was.

She'd never spent time alone in the house since moving away.

'I'm on my own,' she said aloud to the living room. Her words echoed against the walls, which were bare of the usual furniture. It had all been pushed into the middle instead, and covered in sheets, except for the sofa and chairs which were uncovered so the girls could still climb over and sit on them during the evenings. 'Hello,' she said, her voice sounding alien.

When she was alone in her house in Harwell, it was rare for Emmy to talk to herself. Not unheard of, but rare.

All of a sudden, she imagined her mum, and wondered if she ever talked to herself. Did she ever talk to Emmy's dad?

'Dad?' she tried, barely above a whisper.

Nothing happened.

*Face your demons*, she told herself, and then said aloud, 'Sorry, Dad, not calling *you* a demon.'

Emmy went over to her dad's chair and climbed in. She sat for a while prodding the arm rest. She cleared her throat and spoke again, pushing away the feelings of silliness; she needed to stop caring so much about what other people thought about her actions, especially when there weren't even any people in the room.

'Dad, sorry I didn't come and visit more. I hope you ...' She took a pause to collect her thoughts, and a couple of small tears dropped on to the worn leather of the seat. 'I hope you know you were a really lovely dad.' And with that, she cried for a while, unexpectedly, unashamedly.

'Thanks for meeting me,' Noelle said, overly chirpy, as if she were afraid Jenny would have reverted back to anger.

'Thanks for the invite. I haven't been out for coffee for what feels like ages.' Jenny beamed, putting Noelle's mind at rest.

Bonnie wandered over with a 'Hiyaaaaaaa! Girls' day out, love it. What can I get you?'

'Cappuccino for me, please,' Jenny requested.

'I'll have a mocha, and maybe some of that brownie. No, the shortbread. No, the brownie.'

'I'm gonna bring you both.' Bonnie sat down on the arm of Noelle's chair. She spoke through the side of her mouth. 'Did you guys, like, think about the whole article thing at all?'

'I'm sorry, we haven't spoken about it yet. I'll talk to my sisters when I get back later.'

Bonnie nodded. 'I am low-key so excited that you're even considering it. Guess who came in yesterday.'

Their order wasn't going to be coming any time soon.

'Who?' Noelle asked.

'Maisie Bradleigh.'

Noelle looked blank, as did Jenny.

'Like, Tom Bradleigh's wife. She was in your sister Rae's year at school.'

'Right . . . '

'So she was in here talking about Emmy, and that she's hooked up with PC Jones since she's been back! Swipe. Right.'

This girl spoke another language. 'Maisie was telling you this?'

'Nup, I was eavesdropping while cleaning tables. I am, like, *so good* at eavesdropping.'

'Well, no, Emmy and Jared – PC Jones – were childhood besties. They're not hooking up, they're just hanging out.'

'Gotcha. Sips tea!' Bonnie mimicked holding a teacup with a pinkie out. 'I'll get you those coffees 'n' stuff.'

When she'd left, Jenny looked at Noelle and laughed. 'So that girl knows a lot about your lives.'

'Oh yes, apparently she's a "big fan" of all things creepy and paranormal. Enter: the Maplewood House in the Woods. And by default: us.'

'You are causing a stir in the town. The amount of people who've said to me, "Did you know Noelle and her sisters are back?"'

Noelle couldn't understand it. They were the girls people loved to pretend didn't exist – the stain on the community. If they hid away, as they'd done for the past decade, they were forgotten, like a mark on a sofa cushion that had been turned upside down. But if they showed their faces they got filthy looks, gossipy assumptions, name calling (and not just from the school kids). 'People love a bad guy to blame things on I guess.'

'You're hardly the bad guys.'

'We were the misfits whose parents were hippies. Me coming out hardly did me any favours, when the odds were already stacked against us.' Noelle shrugged, then straightened up and smiled at her first love. 'As far as I'm concerned, it's all in the past. The bullies can't touch me now, I am untouchable. But I don't want to talk about me and my family – my whole life revolves around me and my family at the moment. I want to talk about you. I've missed so much and it's selfish of me, I know, but there's a Jenny-shaped knowledge gap I really want to fill.'

'What do you want to know?' Jenny smiled at Bonnie as she brought over their coffees and Noelle watched her face closely. Being back beside Jenny was unreal. She was a stranger now in so many ways, so Noelle couldn't claim to still be in love with her. But her hand itched to reach out and wipe the coffee foam from the strand of Jenny's hair like it was her own, and her natural desire to make contact had to be put in check.

Noelle swallowed, finding her words. 'What do you do now?'

'I own a homeware shop here in town. It's called Sunshine Life. Come on in, if you need anything decorative for the big refurb!'

'You own that place? It's gorgeous. I saw the things in the window, you know the things . . . with the dangly things?' Noelle hadn't made it inside yet, but she wanted to. There were a few places that had popped up in town that didn't used to be there. Maybe she should be focusing more on the new, and out with the old. 'And do you still live out by the river?'

'I live above the shop, actually. Sometimes I feel like I'm spending too much time there because my home is decorated with all the excess stock, so I need to get out whenever I can! Mum and Dad still live out there though. That's where I saw you in the car.'

Noelle stirred at her mocha, the chocolate flakes marbling with the dark coffee. 'And do you live with anyone?'

'No,' Jenny answered. Noelle looked up to find Jenny looking at her with a pained expression. 'I don't want to cross a line here; I'm glad we're back in touch and I'd actually really like to have you back in my life again in some way. But I need you to know I haven't been waiting for you, like a spinster Miss Havisham.'

'Oh, I didn't think—'

'Maybe you didn't think that at all, but I just wanted us to be on the same page. I have a really good life here. I rebuilt the relationship with my parents, Maplewood has actually become a lot more accepting and is a nice place to live. Mayor Reynold has done a great job on the town, which surprised a lot of people. And I know some of the townsfolk are going through some kind of an odd regression with you three being back, but it's just the novelty, it'll die away.' Jenny paused to study Noelle's face. 'My point is that I didn't decide to stay because I was waiting for you. I'm not *not* with someone at the moment because I was waiting for you. This is *my* life.'

Noelle felt herself well up a little. She remained looking down, blinking often, until the feeling had subsided and she looked up. 'I'm so happy to hear you say that,' she answered, and she meant it. 'All I've wanted is for you to be happy, and you are. I would love to get back to being your friend again, but if that ever takes away even a little bit of your happiness, I'll back right off.'

Jenny smiled back at her. They were going to be okay. A moment later she said, 'I see Willow sometimes, you know.'

'You do? No, I didn't know.'

'I asked her not to tell you, but I always thought she might have anyway. Your mum has always been so kind to me. I hope you don't mind us staying in touch. I didn't want you to know because in truth I didn't want to give you the satisfaction of thinking I was stalking you or something.'

Noelle laughed, and they ordered a couple more coffees – a good sign that they were okay to settle in for more getting to know each other. 'That's fair enough. I'm surprised she hadn't told me though, she's not great at keeping secrets.' As soon as she said it though, Noelle wondered to herself, *or is she*?

Over in the Poshville side of town, Rae was wandering about Gabbi's living room looking at all the paintings. 'Was it nice to have your niece over to stay?'

'Yeah, it was lovely,' Gabbi said in a very unconvincing tone.

Rae raised her eyebrows.

'It *was* lovely, I like her a lot and she's a really easy-going kid. But bloody hell it made me feel grown-up.'

'You run a town!' Rae said.

'Yeah, but this felt worse than that. It was like the old me wanted to leg it from the responsibility.'

Rae could understand that. She wasn't ready for kids either, and maybe she would never be. 'So you were just given all of these?' She looked back at the paintings.

'Yep, some of them are gross aren't they? I love the one of the Dartmoor ponies though, that's cute. Do you want to take any for your house? Just kidding, I probably shouldn't give them away.'

'Talking about the house, guess what we're planning for a couple of weeks' time?' She sat back down on the uncomfortable sofa and commanded Gabbi's attention away from her paperwork.

'An unveiling?'

'No, not an unveiling. What, are you going to come and cut the ribbon? A party!'

'Oh! Really? At your house?'

'Yes, a Halloween party.'

'Is this like a small housewarming that happens to fall on Halloween?'

'No, Gab, a proper Halloween party, with decorations and scary pop-up skeletons, and everyone has to dress up. We're going to invite the whole town – well, some of the town – because what's a better cure for hostility than laughter and alcohol?'

Gabbi was watching her in the amused way she probably watched her niece when she was playing make-believe. 'What?' Rae demanded.

'Tell me again why you're doing this?'

'To make people see that we aren't who they think we are. Instead, we are awesome.'

The mayor nodded. 'Let me ask you this. How is a Halloween party going to prove to everyone you *aren't* party animals and you *don't* live in a haunted house and you *didn't* grow up as witches?'

Dammit. She had a really very good point. 'All right, Debbie Downer, no wonder you're the mayor,' Rae said, stumped. 'No, wait, this is still a good idea. We'll be making light of it all, showing them how silly they've been. Perhaps we'll go a little easier than I was planning on the decorations, let them see that it's a beautiful house on the inside, not a dingy, grimy ghetto like they've built up in their heads. Yes, it shall be a classy Halloween party.'

'That makes a little more sense,' agreed Gabbi.

'You're coming, of course.'

But Gabbi shook her head. 'I can't, I think it would look bad if I attended a private event like this.'

'But it's going to be classy!'

'And as mayor, I can't tell you how much I enjoy a tasteful event,' she smiled sweetly before rolling her eyes. 'I know that makes me sound like a bitch, and thank you so much for the invite, but I just really can't. Jesus, I tell you, Rae. Sometimes all I want to do is go over to one of the parties the school kids are having and go absolutely wild. I want to drink all their booze, smash up a road sign, dance on a table. I'm bored of canapés and wearing suits to "soirées". I want to wear a fucking miniskirt. And have my tits out. Not for any boys, for *me*.'

Rae sat back, a huge smile on her face. 'Gabbiiiiii, welcome back!'

Gabbi composed herself. 'But that's not going to happen. Not here in Maplewood anyway, and not if I want my political career to continue. Maybe one day you and I could go out in London, incognito, but for now, I wish you a very pleasant Halloween party; I shall be handing out little bags of sweets to the trick-or-treaters, and anti-littering leaflets to their parents.'

'Fine.' Rae stood up and gave her old friend a hug. 'I'll drink a snake bite for you.'

'Be sure that you do.'

'I'd better leave you to it for now and get back to my manual labour. Catch up again soon?'

'Definitely.'

As Rae was leaving the house and walking down the driveway, she turned back, and looking out of the window at her was Gabbi. When she caught Rae's eye she waved, and then mimicked dancing on a table, holding a cigarette in one hand and her boob in the other. Rae laughed, and then crossed paths with a very surprised-looking postman.

It felt like hours that Noelle and Jenny chatted over coffee. Talking to her was easy, despite everything, and Noelle wondered more than once at how on the same page her head and her heart were.

They left The Wooden Café and paused outside to say goodbye.

'I know I keep saying it,' started Noelle. 'But it's really nice to be spending time with you again, J.'

'Just nice?' Jenny asked, and Noelle's heart did a small bounce. Was that flirting?

'More than nice. Really very extremely good, actually.'

'Well, I thought so too,' she agreed. 'But don't get any ideas.'

'I won't,' Noelle answered. *Too late.* Noelle's intention wasn't to start up anything with Jenny again, it was too complicated, they were too out of touch. But she missed everything about her. She wondered briefly if it would be cute or weird to learn the Bieber 'Sorry' dance routine to try and win her back . . . 'Can I see you again? As friends?'

Jenny tossed her hair back as she laughed. 'What am I getting myself into? Yes, that would be nice. As friends. I'll come over and help with some renovations on my days off, if you like.'

'I would like that!'

Jenny left towards her shop, while Noelle walked the other way to meet her sister. If she'd told herself a few weeks back that she would be here under the autumn sun, smiling and flirting with her first love, she would have laughed herself out of her courtroom.

Rae waited for Noelle outside the nicer sweetshop, where she'd stocked up on some nibbles to help get them through the last of the bedroom clear-outs, which they *really* needed to get on with.

The centre of Maplewood was preparing for Halloween, in the understated way a rural market town in

England does. Pumpkins carved into grizzly grinning faces were popping up on doorsteps and windowsills, and cut-outs of black cats and witches decorated windows. As Rae stood there admiring the scene, Kelvin wandered past. He stopped and grinned at her. 'Still here, Rae?' he asked, unnecessarily.

'I could say the same to you,' she answered. She looked at his chubby head and sweaty body. He really hadn't blossomed, this one.

'I've got a joke for you, right. How long does it take three hippies to paint a house? Dunno? Go and visit the Lake sisters in a year or so and they'll tell you!' He guffawed.

Rae stepped back to avoid being showered with spit. 'You should really spend more time looking at your own life than looking at ours. It's kind of weird.'

'It was just a joke, man, chill out.'

'I'm very chill, man. I just think you're kind of obsessed. Why do you even care what we're doing?'

'I dunno, maybe because we're buds.' He looked at her like she was a right thicko.

She was shocked. 'We were never buds.'

'We were buds with everyone.'

'You were popular, and people worshipped or feared you. Did you think you were everyone's friend, though?'

'Yeah, course.'

'But you tortured people. Me and my sisters, to name a few.'

'It was a joke. God, are you on your period or something?'

Rae threw her hands in the air. 'I'm not on my period, I'm just trying to have a conversation with you. Do you even realise you were a massive, dick-for-brains bully?'

'Shut up was I.' Kelvin was clearly getting uncomfortable now and he started to walk away. 'I wasn't a bully. You're the bully. Bitch.' He walked off grumbling.

But it was a good thing. Rae realised you can't win them all. And while she wanted the Halloween party to mend some fences and maybe even make this a nicer place for her mum to live, going forward, she realised she didn't have to bow down to the bullies. Kelvin and Tom did not need an invite.

# Chapter 16

Back at the house, Jared was lying on his back at the edge of Rae's room, a block of wood wrapped in sandpaper in his hand, and flecks of silver paint from the skirting boards settling like dust on the carpet, his clothes and his face. On the other side of the room, Emmy was sanding the door frame.

'So you never knew your parents were Wiccans at all?' he asked.

'Nope. Hippies, yes. "Earthy", yes. But to us they were always just grown-up versions of Noelle.' She paused to mop her brow before she sweated dust into her contacts. 'I did think they might be naturists though. I never saw them in the nude, unlike poor Noelle, but I always thought they both seemed very sun-kissed all the time, and I never saw any noticeable tan lines.'

Emmy had invited Jared over after her impromptu crying session. Being alone in this version of home didn't seem to do her any good, and, anyway, she wanted to get his thoughts on the Halloween party. Plus, he'd helped out when they'd all painted their rooms these garish colours, all those years ago, so it seemed only fair he helped them slick on the twelve coats it would take to cover them up. Plus, he was yum. She might have mentioned that?

She left the door frame partially done and joined him, slumping down to sit on the floor beside him and brushing the silver out of his hair. She caught herself midway through, still surprised at how comfortable she felt doing such an intimate thing with Jared after all these years. He was still part of her, that was cemented.

Emmy was lying to herself, though she really didn't want to admit that she was wrong and that she was excited about something Maplewood had to offer. She was trying to play it cool, trying to focus on the job at hand, because she Wasn't Here For Fun. But a fraction of her mind couldn't stop thinking about Jared.

'I have to ask you something.' She pulled her hand away, and he sat up, cross-legged next to her. *Focus*. 'If we had a Halloween party, here, and invited all these people that are apparently gossiping about us, to try and bury the hatchet, would you think it was a good idea?'

'You're having a party? Willow's going to be mad . . . '

'I know, but Mum is the least of my worries right now. So, what do you think, and would you come?'

Jared leaned his heavy body against hers and thought about it. 'I don't think lying low is going to resolve anything. On the battlefield – Maplewood being your battlefield – there are only three ways to win the war. One: going into hiding and waiting for it to be over. And that's not really winning, plus how will you ever know for sure it's over? Two: surrendering. And you'd be disappointed in yourselves if you did that, because it's letting them win. Or three: calling a truce. In the form of a Halloween party.'

'So you think it's a good idea?'

'I do.'

'What about actually winning? Couldn't we do that instead?'

'I think calling a truce is winning, in this particular war. Because it's not actually a war, and your mum's going to be still living here, as is everyone else, even though you'll be leaving again.'

Emmy sighed and met Jared's eye, who pouted at her.

'Do you have to leave again?' he asked. 'I don't have any other friends.'

She shoved him. 'That's not true, you have lots of friends, you always did. You don't need me any more.'

'You're right, you suck at Sonic the Hedgehog anyway, from what I remember, so why would I need you?'

'Will you come, then, on Halloween?'

'I wouldn't miss it. I don't know how wild you're planning it to be, but I'll have to head home early-ish, or at least not drink. I have an early shift the next morning.'

'Okay. Will you dress up?'

'As what?'

'Anything you like. We're going as the witch sisters from *Hocus Pocus*.' Emmy of now and Emmy of the past were equally excited about this.

'How appropriate. Could I go as a cop? Then I could just sleep in my clothes and go straight to work.'

'I'm sure that would please a lot of the female guests,' Emmy smiled, getting up to resume work. 'I'm so glad you're going to come along,' she added.

'Me too.' He grinned at her, lying back down on the floor. 'Wow, a Halloween party at the house in the woods. I hear that place is haunted.'

When Rae and Noelle arrived home, they came bearing lunch, and to the delight of Jared they had enough for everyone.

Over pasties and pastries, the four of them sat facing the laptop, ready to make the party guest list.

'How do we actually invite people,' asked Emmy. 'Are we going to post invitations to their houses? Email them?'

'No, thicko, we'll just do it all through Facebook, we'll set up an event.' Rae pulled the laptop towards her and started tapping on the keys.

'Nooooo, no, no, no,' Emmy cried. 'I've seen the news, I know how out of hand those Facebook parties get. I read that one kid had forty thousand people descend on his home because he put it on Facebook.'

'We're not going to make it free for all, it'll be a closed, invite-only event. And we'll be the only ones allowed to invite people. Relax, dork.'

'You are full of the name-calling today, moron,' Emmy retorted.

'Ahh, the serene sounds of the Lake sisters,' commented Jared, closing his eyes as if it was the most relaxing thing in the world.

Rae flipped open Noelle's legal pad and started writing. 'So thus far we know we're asking you, Jared, Jenny, I've asked Gabbi and she's a no, but I'm going to put her on the list anyway … Bloody hell, who else? Annette?'

'I have an idea!' Noelle piped up. 'Let's look at that

Facebook page Bonnie showed us, about our house being haunted.'

'We're kind of in the middle of something . . . ' said Rae.

'I mean to find people to invite. Let's look at who's liked the page, and if we see familiar names – people that we once knew – we then see if their profiles say they still live here, and if so, boom. Added to the guest list.'

'Do you really want a bunch of wannabe paranormal investigators in your home?' Jared asked.

'I think if it's people we know they're more likely to be the Nosey Noras than the ghost-hunters,' she replied.

'All right, let's take a look.' Rae navigated to the page and the list of people that had liked it. 'There's a few names I remember, but not many . . . some faces though. I guess some of them have married and changed their names.' She let out a whopping sigh. 'I feel like I'm trying to organise a high-school reunion, only I don't remember any of the people from high school.'

'I remember some of them,' Emmy said, leaning closer. 'Those two girls were the ones that tried to form a girl group and they held auditions in the sports hall. I so, *so* wanted to go, but I would have been laughed right out of there.'

'Well, they didn't make it big and it seems that

one, Becky, is still living here in Maplewood. She's on the list.'

'Look at that comment, under the photo.' Noelle pointed at the screen. She read aloud, '"I was in the same school year as one of the kids that lived in this house. They were WEIRD. When their parents came to parents' evening it was like the Addams Family had walked in." That's not true, we weren't Goths, apart from Rae for a period.'

'That comment had twenty-six likes,' said Rae.

Noelle continued, 'The reply has thirty. "Yes! My mum was always telling me to stay away from that end of town! I grew up afraid of the woods because of them."'

'Good,' Rae stated, adding the names to the list. 'We wouldn't have wanted people with no balls hanging around anyway.'

Noelle sank down on to her hands. 'I knew we were unpopular, but I thought it was because we were eccentric and they thought Rae was always causing trouble, and because I was gay. I didn't know everybody thought we were *creepy*. We weren't creepy. We were actually really nice.'

'Let's not lose focus,' Rae said, rounding up her sisters. 'There seems to be a million intertwined reasons Maplewood didn't give us a fair shot. Now we're going to reclaim our place here and show them what a beautiful, welcoming, bright and not-at-all-creepy house this is. Aside from a few Halloween decorations. And we will be so nice and so charming that they're going to hate themselves for the lost years where they could have been our friends and made the most of our bomb-ass woods. Ain't that right, Jared?'

'Word.'

By mid-afternoon, with the help of Jared – who actually was in the know about who in the town would benefit from a wake-up call in the form of a party – the guest list was sorted. The Facebook party invite was set up, and with a flourish, the three sisters laid their fingers atop each other and hit ENTER.

Now all they could do was wait, and see if the least popular kids around would have anyone agree to come to their party.

Another week of frantic decorating passed and the house was really starting to take shape. Noelle was doing a great job on the outside, when the weather permitted, and the entire exterior was now painted a bright cream, which was pretty against the woodland backdrop. And Noelle had only had one major incident where she'd had to peel Vicky off the side of the building when she'd brushed up against the wet paint, but a gentle bath and some baby shampoo and she was back clucking about outside in no time.

The porch was built and varnished and the older windows were sparkling clean (at least from the outside). Noelle just had to tackle the driveway, so that it actually looked like a driveway to unsuspecting visitors, rather than a path to nowhere, and do a little plant pruning, lawn mowing and general prettying around the garden.

Inside the house, a transformation was also occurring. The kitchen and living room did, Emmy reluctantly agreed, flow better without the big heavy door that had separated them. And thanks to the electrician who'd called his plumber pal over to 'whack in an extra radiator', the house was toasty-ish. The spotlights were looking good and the paintwork was all complete. Now all that was left to do was rip up the old carpets, build the window seat, take delivery of some new furniture, and finish the Grand Clear-Out, which at the moment felt like it had barely started. Instead, boxes and piles and memorabilia and crap were just being shunted out of the way in every room.

They had a week before the party, and Rae, Noelle and Emmy had tasked themselves with tackling the last of the crap in Rae's room first, since the twin beds were arriving the next day.

They sat on the floor, drinks and snacks beside them, and as they picked through boxes of paperwork and dusty Alanis Morissette albums, they entertained themselves with Truth or Dare. Rae's idea.

'Okay, Noey,' Emmy said, picking up a dead cat – oh, no, it was a monster-foot slipper that was covered in dust and something syrupy. She gagged and chucked it in the bin liner. 'Truth or dare?'

'Truth,' she answered with a smile. Noelle loved telling the truth.

'Did you ever lie in court so you could win a case, because you knew the environment would be better because of it?'

'No!' Noelle gasped, then thought. 'But I have omitted information because I knew it would really muddle things. Rae, your turn.'

'Dare.'

'Ooo, okay.' After a long period of Noelle staring into space while the others just cracked on, she suddenly snapped her fingers. 'I dare you to hair-mascara your hair and wear it that way for the rest of the day.'

'Easy,' scoffed Rae. 'Just call me Harley Quinn.' She pulled her hair into bunches and grabbed some very crusty hair mascaras from the shoebox of old make-up and slicked red on one side and blue on the other.

*Dammit*, thought Emmy, she still looked good.

Rae turned, triumphant, onwards. 'Emmy, truth or dare?'

'Truth, please, maybe.'

'Do you ever wish you'd kissed Jared?'

Emmy rolled her eyes. 'This is like déjà vu, you used to ask me this every time you made us play Truth or Dare.'

'And you always lied, so now I want the truth.'

'What makes you think I was lying?'

'Because when you lie you blush and your eyes start stinging and you have to take your glasses off or your contacts out and rub them for about ten minutes.'

'No, I don't wish I'd kissed Jared,' Emmy replied. Her eye started to twitch.

'It's happening, it's happening,' pointed Noelle with happiness.

'Fine, fine, *fine*, yes, I wish we'd kissed.' Her sisters whooped their heads off, but when she managed to get them to calm down she added, 'But not because I fancied him, because it would have been nice to know what a kiss felt like, not just from my Mark Owen poster.'

Noelle went back to looking through Rae's old school work, satisfied. 'That's fair enough.'

Rae however, had turned to face away and was mimicking snogging someone with their hands all over her back while she moaned, *'Mmm, Jared, I love your wet-look gel.'*

'Shut up.' Emmy grabbed a tub of body glitter from the shoebox and threw it at her older sister.

'Ow.' Rae stopped and picked it up. 'I don't know why this is in here, this must be yours. Body glitter was so not my thing. Noelle's turn again!'

Emmy held up a hand. 'Let's switch who asks who this time.'

'Can I ask Emmy one?' Noelle grinned.

'I just went! But, fine, let's get this over with. Dare this time though, because I'm not using a dare on Rae's turn asking.'

'Hmm . . . I had a truth in mind, but okay, a dare . . .' Noelle went back to staring into space.

Emmy could handle putting on hair mascara or something similar, this was going to be a breeze. Until . . .

'Oh, I don't know,' Noelle shrugged. 'I dare you to kiss Jared at the Halloween party.'

'No!' she cried.

'YES!' yelled Rae.

'You can't pre-date a dare!'

Rae jumped in. 'Of course you can, and you have to try now. Bravo, Noelle, I didn't know you had it in you.'

'But it's not going to be a kissing type of party, we're not in school.'

'As if you ever kissed anyone at a school party.'

'Thanks for that, Rae. Besides, he's not planning to even drink because he's got a really early shift on the first of November, and he doesn't even fancy me any more.' *That's right, bitches*, thought Emmy, and her chest swelled with smug pride. *Oh, Emmy, you sex goddess.*

'WHOA. He doesn't fancy you *any more*? Where did that come from? Did you and Jared already have a "thing"? Did you already bump your nerdy uglies together?' Rae was practically drooling.

'No, didn't I tell you?' Emmy preened a little.

'Tell us what.'

'I thought I told you ... what Jared said to me ...' She preened a little more. It wasn't often she was the one with any juice to share.

'I'm going to kick you in the fanny if you don't hurry up and spill,' Rae said kindly.

'He might have told me he used to have a bit of a crush on me, once upon a time.'

'Really?' Noelle beamed and tilted her head and went all soppy-Disney-princess.

'*Really?*' Rae burst with incredulousness. 'I mean: cool, really?'

'Yes, really. He said he never said anything because he thought I knew and wasn't interested. I, girls, had a secret admirer.'

'He fancied *you*,' Rae said, in the way really only sisters can talk to each other. 'I'm not being a cow, but you weren't ... Whatever, I'm happy for you. I always knew you were awesome and actually quite funny, I just didn't realise there were other people outside our own four walls that realised that too.'

Emmy made a face at her and then leant back on her hands. 'Hey, I have a truth question for the room. Does anyone feel sad about what we're doing?'

'Sad?' asked Noelle.

'Sad in a sentimental way. Because we're stripping our family home of, well, our family.'

'Hmm.' Noelle thought for a moment. 'Well, now I do. But it'll still be ours, just a bit scrubbed clean.'

'The house is growing up,' Rae said. 'Just like us. How about you?' she asked Emmy back.

'Nope,' she said with a shrug.

'Nothing melting those icy walls around your teenage heart yet?' Rae teased.

'Nothing.' Then she remembered her outburst last week when she was alone, when she'd climbed into her dad's chair. But she'd just been tired and overworked, and outside her comfort zone. The icy walls were intact, thank you very much.

Emmy's eyelid twitched.

# Chapter 17

'Emmy? Noelle?' Rae called for her sisters from where she was sat on the living-room floor trying to figure out how to build a window seat. Emmy came down the stairs and Noelle and Jenny came in off the porch where they had been flirting like teenagers whilst putting together some flat-pack furniture bought at Jenny's shop.

'You hollered?' Emmy asked.

'Check this out.' She moved to the side, and under the window, where she'd ripped up the carpet, was a huge mural of a circle with a crescent shape on either side.

'What's that supposed to be? A boiled sweet in a wrapper?' Emmy tilted her head.

'Is it a crab?' asked Noelle. Jenny squinted beside her.

'No, I googled it,' Rae said. 'It's a triple moon – a Wiccan symbol called the Triple Goddess. Apparently, it represents the maiden, the mother and the crone.'

'Hey, it's like the three of us!' cried Emmy. 'Noelle's the sweet flower-girl maiden, Rae thinks she's our mother and – oh.'

'You're the crone!' squawked Rae.

'I think this is kind of cool,' said Noelle, crouching down and running her hand over the age-old paintwork. 'This should be the pattern we use for Mum's stained-glass window.'

'That's a really good idea, actually,' Emmy said.

Rae looked up. 'You know what I've been thinking? It's pretty clear that Mum and Dad were indeed into all this stuff, and good for them. But how did they go from having the town storm their house in the night with burning pitchforks, to Mum being feared enough for people to keep a respectful distance?'

'Jenny.' Noelle turned. 'Do you know, as someone who lives here full-time?'

Jenny shrugged. 'I don't know. For as long as I can remember, people have been that way around your mum. So any change in the weather must have happened before I came along. Maybe before you all came along.'

Hmm. That was something for the sisters to think about.

'Something else I want to know,' added Emmy, 'is exactly what everyone thinks is so creepy about this house?'

'Welcome to Creepy History 101 with me, Professor Bonn-izzle!' Bonnie stood by the living-room fireplace, facing the sisters.

'Thanks for coming, Bonnie,' Emmy said, wondering what they'd got themselves into. But this girl had already done all the research, so who better to fill in the blanks? Well, who better on short notice, when this was really only an excuse to further procrastinate from DIY?

'No problem at all, and you're going to let me put some of this stuff in the article, yeah?'

'Yep. Deal. Maybe we could just read it first, before you submit it, okay?'

'Dealio.' Bonnie addressed them all. 'What makes a house creepy? According to research by . . . me . . . three factors: location, appearance and rumours of weird things. So, for this house, you've got all three boxes ticked. Location-wise, you're in the woods. *Trapped* in the woods. You don't need me to tell you why that's creepy, you're *Blair Witch* era.'

The sisters nodded at each other; she had a point.

Bonnie continued, 'Appearance. This one you're working on, but before now this house has been a little rough around the edges, no offence. And everyone knows a crumbling old house is bound to be full of secrets. And, finally, weird things. It doesn't even have to be ghostly apparitions; literally any weird things can help add to the drama of a creepy house. Your mum and dad were witches or whatever, and that's – rightly or wrongly – been documented in newspapers. Hey presto, badda-bing, you have a creepy house.'

'And people just love a haunted house, I guess?' Noelle added.

'Exactly. Just look at theme parks. I'm telling you, this Halloween party is an awesome idea. Give them a chance to nose around and they'll love it, and suddenly you'll have a hundred new best friends.'

Did they want a hundred best friends? The sisters caught each other's eyes. They had been complaining about not having friends here, but a hundred seemed like a lot of effort.

'Finn can't make it to the party,' Rae said, unable to keep the irritation from her voice. It was the day

236

before Halloween, and he was due to drive down that night.

She walked across the room and flopped down on the sofa next to Noelle, who was looking through a photo album, on a break from building the window seat while Emmy went to the garage for more tools. 'You're always looking at photos of Jenny, why are you so weird and obsessed?'

'Okay,' Noelle said, pushing the photo album aside. 'Wanna talk, Rae?'

'No. This is about a grown-up relationship, not some bloody little high-school romance like you're trying to rekindle.'

Noelle nodded and stood up, moving to the front door. 'Emmy?' she called outside. 'We have a sister-bitch situation occurring in here.'

Rae mumbled something about Noelle telling on her just as Emmy walked back in the house, carrying two hammers. 'Okay, let's defeat the window seat! What's the problem?'

Noelle filled her in. 'Finn can't come to the party, so Rae's taking it out on me.'

'Why are you blaming Noey?'

'I'm not, I just asked why she was obsessing over her ex-girlfriend like some reject from *Ex on the Beach*. Not everything's my fault.' Rae pushed her face into the cushion. She was quite aware she was being a massive cow. She should apologise. Instead, she reached out and knocked a book off the coffee table.

Emmy sat down next to her and smacked her on the bottom. 'Oi. Pack it in. So, Finn isn't coming down to visit?'

Rae knocked a pen on to the floor. Deliberately.

Emmy's voice softened. 'That sucks. I know you were looking forward to seeing him. What happened?'

Rae sat up and sighed. 'He can't get away from work. It's ridiculous. Surely he can get just twenty-four hours off to come and see his wife? What a dick.' She rubbed her face. 'But I know he can't. He wants to, but he can't. I just miss him *a lot*. He's going to try and make it down as soon as possible in the next couple of days.'

Emmy rubbed her sister's back, while she sat miserably for a while.

'I wasn't looking at photos of Jenny, you know,' Noelle said in a quiet voice. Rae looked over at her. 'I was actually looking at photos of us. From an Easter holiday we took to some caravan site up country. Look.' She turned the photo album and there was the whole family posing at the door of the caravan.

It was 1994. Noelle was around the age of six, Emmy eight, and Rae about ten. Noelle and Emmy were in matching pea-green sweatshirts, their big glasses reflecting the flash from the camera. Noelle was in the foreground, a huge grin on her face, holding on to a Barbie doll in a swimming costume, whose hair had been chopped at an angle. Emmy and Rae hung from the door frame, arms wide like they were in a Hollywood musical. Rae wore a Garfield T-shirt tucked into some humongous culottes, her face clean of all the make-up of her future (apart from a cheeky slick of brown lipstick she'd got from the front of a magazine).

Their mum and dad stood behind the girls, only their heads visible in the doorway. They were smiling, like they always were.

Emmy grinned. 'We did take good Easter holidays, didn't we?'

'They were really good. A beach and a caravan, and we were happy as anything,' Noelle agreed.

'We never went very far, you know,' Rae said. 'It felt like we were in the car for hours, but we were only going to Cornwall, Somerset, North Devon, maybe Wales.' She looked at her sisters. 'I don't mean that as a bad thing, I'm not being ungrateful. We had some really good times, even though some other kids were flying off to Disney World or swanning about at a Eurocamp.'

'I kept going on those Easter holidays to the bitter end,' said Emmy. 'Right up until uni. And one year after, since Noey was still going.'

Rae took a deep breath. 'We should do one next year. The three of us, with Mum. Let's just rent a caravan for a week, down in Cornwall somewhere.'

'That sounds really good, actually,' Noelle nodded.

'I'm in too,' said Emmy.

'Then it's sorted. And Noelle, I don't think you're obsessing over Jenny. I think you're actually being quite cool about it all. So sorry for being a huge c-word to you.'

'Thank you.' Noelle reached over for the Magic 8-Ball. 'Should I forgive my sister and stop obsessing over my ex for the rest of the day, so we can plan a total rager of a Halloween party with all our frenemies? ... Oh. "Don't count on it."'

Emmy took the Magic 8-Ball off her sister and put it down with a smile. 'Shut up, ghost of Dad. You just don't want us to throw a party.'

'I can't believe so many people are coming tonight.' Emmy fluttered about, Ashanti blasting out of the stereo that Halloween morning. The sisters were all up at the crack of dawn (though dawn was getting later and later these days) and were scampering about in their PJs touching up bits of paintwork they'd missed, hanging garish orange and black banners in the windows, and googling recipes for blood-coloured punch.

Noelle sauntered past with a witch's broom. 'The response has been great, people seem genuinely excited. Maybe they don't hate us any more after all.'

'Those arseholes are going to be so gutted when they see our house isn't haunted,' Rae said, tying a ghost balloon to a lampshade. 'Like, actually haunted I mean.'

Noelle then pulled a big bag out from the living room. 'I bought loads and loads of fairy lights at the shop, so we can keep things really light and bright and pretty. I was going to go with candles but I thought it was a bit too "Wicca".'

'Thanks for agreeing to this,' said Rae, stopping and pulling them both into an un-Rae-like double hug. 'I really think we're going to move past the pettiness and bury a lot of hatchets with this party. Tomorrow, one: we'll see if Emmy managed to do her dare of kissing Jared, and two: we're going to wake up and, for the first time in Maplewood, feel like grown-ups.'

# Chapter 18

'One, two, three, drink!' Rae commanded. It was past seven. The invite had said seven. Why was no one here yet? Had they never intended to show up? She was rapidly losing her nerve and her patience, so was resorting to Dutch courage. She grabbed the bottle of vodka. 'One more?'

'Rae, they'll be here,' said Noelle, but she accepted another shot anyway.

'Yeah, who shows up at a party on time anyway?' added Emmy. *No really, who does? I genuinely don't know. Should I call someone?* She went to the stereo and restarted the playlist. No point in wasting good Michael Jackson.

Right on cue for the opening wolf howl of 'Thriller', the door opened and in leaned Jared, dressed as a werewolf. He howled in perfect synchronicity. 'What do you think of my costume?' he asked, coming inside.

'Looking good, Jared.' Rae admired his slashed T-shirt and Wolverine-style stuck-on sideburns and fuzzy hands. 'Very *daring*.' She winked at Emmy, who shook her head. 'Out of interest, will you be keeping the fangs in all night?'

'Probably not,' he grinned, showing off the full set. 'It took me a long time to get over my childhood lisp and this is just bringing it back full circle. Are you guys doing shots?'

'Want one?' Emmy asked, tugging at the neckline of her dress, which was determined to keep slipping down and show more cleavage than anyone needed to see. She slid a glass towards Jared, feeling shy under his gaze. '*What?*'

'I was just trying to remember if I've ever seen you in a dress before.'

'Oh, shut up, this isn't *She's All That*. Of course you have. Now drink with us.'

He laughed. 'Okay, but I'm only having a couple tonight.'

'I know, I know, you have to get away early for work tomorrow.' Emmy made a raspberry sound at him. Oops, this vodka was going to her head quickly!

As 'Thriller' turned to 'Bad Blood' they heard a

commotion in the driveway, and moments later in walked Bonnie, followed by several other wide-eyed teens and a large group of the familiar faces from the Maplewood House in the Woods Facebook page.

'Here goes,' whispered Noelle.

'GIRLFRIENDS,' bellowed Bonnie, who was kind of in a bat costume but mainly just a few bits of black fabric. She handed over a fresh hamper from The Wooden Café. 'Thanks for the invite, you have no idea how cool it is to actually spend Halloween in this house. You are legends, and anyone that doesn't think so is a *TWAAAAAAT*.'

The teens behind her whooped in unison. They also seemed to be dressed as bats, or vampires, or cocktail waitresses in a Vegas hotel.

'Ooo,' said Bonnie, clocking the bottle of vodka, before locking eyes with Jared. She moved to the side. 'Ooo . . . *Appletiser*.'

He smiled, then turned back to the sisters. 'So, do you want me to reintroduce you to anybody?' he asked, as a couple more people came stealthily through the door.

'That's okay,' replied Emmy. 'There's no time I shine more than walking up to people that don't like me at parties.'

He squeezed her hand, and off she went, flanked on both sides by her sisters.

'Thanks for coming,' they accidentally said in unison to the haunted house Facebook group.

'Hey girls.' Becky the ex-girl-bander stepped forward and gave Emmy a one-armed hug. 'Cool party. I can't stay long because the kids are at home with their dad but I so wanted to say hi.'

'Did you? Is that why you came?' Rae answered but Emmy dug a fingernail into her arm.

'Of course. Wow, this house is actually really nice inside. You're going to laugh but I always kind of thought it might look a bit like the *Rocky Horror Show* house in here.' She laughed, and the sisters joined in.

'That's so funny,' Rae said through gritted teeth. 'And did you tell everyone that?'

'What? No. Well, just you know, when you're a kid you're always gabbing about something.'

'What would you like to drink?' asked Noelle, leading Becky away.

'It's filling up,' Emmy commented to Rae as they moved on towards another group. 'Do you recognise everybody?'

Rae nodded. 'Most people. This was a good idea, wasn't it?' She faced her sister in a sudden panic. 'We haven't made a massive cock-up? What if they're all like Becky, or what if someone draws on the walls – it took us so long to paint.'

'Rae, you sound like me, calm down. There's no turning back now, and people look happy, not anarchic. And Becky was ... Well, she was tactless and whether she meant to or not she was throwing shade all over the place, *but* she was surprised. She admitted she was wrong. That's what we wanted, no matter how people got there.'

'This is true. We should just have fun. Will you have fun with me tonight?'

Emmy scrunched her nose.

'I'm not talking incest, you bloody weirdo, I'm talking about letting our hair down and having ourselves a party.'

Could she do it? Could Emmy let her hair down for a change? She wondered what that would even look like – but yes, she thought she might be willing to give it a try. In the spirit of distancing herself from the girl she had been when she was growing up, of course.

Noelle reappeared at the perfect time with three bottles of beer. 'You called for a party?' She then whispered to Emmy, 'I know this is a lame thing to say, but if you see anyone put a beer or wine bottle in the normal bin can you fish it out and put it in the recycling?'

Emmy laughed and cheersed her sister, just then catching Jared's eye from across the room. He raised his bottle at her and she brought her own to her lips.

Talking of letting her hair down. She might be in her thirties now, but . . . it still wouldn't be cool to back out of a dare, would it?

Less than two hours later, and the party was swinging. Noelle and Emmy squeezed through the throng of people laughing and dancing in their living room. *Their* living room. 'This party is so beautiful,' Noelle said over the music.

Emmy was feeling wonderfully merry and had been throwing and catching glances and smiles with Jared all evening. It was like living out a scene from one of her *Sugar* magazines. 'Is Jenny having a good time?' she asked Noelle, wanting ALL the love to be in the air.

'Yes, I'm so relieved. We're still in the friend zone, but it's awesome.'

'Would you like to kiss her up?'

'Yes!' Noelle laughed. 'Have you seen how she looks in that Britney *Toxic* costume? God, I really, really want to kiss her and stuff, and I think she wants to as well, but I guess we'll see what happens. That costume though, she's killing me . . . '

They went their separate ways, and Emmy stepped on to the porch to cool down a little, surprised to see

Rae already out there on the driveway. She was about to call out when she realised Rae was hissing at a couple of people. 'Just leave, you nosy slags, I know you've got some secrets too!'

Rae stomped back towards the porch and only looked up when she was about to ascend the steps. 'Hi Em!' she said, stooping at the top step to retrieve a drink she'd left in limbo.

'What was that about?'

'Nothing.' Rae sidled round her and went back inside.

'Who were those people?'

'Just a couple of people from school. From your year, actually. Let's just say they weren't here to build any bridges. Another drink?'

'What secrets do you know about them?'

Rae laughed. 'I've got nothing, but everyone has secrets of some form, so it'll pique a nervous curiosity, if nothing else.' She was certainly her mother's daughter at times.

'This was such a good idea,' Emmy said, the occurrence already forgotten. 'I might breakdance – do you think I should breakdance?'

'Maybe save that for the late-night crowd.' Rae led her back inside.

Emmy nodded and smiled into her drink. Teenage Emmy *had* been a good breakdancer. She mentally high-fived that version of herself, who maybe really wasn't so bad, now she was coming out of her shell. She had amazing taste in music for one thing, and Emmy let out a loud *whooooo!* As 'Everybody' by Backstreet Boys began to boom out.

'*Whoooooo!*' screamed Rae, as she slid down the bannister chugging a beer. The crowd went wild and she put her bottle on her head as a victory. She wasn't sure who'd started the bannister-slide drinking game, but she loved them for it.

She was partying with old strangers who were now becoming new best friends, for tonight at least. Seeing all these vaguely familiar faces from her past, here in her house now, was laughable, but everybody was having a good time; the past was in the past, and the present was all about fun and forgiveness.

But then she was getting pretty steaming, so she loved everyone right now, including Big Daddy the spider, who'd come in to see what all the fuss was about. Everyone was ignoring him, thinking he was just a Halloween prop.

'I see you and your cheeky seven legs,' Rae gurgled up at him as he sat above the living-room doorway-with-no-door.

'Do you know what's good about being old?' she said to nobody in particular.

'Viagra!' answered one chap dressed as a devil, who wandered through eating some cheese.

'Us old people don't come to a house party to trash it, we just have a really good, really civilised time. AMIRITE, MAPLEWOOOOOOOD?'

The living room whooped without knowing what they were whooping at.

God, she missed Finn.

*Nope, nope, nope.* No, she didn't. Time for another drink; hello, parents' drinks cabinet! Hello Sourz Apple!

Noelle and Jenny squeezed on to one end of the old sofa that was pushed into the corner of the living room. Bonnie and her friends were taking selfies on the other end, and there were so many of them that they kept bumping into Jenny's back – until her Halloween punch sloshed over the side of her glass and landed on one of her legs.

Jenny gave a tipsy chuckle, and moved closer to Noelle, so that her legs were flopped over Noelle's lap. *This is too much*, Noelle thought to herself, knowing they were on dangerous territory. They had been for days, and the minute they'd both allowed themselves to be loosened by the drinks there was no turning back. Noelle didn't want any broken hearts on either side – but the music, the liquor, the heat all mixed well with the fact that the one who got away was right back where everything started.

'What are you doing?' Noelle asked, softly.

'What are *you* doing?' Jenny asked in return. 'Take your eyes off my lips.'

'Take your legs off my lap.'

'You take them off.'

Alcohol. Oh, alcohol. Noelle and Jenny were pleasantly intoxicated in teenage heaven.

Jenny shuffled a little closer as the Bonnie brigade squeezed an extra person on to the sofa down that end. She studied Noelle's face. 'I've forgiven you, you know,' she said over the music.

Noelle beamed and squeezed Jenny around the middle. 'Thank you.'

'But that doesn't mean we're getting back together.'

'I know.'

'I'm over you,' Jenny said, but there was a smile on her face, and she played with Noelle's hair as she said it.

'I'm over you too,' Noelle said. 'But if you wanted any kind of closure, just say the word.'

Jenny laughed. 'Closure?'

'You know, one night only, for old times' sake.'

'One night only? I don't think that's a good idea.'

Noelle smiled at her first love. She was right, of course. 'Suit yourself.'

Jenny snickered into her shoulder and kissed her neck. Noelle held her warmth close and it was everything, like it always had been.

'One night only?'

'Closure,' nodded Noelle.

Emmy was in her element. She felt alive in a way she never usually did, in public at least. She was dancing to Haddaway in the centre of the living room and everyone else wasn't sniggering at her or moving somewhere else, they were right there dancing alongside her. She even threw out some amazing moves she'd learnt from *NSYNC and got a few cheers.

She felt someone run a hand down her arm and turned to see Jared. '*What is LOVE?*' she yelled at him. She pulled at him, tossing her hair from side to side, and tried to entice him to dance.

He leaned in close to her ear. 'Em, I'd better go.'

'Noooooo.' She pulled away and looked over at the clock under the TV. 'No, it's barely eleven. Stay with me for a while.' She went back to dancing, but held both his hands in hers.

Jared stuck out the song and she loved that he really let himself get into it. Jared had never been one to try and play it cool, and that made him all the cooler in her eyes.

As 'What Is Love' merged into 'Mr Vain' (which left the ridiculously young Bonnie brigade confused for a moment, before they went with it anyway), Jared extracted himself. 'I've really got to leave,' he laughed.

But she hadn't kissed him yet. If he even wanted to. She just knew she didn't want to lose the momentum while the adrenaline was finally pumping through her body. She stood on tiptoes to reach his ear. 'Do you have time for a quick walk?'

'Sure, are you feeling okay?'

'I could just do with cooling down.' *Girrrrrrl, wasn't that the truth. I am so pissed.*

They stepped on to the porch and Emmy pulled her frizzed, sticky hair from her neck and beamed at Jared. 'Did you have a good time?'

'I did, did you? *Are* you?'

'I really am – I am a party animal!' They climbed down from the porch and set off on their usual walk around the house and into the woods. 'Wow,' she said as they became cloaked in the trees. 'The music's pretty

253

loud, I didn't realise. The cops'll be around in a minute,' she nudged Jared and snickered.

'We're definitely going to be getting some complaints about you three this evening,' he grinned, slinging an arm around her neck.

In answer, she danced along under the weight of his bicep, jiggling her shoulders and bopping her head, the biggest smile on her face.

'I love you like this,' he laughed.

'You do?' She loved him like this too.

'You were always so natural around me, laughing at what you wanted to laugh at, dancing how you wanted to dance, reading anything that interested you and then telling me all about it in so much detail. I basically read the Baby-Sitters Club through you.'

Emmy stopped walking (didn't stop dancing) and examined his face, unable to keep the smile from hers. 'I have never felt as comfortable around anyone as I have around you. My sisters are my comfort zone, but seeing you again is like . . . waking up.'

'Wow,' he replied, and he put his hands in his pockets in a way that made him look fifteen again.

'Are you drunk?' she asked all of a sudden.

'A little bit. A bit more than I intended to be. Are you?'

'Yep. Do you want to go to the den?'

In the distance, nineties dance music mixed with

the wind rustling the last of the autumn leaves to provide the soundtrack to the two of them standing face-to-face, weighing up just how heavy that loaded question was.

'I mean, we can't stay out here,' Emmy eventually whispered. 'It's Halloween. And I hear this house is haunted.'

Jared nodded his head. 'That's a good enough reason for me.'

They continued down the path-that-was-barely-a-path. After a moment, Jared took Emmy's hand and the way it made her head rush was akin to a long gulp of champagne.

At the entrance to the den, and under the cover of the pine trees, they sat down clumsily on a pile of leaves.

Jared reached over and moved a piece of hair back off her face. 'What are we doing?'

'Letting our hair down.'

They moved closer to each other, the leaves crunching beneath them. As their faces closed in she looked at him in close-up. She'd never seen him in close-up before. It was nice.

She felt his breath on her lips for a moment and she savoured it, even in her tipsy state. Every part of her, everything she had been, everything she was now, wanted this to happen. She was drunk but in control. At his mercy, but the one calling the shots. She felt strong and real and present.

And then as Jared's lips met her own, her mouth curved into a smile and she kissed him back, slowly, images of honey, champagne, moonlight, his biceps, Haddaway and a hundred sweet memories she'd pushed aside saturated her.

She *had* been happy here. Not all the time, but she was all of a sudden so aware that the happy times didn't need to be treated as less important and less meaningful than the sad times.

Emmy shuffled in closer still, resting her legs upon his.

Kissing Jared was fun and strange, serious but also funny, exactly what she needed and probably something she'd regret come morning. Finally, she forced herself to come up for air, and rested her forehead against his.

'That was my first kiss,' Emmy breathed.

'It was?' he asked, his eyes snapping open.

'No, I'm just kidding.' She was so funny. And then they both went back in for more.

The doorbell rang and Rae picked her way through the guests, a WKD in hand. 'Who rings the doorbell at a party? Just come in!'

'That's why everyone hates you,' hiccuped someone

as they sauntered past. 'They call you no-doorbell-dolly. No, they don't, I'm sorry, are there more Wotsits?'

Rae opened the door to someone dressed in full Ghostface-from-*Scream* cloak and mask. 'Trick or treat, muthafuckerrrrrrs!' squealed a tone of voice Rae hadn't heard for years. She leapt out of the front door, closing it behind her and pushing Ghostface back on to the porch.

'Now I know that's not our upstanding town mayor under there?' Rae cautioned.

Gabbi whipped up the mask. 'It is! It's me!' Her eyes were bright and her eyeliner thick, just like the old days. 'But nobody's going to know because of my incredible costume.' She danced and grinded around Rae.

'Okay, how pissed are you right now?' Rae swigged from her bottle, knowing maybe she should be the sensible one here, but the loosey-goosey tipsy part of her was trying to claw its way out and embrace its childhood friend and go hell for leather.

Gabbi pulled the mask back down as someone popped their head out the door looking like they were going to be sick, but then obviously felt better and went back in. 'Pissed enough to want to relive the good times and let my fucking hair down FOR ONCEEEEE, but not pissed enough to take this costume off and let anyone know it's me. If you see me trying to do that, you have to punch me in the tit – okay, Rae?'

'Gotcha.'

'Seriously. Like you know we used to be on boob watch for each other when we'd go on nights out? If one of the bongo-bongos was about to jump ship we'd alert the owner to hoik them back in?'

'I remember it well. Often they came out anyway.'

'Tonight, imagine my face is a boob. If it starts to come out, shove that squishy bad boy back under its cover. I mean it, Rae. I'm going to be drinking more, and even if I want to take this mask off and sing 'Earth Song', you have to stop me.'

'How are you going to drink with it on?'

'Ohhhhhh shit.' Ghostface flopped down on to the porch.

'We have straws! We have straws, don't panic.' Rae helped her up. 'Come inside, we have music and dancing, and people are actually beginning to let loose. In our house!'

Mayor Reynold didn't take much convincing. In she twerked, and within seconds was grinding against the Viagra man from earlier while the Vengaboys *Boom Boom Boom Boom*-ed on the stereo.

A part of Rae knew this was a bad idea. She knew no good could come of it. But as was so often the way, she also told herself that, really, what's the worst that could happen?

# Chapter 19

Emmy woke up with a jolt, her eyes shooting open but her brain struggling to make sense of the world around her. She was cold, the ground firm but damp beneath her. She was outside; her view was of leaves in extreme close-up and the bottom of tree trunks. The light was blue – not bright, more of a muted indigo – which suggested to Emmy that the sun hadn't risen yet. Her body was facing the ground, and something heavy was pushing her there.

No, not pushing her ... Spooning her.

She gasped and lifted her head so she could twist her neck, ouchhhh her stiff and aching neck. Next to her, surrounding her, and sleeping as soundly as if he was in a California King, was Jared. She gasped again, and without pausing to think shot out her right hand, as much as she was able to, to feel his crotch.

*Good, jeans still on.* So they'd probably not had sex.

Unless they'd had sex and then got dressed again afterwards? They had clearly thought it was a good idea to sleep in the woods, perhaps they had also thought through the ways of avoiding hypothermia. They were both sensible, after all. Nerds *would* avoid hypothermia. God, she loved being a nerd. Getting dressed après-bonk was a good start in beating the chill-factor, even if going inside would have been way more sensible.

No, no, they hadn't had sex, she wasn't that drunk – and now that she'd been awake for fifteen seconds, it was all coming back. They had smooched, a lot, and they had discussed having sex and, as much as Emmy was *pretty certain* she'd been the one egging him on, she was also a girl who liked her sleep, and she'd given up pretty quickly in favour of a good old snuggle among the worms and the—

*Ohmygod SPIDERS!* Emmy hurled Jared's arm off her and leapt to her feet. He awoke, sat straight up, and took about the same fifteen seconds to look around and figure out where he was and why he was here and whether or not his jeans were still on.

When he looked like he'd finish processing, Emmy hissed at him, 'Jared, get up.'

'What time is it?' he asked.

'I have no idea. Five? Six? The music's not playing any more so I think the party's over.'

'Shit.' Now it was Jared's turn to jump up. 'Oh crapbags, I've got an early shift. I'm going to need to get home.'

They scurried up towards the house as quietly as they could, Jared peeling at his stuck-on werewolf fur and Emmy trying not to think about all the kissing and stuff for the moment.

They reached the front of the house, where they had to cross a moat of orange pumpkin pulp and what appeared to be the site of a jack o'lantern massacre.

'Someone didn't like your decorations,' Jared commented.

'The weird thing is, we didn't have any pumpkins . . .'

Up the porch steps to a front door that was wide open. Emmy was about to enter when Jared moved her gently to the side and walked in first, the torch on his phone held high, in full police mode.

The hallway was dark and quiet, and freezing cold, any body heat created by the party long departed through the front door.

Emmy was afraid to look inside the living room. Not because of lurking murderers, but because she couldn't bear to see it if the freshly painted skirting boards were covered in drink, or puke, or whatever else might be in there. The skirting boards took sooooo loooong.

But Jared needed to get going, so she had to let him perform his sweep as quickly as possible.

The two of them entered the living room, where the lights were still on. Bonnie was curled up on the sofa like a cat, fast asleep under a blanket. Emmy peered at her. Thank *fudge* she didn't look or smell like she'd been drinking, but young people are so resilient and pretty these days that while Emmy probably looked like the dead mother from *Psycho* right now, Bonnie could have been on the most almighty drink and drugs binge for all her face showed.

The rest of the living room looked . . . okay. Somebody had clearly knocked a glass of red wine down one wall, and there was a lot of rubbish everywhere, but it could have been much worse. The iPod dock was paused on 'Ni**as in Paris', which Emmy thought was quite impressive. The hip-hop set made up hours seven to nine of the playlist, so the party had ended pretty late.

The kitchen hadn't made it out alive quite as easily. There was a bra hanging like a sling-shot from the oven extractor fan, and on the opposite wall was a variety of food mess. Some hadn't made it as far as the wall. She guessed there'd been some kind of competition. Someone must have had the munchies too, because there were both burnt and raw defrosted chips dotted about. There was also a large black stain above the hob which suggested there'd been a mild fire at some point.

They crept back into the hallway and Emmy listened for a moment for any sounds coming from her sisters' rooms. Somewhere in the house there was soft snoring, but that was it.

'Do you want me to look upstairs?' Jared whispered.

'That's okay, you have to go. Thanks for coming in me. Coming in *with* me.' *God*.

She walked him out of the house, where the sky had lightened a shade. 'That was a hell of a Halloween party,' he said, distracted by the impending dawn. 'I'll catch up with you soon.'

Jared stepped away from her with a little wave before whipping back around. 'God, sorry,' he said, and kissed her lips, just once, cupping her face. 'And sorry for my morning breath – my mouth must taste rank. I will catch up with you, really soon.'

And with that he really did go, taking off down the driveway in a light jog.

The thought of jogging right now made her want to hurl.

But on the bright side, his mouth really hadn't tasted bad at all.

Emmy went back inside the house and shut the door, then turned the heating up. She made two cups of tea and then took one over to help her rouse Bonnie.

'Bonnie,' she sang. 'Wakey wakey.'

Bonnie opened her eyes, smiled at the cup of tea and then reached over the side of the sofa and picked up a black box, studying it.

'What's that?'

'It's my ghost box. It has a radio for ghosts to communicate through, and a built-in thermometer. I bought it on eBay. Wow, there were some real cold spots here in the night!'

'The door was left open, that's probably all that did it. I grew up in this house, Bonnie, I can tell you it's not haunted.'

Bonnie looked crestfallen. 'But it's Halloween.'

Emmy didn't have the strength, stomach or head to argue, as the first signs of the hangover from hell were arriving. 'Okay, maybe it's haunted at Halloween. I hope you found something. But I think you'd better head home, your parents might be worried sick.'

'No, it's okay, I told them I'd be staying over at the party I was going to.'

'Did you now?'

'You guys are really cool, I didn't think you'd mind.'

Emmy took a long, careful sip of tea. Had she just been inducted into the Maplewood Cool Club? She was now more powerful than she'd ever been.

Was she about to throw up?

. . .

No, not yet.

'Really, though, it's getting light now and my sisters and I are going to have a lot of cleaning up to do. Would you mind heading on home? We can meet again soon if you need any more stuff for your article.' Plus, Emmy really wanted to flop down on that sofa.

'Sure!' Bonnie drained her tea and hopped up with the energy of an NBA cheerleader. It made Emmy's nostrils flare. 'See you later, alligator; happy cleaning.'

'See you soon, baboon.'

Bonnie thought for a moment. 'I haven't heard that one before. You're funny.'

*YES, I AM.* 'Wait, Bonnie?'

'Yep?'

'Did you drink while you were here?'

'*No.*' Bonnie side-eyed her and scarpered.

Emmy finished her tea with her head resting against the tatty old sofa cushions. The seat had been left warm from Bonnie and she was very tempted to just relaaaax, and maybe have a teeny tiny snooze.

No. She opened her eyes again. What she needed was to get out of these damp clothes, shower and get cleaning. They were on a countdown now with about ten more days to finish the house completely, and only two days before the new carpets were being fitted.

If she could crack on with the clean-up today, tomorrow could be about moving furniture and touching up any paintwork, then the carpets would arrive and then they could probably take the rest of the time a little easier. So she stood up, held her head for a moment and then headed upstairs to the bathroom. *I will not think about Jared yet. I will not think about Jared yet. I am a very busy woman. Jared Jared Jared.*

Emmy stopped on the landing, which was dark, and listened outside her sisters' bedrooms. All was calm and peaceful. It seemed the party hadn't made it to the upstairs of the house, which was a relief.

*Jared. Kissing Jared. Spooning with Jared. Jared.* She tried not to think as she crept into the bathroom and closed the door.

And then she screamed, waking the whole house, almost causing herself to puke and then have a heart attack, and causing the person lying in the (thankfully empty) bathtub to scream back at her.

'Get out!' she screeched at the man dressed as a devil.

Emmy closed the door and locked it behind her in a flash. She could hear the landing outside come alive with voices, and saw a light switch on and pool under the bathroom door. There was definitely a handful of voices, and not just those of her sisters – but after reassuring them through the door that she was fine, she switched the shower on, full and hot, ready to drown them all out and deal with whatever was happening out there afterwards.

The warm steam and soft water, combined with the strawberry-scented shampoo, lulled her into a false sense of feeling hangover-free for a few minutes. She kept her eyes closed and massaged her hair, thinking about last night.

So, her and Jared, hey? It happened. It was strange to think about after knowing him so well, but at the same time he seemed so new to her. Shouldn't she be cringing? Embarrassed by her actions, worried about the next time they saw each other? Because she wasn't. She just felt calm, and happy. She felt at peace. And not because a boy had changed anything in her, but because she was more comfortable in her own skin after last night. She'd found happy in a hopeless place.

Steam-cleaned and seemingly free of leaf mulch, Emmy gulped some water from the tap and exited the bathroom, noticing a sticky black stain on the floor, and ... hair? Whatever. The landing was back to quiet again. She entered her bedroom with trepidation, relieved to see it free of food-fight remnants, pumpkins or strangers. It did look like someone had been in here, though – her humble box of 'keep' items had been opened and nosed through, but it looked like nothing had been taken.

After a very brief lie-down that lasted two hours, she was up and dressed and feeling like death. But she was ready to crack on.

Out on the landing she tapped on her sisters' doors. 'Get up, party animals, we've got a lot of cleaning to do.'

Rae appeared downstairs sooner than she'd expected, and the coffee pot was still brewing. Emmy hadn't cleaned anything yet, but had done a lot of staring at the mess.

'Morning,' she rasped.

'Morning,' Emmy replied. 'Coffee?'

Rae sat on a bar stool. 'Yes, please. This doesn't look too bad.'

'You were expecting *worse*?'

'Dunno.' Rae was still in her costume and full, but smudged, make-up. She watched Emmy, until Emmy handed her coffee and a sponge.

'Did you have a good time at our party?' Rae asked.

'A really good time actually, everyone seemed to be having fun and being friendly. From what I saw while I was in here, anyway.'

'You weren't here all the time?'

'Weren't *you* here all the time?' Emmy replied.

They watched each other for a moment, before Rae answered, 'I was here the whole time.'

'Me too.' Emmy picked up the bin and a large spatula and walked over to the food pile slumped at the foot of the wall. 'Let's clean.'

'Do we have any food? Edible food?' Rae dropped the burnt and the raw chips into a bin liner one by one.

'The fridge door seems to have been left open, so don't have anything in there. There's UHT milk on the side. And Bonnie brought another hamper with her so perhaps there's something in there.'

'Bonnie and her crew of young 'uns seemed to enjoy themselves,' Rae said, plucking a box of rosemary-infused crackers from the hamper and dipping one in her coffee.

'You know she was asleep on the couch this morning when I came in.'

'Came in from where?'

'… The kitchen. I came down to grab a drink.' Emmy knew she was being cagey but a) she didn't want to deal with all the squeals and the shouts of 'I knew it!' yet, if she said what she and Jared had been up to, and b) Rae was being cagey with her – and yes, she was that petty.

'Good morning, sunshines!' beamed Noelle, flowing into the room and helping herself to coffee. 'Whoopsie daisy,' she said, sitting down on a potato waffle.

'Good morning to you,' Emmy replied.

'Why the fuck don't you have a hangover and look as shit as we do?' asked Rae.

'Oh, I do, I look awful,' Noelle said, her cheeks rosy and her skin clear and her hair tousled and beautiful. 'Did you all have fun last night? It was a success, wasn't it? I had a good time. Okay, see you in a while.' She hopped back up, topped up her coffee, filled another mug with more coffee, nabbed the box of crackers and went to leave the room.

'Wait, wait, wait,' said Emmy. 'Come back, we've got cleaning to do.'

Noelle smiled at her and carried on out the door. 'But Jenny's upstairs.'

Emmy and Rae squealed in exactly the way Emmy didn't want them squealing at her, and there were overlapping shouts of 'Come back', 'Oh my god', 'Jenny's in your bedroom?', 'You dirty BITCH!'

'Okay, okay,' Noelle said, popping her head back in

the room. 'Let me go and have a coffee with her and then I'll be back down to clean forthwith.'

'Well, I never,' said Rae. 'Hooking up with her childhood sweetheart. Who knew our little Noey was such a firecracker?'

'Ha ha ha, yeah totally. Right, I'll focus on here and you go and start on the living room.'

'Fine.' Rae stood up and grabbed the sponge and the bin liner. 'But when I'm feeling two degrees above rough we need to talk about this.'

'This?'

'That.'

'Me?'

'Noelle.'

'Right.' And Emmy was alone. Just her and the pounding sound inside her head.

A couple of hours later, and the house was still a tip. Jenny had gone home, and Noelle, Emmy and Rae worked slowly and silently, scooping things into the bin, wiping things off the wall, taking things outside to Febreze them, and then coming back inside and having to clean the hallway floor from pumpkin pulp yet again. It turned out that was something to do with Rae and a competition to hurl them from the upstairs window during the early hours of the morning. Rae couldn't remember who'd brought them, or how they got fifteen pumpkins down the drive, through the house and upstairs.

The doorbell rang and they all winced at the noise. Rae glanced out the window on her way to the door. 'It's just Jared,' she said with zero enthusiasm.

'Jared's here?' Emmy pulled off her rubber gloves and went running after her.

Rae opened the door before Emmy arrived. Outside was a police officer in full uniform, and behind him was a police car, and another police officer who was staring up at the house, hands on hips. 'It's not Jared. Soz,' she said, which was aimed at Emmy but she couldn't be bothered to turn her head. 'Hello.'

'Morning, madam.'

'Morning back atcha.'

The police officer consulted his pad. 'Are you perchance Miss Lake?'

'I am,' Rae answered. 'Ms Lake, actually, is what I go by now.'

'And are you Ms Lake?' he addressed Emmy, who stood by her sister.

'I am.'

'And are you, also, Ms Lake?' he asked Noelle, who had muscled her way to the front.

'I might be,' she replied. 'What can we help you with, officers?'

The police officer glanced back at his colleague who gave a discreet shake of her head. He faced the sisters again. 'I'd like to ask you a few questions relating to your whereabouts last night, if I may.'

Noelle smiled at him. 'We were all here, the whole day, and then the whole night. We were hosting a Halloween party, and there are maybe thirty-odd people that could vouch for us being here the whole time.'

Rae held her breath. Emmy's eye began to itch.

The police officer looked at all three ladies. 'Is that so?'

'Absolutely,' Noelle answered, unaware that her sisters would like her for once to be less self-assured around law enforcement.

'Might my partner and I come in and have a sit down while we do this?' he asked, pleasant enough, but Rae was pretty sure this was some sneaky way of getting into the house without a warrant.

Luckily, Emmy spoke up. 'I'm not being difficult, but there is literally nowhere you'd want to sit in there right now.'

'Perhaps we could move this to the station then.'

That didn't sound like a question.

'Is that necessary?' Rae asked.

'When was the last time you saw the mayor?' he asked Rae directly. 'You and she are old friends, I gather? Or at least you were. I can't imagine you're happy about her being part of "the establishment" now.'

'I'm very happy for her,' she answered.

'And you last saw her . . . ?'

'Maybe a couple of days ago?'

Noelle felt her smile crack at this, just a touch. She knew her sister. And her sister was hiding something.

The police officer wrote on his notepad. 'You didn't see her yesterday, or today?'

Rae shook her head, as did her sisters.

'So, you had a party last night?' asked the other police officer, coming up behind her partner and looking over the sisters' heads into the hallway. 'Were you drinking?'

'Of course,' Rae answered.

'Of course? Drink often then, do you, madam?'

'Like a fish, but I don't know what you're implying.'

Police Officer One was clearly getting tired of standing in pumpkin juice, so he got to the point. 'Mayor Reynold had her house vandalised last night. Today we can't get hold of her. We have reason to believe you ladies might be involved. That is what we're implying, and that is the tip of the iceberg of why we'd like to speak to you down at the station, if you could accompany us.'

The three sisters blinked and opened and closed their mouths like salmon that were severely hungover. Eventually, Rae said, 'We didn't vandalise her house, she's my friend!'

'If you could accompany us to the station perhaps we can clear all this up.'

'Are we under arrest for anything?' Noelle asked, folding her arms over her chest.

'Not at this time. Your cooperation would simply be appreciated.'

'Will Jared be there?' Emmy spoke up. 'PC Jones?'

Police Officer Two nodded, her eyes on Emmy's face.

'Can we just grab our bags and wash our hands? And Rae, you should get changed.'

'Emmy—' both Rae and Noelle started to protest, but the police officers nodded them inside and went to sit back in their car.

Emmy stopped them when they were in the hallway. 'We'll ask to speak to Jared when we get to the station and we'll get it all cleared up. I think we should just cooperate. We don't know anything, so it's no big deal, right?' They nodded. 'Right, Rae? You don't know anything?'

'I might know something,' she whispered, leading them further into the house and away from the door.

*Great*, thought Emmy. *Off to prison we go.*

Rae walked them upstairs and stood outside her bedroom. She faced her sisters. 'Just don't make too much noise okay? No screeching, or . . . laughing.'

She opened the door and inside was Mayor Reynold, sat on Rae's bed and turned away from them, wearing a pair of Rae's PJ bottoms and one of Rae's hoodies pulled over her head. 'Good morning, everyone,' she said, her voice scratchy, refusing to face them.

'Gabbi? Are you okay?' Noelle asked, stepping forward.

'I cocked up,' Gabbi said, turning slowly. 'Massively. Don't laugh.'

When she looked at them, it was like looking through a tunnel (the tunnel being the hood) into the past (the past being Gabbi's teenage Goth-phase face staring back at them). Gabbi pulled down the hood.

Emmy and Noelle gasped. Rae couldn't help but start to shake with silent snickering, doubling over.

Gabbi's hair had been dyed jet black, and a large, shaved undercut had been shorn into the side above her right ear. Her nose had been pierced, in a very off-the-books kind of way, and what appeared to be an emerald earring dangled from the enflamed and bloody nostril. But the worst thing, the reason for her sad eyes and Rae's endless cackling, was the writing scrawled up one cheek, across her forehead and down the other cheek in thick black lettering.

*MAPLEWOOD IS FULL OF ...*

Maplewood was full of something unrepeatable, so said their mayor's face.

'Rae, will you shut up and get dressed,' Emmy hissed, then turned back to Gabbi. 'Did my sister do this to you?'

'Hell no, she did this to herself!' Rae cried.

'You shut up,' Emmy said. 'What happened?' she asked Gabbi.

'I came to your party, and I was drunk, and then there was more drink, and I don't remember a huge amount after that but I do remember Rae and I finding an ancient Body Shop henna hair dye in her room in the early hours of this morning, and I remember thinking I really loved my old black hair.'

'So you did this here? What about the nose, and the ... words?'

'The words were funny at the time and we had a bit of henna left over. I don't remember about the nose. It's all really fuzzy.' Gabbi flopped backwards on to the bed, pulling the hoodie over her again.

'Don't look at *me*,' Rae said, finally pulling on some jeans. 'I was as pissed as she was. We went *at it*.'

'So this is written in henna?' Noelle clarified, picking up a bottle of cream cleanser and dabbing a bit on Gabbi's cheek. Nothing happened. 'I don't think it's going to be easy to get this out.'

Gabbi made a groaning noise.

'Come on,' Rae said. 'Let's leave her to recover, we'll figure this out when we get home.'

'Where are you going?' asked Gabbi, without lifting her poor damaged head.

'We've got to go to the police station—' Emmy started, but was cut off by her older sister.

'Something about complaints about the party. No big deal, we'll be back in a while, you lie low here. Oh, if you could call the station though at some point soon – they just needed a quick word with you about something. 'Kay, bye.'

Leaving Gabbi they headed down the stairs, where the police were waiting for them. The three sisters jumped into Rae's car with a 'We'll meet you there!'

Starting the engine, Rae said, 'No way we're being carted over there in a police car.'

'Why didn't you tell Gabbi about her house?' Emmy demanded.

'The poor thing's in mourning for her face and hair right now, I didn't want to be the one to break the news about her house as well, at least not yet.'

'Those words though . . . ' said Noelle from the back seat. 'Does Gabbi really feel like that?'

'Nah,' said Rae. 'She was just letting her hair down. Or chopping it off completely, ha! We all like to have a vent about work sometimes.'

'I've never called my colleagues *that word*, at least, not on my face.' Emmy pulled down the sun visor to look at her own face in the mirror. Ugh. She still looked grey and like she could vom at any moment.

'It'll be fine,' Rae said. But inside she wasn't so sure. What the hell *did* happen last night?

# Chapter 20

The three wise monkeys were seated in the pale-blue waiting area of the Maplewood police station. See no evil, Emmy, was leaning her head back against the wall with her eyes closed against the bright fluorescent lights. Hear no evil, Noelle, sat up straight with a smile on her face; the confident lawyer, who'd just got some, and was refusing to hear that anything bad was happening. Speak no evil, Rae, leaned forward with her elbows resting on her knees and her hands clamped over her mouth, lest she blurt out the location of the mayor and/or start laughing at the memory of her friend's face, and/or puke on the police station floor.

Jared appeared eventually, looking flustered. He spoke to someone behind the desk, gesturing at the women and his voice rising until they heard him bark, 'Just leave it with *me*.'

Behind the desk, Police Officer Two stirred her coffee, shook her head at Jared, glared at the sisters and walked away. Jared came over to them.

'Emmy, Rae, Noelle, could you follow me, please?' he said formally.

They followed him down a corridor to what seemed to be called, on US crime dramas, an interrogation room. Rae looked around, disappointed in the lack of a two-way mirror.

Emmy kept her eyes on Jared, watching the way he walked, the line of his face, the pink in his eyes. He looked tired, and she couldn't help but be a little smiley because she knew why and nobody else did. Apart from him.

Jared took a seat on one side of the table, and gestured for them to take seats on the opposite side. Emmy noticed his discomfort. This was how he used to get around Rae and her friends, once he'd hit puberty. Trying to be in control, but actually caught up in his own confusion of what his role was in this altered dynamic.

'Hi,' she said first, nudging his foot to help him ease up.

'Hello, again,' he replied, but to all three of them. 'Who knew I'd be seeing you all again so soon.'

'Did you enjoy the party?' Noelle asked.

'Definitely,' Jared nodded, avoiding looking directly at Emmy. She was okay with that, he was just trying to keep it professional in his workplace, she could do that too.

*I snogggggged him.*

'I'm sorry about this,' he started, picking up the folder in front of him. 'We need to ask you a few questions. I asked if I could talk to you initially, once I heard you were being brought in. So, um ... '

Jared loosened his tie and Emmy looked at his neck. *For god's sake, focus. It's just Jared's stupid neck.*

He continued, 'There's been an incident. Um, Gabrielle – Mayor Reynold – her house was vandalised at some point during the night.'

'Vandalised how?' interrupted Noelle.

'A window broken, some pot plants pushed over and smashed, silly string and toilet roll flung about, a bit of graffiti.'

'You do remember that last night was Halloween, right?' Rae asked. 'That sounds like exactly the kind of thing people do when they're trick-or-treating.'

Jared gulped and all three of them looked at her. 'Is it the kind of thing *you* do when you're trick-or-treating?'

'I don't go trick-or-treating, I'm thirty-three! All I'm saying is, why are you questioning us, when Maplewood has quite a lot of kids and I'm sure there are a high percentage of shitbags among them.'

'I know, I know,' he said. 'Look, there've been some complaints related to the party – noise complaints, mainly – so my Sergeant already had it on his radar this morning that it was a pretty wild do. That, combined with a few reports we've had since you've been here – which I don't agree with at all – means that when the call about the mayor's house came in they looked straight to you.'

'Who reported that the house had been trashed?' Rae jumped in, as Emmy was about to demand to know what other complaints they'd received about them.

'A passer-by.'

'We were at our party all night – at our house which is on the other side of town – and we have a houseful of people that could vouch for that,' said Noelle.

Jared nodded and wrote down some notes. 'Okay, so Noelle, you know that there's at least one person that could attest to you being at home from late last night until about seven o'clock this morning?'

'Yes, absolutely. Same with these two.'

Rae and Emmy side-eyed her.

Jared took a deep breath. 'Emmy,' he said, finally meeting her eye. He smiled. 'I can vouch for you, if needed.'

'Can you?' shrieked Rae. 'For all night?'

Emmy shrugged, a blush creeping in.

Rae's eyes grew wide. 'Did you bone each other? You dirty little boners!'

'We did not bone, will you shut up for two minutes,' Emmy hissed.

'And Rae, what about you?' Jared asked, trying so very hard to keep things professional.

'Who did I bone? Nobody.'

'No, um, were you at the party all night?'

She shrugged. 'Yep.'

'Was that an "I'm not sure" shrug or a definite yes?'

'I was there,' she said, then shrugged.

'Right,' he said. 'It's just that, when we arrived at the mayor's house, the door was wide open, and she didn't seem to be at home. Did she come to the party?'

'I wouldn't vandalise my own friend's house,' Rae said in reply. She was pretty sure she was telling the truth . . . Why would she do that to Gabbi?

Emmy shifted in her seat, the hard plastic as unforgiving as her hangover. 'Come on, Jared, you know we haven't done anything wrong.'

'This is clearly a case of Maplewood bullshittery,' Rae scoffed next to her, peeling fragmented pigments of last night's lipstick from her mouth and dropping them on the table like a pink pile of ash. 'This town ain't big enough for the three of us.'

Jared mirrored Emmy's shuffling, uncomfortable under the gaze of the three sisters. 'It's just ... We found this taped to the door.' He pulled a piece of paper wrapped in a clear plastic bag from within his folder, and slid it across the table. It was a note, written in biro.

Rae read it aloud. '"I've got your mayor, assholessssss, she's mine now. Goths rule. You suck. Fuck you. I love No Doubt."' Below the writing was a big kiss print, in bright pink lipstick. Rae put down the letter, swept the lipstick peelings from the table into her hand, jammed them in the pocket of her jeans and looked up at Jared. 'I've never seen this in my life.'

'You didn't write this?'

'Nope. I don't like No Doubt.'

'Weren't they your favourite band?'

'... It was a band? I had no idea. No diggity. Noooo doubt.'

'Is this your lipstick mark?'

'Nope. Who are you – Miss Marple?'

'No ... I'm a police officer. Do you know where Mayor Reynold is?'

'Yes, she's locked in our basement.'

'Really?' Jared looked at all three sisters, surprised.

'*No,*' Rae cried. 'Of course not, Jared, we don't even have a basement. And I did not trash her house, I wouldn't do that, I'm not the person this town always wants me to be. I'm not the baddie.'

They were all quiet for a while, mulling over their respective thoughts. Eventually, Jared put down his pen and spoke up. 'How can I *not* bring you in for questioning? The misdemeanours are stacking up against you.'

'Please tell us exactly what we've done wrong?' prompted Noelle, who sat up straight, business-face on, the knowledge of the law behind her unwavering smile.

Emmy pushed her hair away from her face, and feeling something against her fingers, pulled a small stubborn leaf from the tangles. She met Jared's eye for a second.

He refocused on his paperwork, a blush creeping out from under his collar. 'I've had reports of theft, criminal damage, threatening language, antisocial behaviour, disturbing the peace, breaking and entering, devil worship, kidnapping—'

'*Alleged* kidnapping,' Noelle interrupted.

'It's all alleged,' sighed Emmy. 'What's this about criminal damage?'

'The window of Annette's Newsagent's was also smashed last night. That's between the mayor's house and yours. Do you know anything about that?'

Emmy and Noelle both looked at Rae, who turned back to them. 'Are you *kidding me*? No.'

Emmy faced Jared again. 'And the devil worship? Nobody's been devil worshipping.'

He shuffled to another sheet of paper. 'That was from a couple of weeks ago. Something about somebody walking their dog past the woods and they saw a, urm, naked woman holding a chicken up to the sky?'

'My bad,' sang Noelle. 'Vicky and I were just catching some rays.'

'In October?' Rae derided.

'It was unseasonably warm that day.'

'Help me out here, ladies,' said Jared, holding his head in his hands. 'You can't keep this silence up. Where is she? Where's the mayor?'

'We don't know,' Rae said firmly. 'We don't know exactly where she is right now, but let me try and get in touch with her and ask her to call you, okay?'

'She's not answering her phone,' Jared replied.

'I think I know where she might be.' That wasn't technically a lie. Rae didn't know exactly where Gabbi currently was in their house, but she thought she might be crouched in the bathroom with her head over the toilet.

'Okay.' He stood up, and the sisters followed suit. 'I'm going to let you go for now, but I expect we might need to speak to you again, probably later today. Perhaps if you're able to get in touch with the mayor between now and then we could look at putting some of this to rest?'

'We'd be happy to,' said Rae, pulling Noelle out the door with her first, leaving Emmy to walk next to Jared.

'Are you still drunk?' Emmy whispered to him as they walked down the corridor.

'No, are you?'

'I don't know. If I'm not drunk I might still be dreaming.'

Jared grazed his fingers against hers as they walked side by side, and she looked up at his warm face. 'This'll blow over one way or another,' he said. 'I'm sure.'

She nodded, but disappointment was starting to sink into her soul. Last night had felt like progress. Like a step forward. This felt like it might be a huge, drunken stumble back.

# Chapter 21

Rae drove the three of them home in silence. Emmy had tried to ask her about last night but she'd shut her up with a stern look that she'd borrowed from their mother. She needed to think, not to be questioned and lectured by her little sisters.

She remembered having a fun time at the party, she remembered Gabbi showing up dressed as Ghostface, and she remembered doing shots with her and howling at the moon in her garden. Then she remembered deciding they needed more alcohol and suggesting they walk into town. They definitely didn't need more alcohol. She recalled dancing down the dark, deserted high street, and both of them being loud and obnoxious. Not Rae's finest moment, but Gabbi had been insistent she be allowed one reckless night because it had been so long.

She didn't remember going to the mayor's house, and although she thought she might have mooned the window of Annette's, she didn't remember causing any damage. This wouldn't have been the first time she was accused of graffiti, though – she was once suspended from school for a week because they thought she'd spray-painted a big swearword on the side of the teachers' lounge. She hadn't, but by that point she'd stopped putting too much effort into defending herself; she was a lost cause – her energy had to go on defending her sisters instead.

But that note was in her handwriting, and her lipstick.

*I am never drinking again*, Rae lied to herself.

Parking haphazardly in front of the house, Rae jumped out first and stomped ahead, trailing goddamn pumpkin pulp into the hallway.

'*Rae*.' Emmy grabbed her sister's arm. 'Will you just bloody talk to us?'

'What? What do you want to know? I don't remember what happened, I was smashed, but I didn't do that to Annette's, or Gabbi's house, I know it.'

Gabbi appeared at the top of the stairs. Showered, but still under a hoodie. Still with a face full of crystal-clear swearies. 'What's wrong with my house?'

The sisters looked up at her. 'Didn't you call the station?' Rae asked.

'No, I can't find my phone.'

Noelle stepped forward. 'Gabbi, we really need you to call the police station. They think you've been kidnapped and are blaming us. Well, Rae.'

'I lost my phone, I think. By lost I mean I think I remember flinging it somewhere.' She descended the stairs and Noelle averted her eyes from the shitstorm that was Gabbi's swollen and painful-looking nose. 'Why do they think you kidnapped me? What happened to my house?'

Her poor friend. Rae felt for her. She'd just wanted a night off and now she was all shaved and punctured and grafittied and her garden had bog roll all over the trees. 'Apparently, it's been vandalised. Only the outside, I think. It sounds like trick-or-treaters to me. One broken window and a load of silly string. And they found a note that suggested you'd been taken, which kind of looks like it was from me. But you and I were together, so you know I didn't do this. Can you just call Jared and let him know that you were with me, and that I haven't kidnapped you, and that you're okay?'

'You can use my phone,' Emmy said.

'No,' Gabbi backed up slightly. 'They'll know I was at your party.'

'So what?' asked Rae. 'It's over now and nobody's

going to care. And you were in a massive cloak and mask so it's not like embarrassing photos are going to surface of you in the *Maplewood Gazette*!'

'Please, I don't want anyone to know.'

'Why?'

Gabbi looked awkward (even more so). 'I'll tell them I'm fine, I'll tell them I'm not interested in pursuing anything with the mess at my house, and we'll leave it at that.'

'Thanks a lot,' said Rae. 'Is it really that much of a political suicide for you to hang out with us?'

Gabbi looked at each sister and they knew it kind of was.

Rae shook her head. 'Well, that's good to know. If you don't tell the police, I will, because I'm not having them or anyone else in this town think I'm some kind of abductor.' She walked past Gabbi and up the stairs, sniffing her own armpit as she went. She needed a shower. And her husband. She'd had about enough of reliving her youth in this lifetime.

In the shower, Rae sang loudly her favourite song from *Madame Butterfly*. This was the real her, she thought as she relaxed into the music. This was her real life now – opera, her home up in London, being a grown-up. Not this childish rubbish, not being on the defensive all the time. She'd been so determined to be the opposite of Emmy, to prove that their past selves were something to be proud of, that she'd allowed herself to forget that life was constantly changing. She didn't have to be exactly the girl she had once been in order to prove she wasn't ashamed.

Back in her bedroom, she tried to call Finn but he wasn't answering. He was never there when she needed him any more, she thought, unfairly. She stomped about the room for a bit, but curiosity eventually got the better of her, and she skulked back downstairs to see what everyone else was doing and whether Gabbi had fessed up to the police yet.

'Wow, you really can sing!' Gabbi said as Rae entered the living room, standing up from where the three of them were leaning over the laptop and applauding.

'Well, I did tell you I was a professional,' Rae grumbled. 'Did you call them yet?'

'I did. Sorry – I was being selfish. Unfortunately, Jared wasn't there and I spoke to this other officer who's a real stickler. He thinks I was speaking under duress and that I'm being held hostage. I told him that was ridiculous, but he said he was going to come by here himself this evening and check on me.'

'Why don't you just go home?' Rae asked bluntly.

'No, I can't. I have people over at my house all the time – work people, cleaners, gardeners . . .'

Rae rolled her eyes.

'They can't see me like this, Rae. Please, let me stay here just until I'm more presentable. Then I'll be out of your hair.'

'Fine. What are you all looking at?'

'Ways to remove henna from your skin,' Noelle answered. 'Do we have any hydrogen peroxide?'

'We're not putting hydrogen peroxide on her face!' Rae said, going over and peering at the screen. 'What about that toothpaste-scrub one? That sounds safer.'

'We tried that while you were upstairs. No change.'

Emmy stood up. 'I'm going to walk into town. I could do with some fresh air anyway before we crack on with the cleaning and decorating. I'll pick up some baking soda and lemons for that other tip, and some thick concealer for you.'

'Can you make sure it's medium-coloured?' Gabbi asked.

Emmy picked up her bag. 'I don't think a slight mismatch in skin tone is your biggest worry right now.'

'I'll come too, if that's okay?' Rae asked.

'Sure.'

'Does anyone want anything else? Gabbi, do you want a hairpiece? Or a nose job?'

'Ha ha,' Gabbi replied, but with a tired smile. 'Actually, if you see any of that colour-stripping

294

shampoo stuff in the hair-dye aisle I'd really appreciate it. And some antiseptic cream. Thank you so much.'

'No black eyeliner today?' Emmy asked her sister as they turned out of their driveway and started a slow stroll into town, which was the best either of them could manage.

'Not today. I think my skin's had enough of ancient make-up. How are you feeling?'

'A tiny bit less death-like. A lot worse than normal though. How about you?'

'Still pretty rough.'

'Sorry Finn didn't make it down yesterday.'

'Me too.' They walked in silence for a while, Rae turning thoughts of Finn over in her head. She missed him too much. 'So, what happened between you and Jared last night?'

'We didn't *bone*,' Emmy answered. 'But we might have kissed.'

Rae did a small cheer so as not to rattle her head too much. 'I knew you kids were meant to be together.'

'We're not meant to be together, it was just a kiss.'

'A kiss?'

'It was kissing – lots of kisses. I don't know, we

were drunk and all my favourite pop songs from the nineties were playing. We just got caught up in the moment.' Emmy couldn't help but downplay it. That was her way.

'Is that all you want it to be? Just a silly moment of teenage-style fun?'

Emmy made a non-committal 'meh' sound, and kept her gaze on the pavement. What did she want from Jared? Was this the start of something? Or closing a chapter in her life? What did she *want*?

'I want happy memories,' she said, and for now that was the best she could do.

'Would you kiss him again?'

'If he was okay with that.'

'Would you start up a long-distance relationship?'

'Probably not.'

Rae nodded. 'I've been thinking about our real lives this morning too. It'll be nice to get back to normal in a couple of weeks.'

Emmy looked at her sister, and a tiny bit of sadness sneaked in. She had thought she was the one dying to get back to normal. Now she wondered if any of them really wanted to be there. 'Is it because of Finn?'

'Just homesick, and under a hangover cloud,' she smiled, shaking herself out of it. She didn't want Emmy to think she didn't want to be there with them.

'*Oi!*' came a shout from across the road. The sisters looked up. '*Oi, you little* . . .'

They were level with Annette's Newsagent's when the lady herself flung open the door and started striding across the road towards them, giving zero effs about the oncoming traffic. Her frail, hunched-over body gave no sign of crumbling as she marched forcefully towards them. 'Stop right there, you little madams!'

Annette didn't stop when she was in front of them; instead she kept going, forcing them back against the wall. Only then did she stop and sneer up at their faces, waving her fingers. 'What did you do that for, hmm? Think it makes you big girls, breaking my shop window, do you?'

'We didn't break your window,' said Emmy, holding her hands out like she was surrendering firearms. Out of the shop doorway stepped the two police officers who had visited their house that morning.

'You would say that, but you've always been nasty little girls. I never had a problem like this before you came back. Angry I wouldn't let you stuff your filthy little pockets with all my stock, were you?'

Emmy was so shocked that she stopped taking it all in. All she could process was how often Annette said 'little', for someone so little herself.

Some people were stopping and having a gawk, and the police did very little to move them along, instead ambling across the road themselves to see what the sisters had to say.

'Hey, we had *nothing to do* with your window,' Rae protested.

'What about the mayor's house?' someone shouted out. 'Where's our mayor?'

'I blame the mother,' Annette sniffed to the spectators. 'And the father. Hippies, you know ... devil worshippers.'

'They were not devil worshippers,' Emmy said, louder than she intended, and bunched her fists up at her sides. The police stepped forward. And all of a sudden there was a thunderous growl as a Harley Davidson motorbike varoomed down the street, skidded, turned and then pulled up next to where they were standing.

The rider stepped off, a huge bear of a man, and removed his helmet.

'FINN!' shouted Rae, joy shooting through her entire body. She leapt up into his arms, kissing his face all over the place.

The police officers raised their eyebrows at each other; Annette could not have looked angrier.

'Finn,' Rae repeated, happy tears in her eyes, as he lowered her down. 'You're here. Why do you look like a Hells Angel?'

'Because heaven's no place for a broad like you,' he boomed, then laughed his head off, waving at Emmy and holding on to his wife tightly. 'Hello,' he said, noticing the police for the first time. 'What's she done?' he teased.

'Is this an acquaintance of yours, Ms Lake?' Police Officer One asked, looking thoroughly chuffed.

'He's my husband. And he doesn't usually look like this, not that it would have anything to do with you if he did.'

'It's my Halloween costume!' Finn said, his huge beam still on his face. 'Just a day late.'

Emmy was equally pleased to see him, especially for Rae's sake – it was impossible not to smile at those two together.

'Not the best timing, bear,' Rae murmured to him. 'I'm sort of under investigation for causing some trouble.'

Finn stood up a little taller, and reached an arm over to Emmy to pull her protectively in towards him too. 'What kind of trouble?' he said, addressing the police officers.

Police Officer One smiled politely. 'We're just investigating a few lines of inquiry following a party at your wife's residence last night, sir.' After gesturing to his colleague that they'd be on their way in a moment, he turned back to Rae. 'I shall see you in a little while, Ms

Lake – I've promised the mayor I'll pop over to see if there's anything she needs.'

'I can tell you now, she doesn't need anything.'

'With all due respect, Ms Lake, you also told me this morning that you did not know of the mayor's whereabouts. And then she called me from your sister's phone, from inside your house.'

Hmm. 'She came over later in the morning?' Rae really wished she'd bothered to get her story straight with Gabbi beforehand. *See*, she wanted to shout, *I'm a rubbish criminal – clearly I have no prior skills in this area. Knobs.*

Police Officer One just smiled, knowing she was lying, and off they went. Annette also crossed back over the road, cursing the sisters and saying they owed her a window. The rest of the rubberneckers ambled on with their days.

Finally, Rae could sink into her husband; and the feel of his beard on her forehead, his large, warm chest and tummy breathing against her and his hand stroking her back brought more comfort than a thousand glasses of wine. And she *loved* wine.

He held her, and she drained a handful of exhausted tears on him – swirled together with some happy and surprised ones. After a while she pulled away, inhaling deeply. 'I needed that. I'm so happy to see you.' She looked over at Emmy, who was leaning against the wall playing on her phone, giving them their reunion moment. 'Emmy and I have to just pop to the shops really quickly, then I can meet you at home and tell you the whole story?'

Emmy looked up. 'I'll get the stuff, you two go home.'

'I did hire a second helmet,' Finn said with hope. 'In case you wanted a ride while I was down. Unless you want me to stick with you both and be a bodyguard against angry old ladies and smarmy coppers?'

'I will be just fine,' Emmy insisted. 'Go.' Rae was struggling, Emmy could see this. She'd seen this many times before, during their childhood. In the past, the pressures of always being the one to protect them all had often been the catalyst for Rae disappearing. Finn had come to her side at just the right time, when Rae could do with a little looking-after herself.

Rae didn't need too much coaxing, and she leapt on the back of the motorbike like she was in *Grease 2*. Her husband was here! She snuggled into his back, and Emmy watched them ride off into the non-sunset.

Back at the house, the doorbell rang – a welcome interruption for Noelle, who was having her ear chewed off by Gabbi. Politicians sure like to talk about themselves, she thought, walking to the door. Behind it was Jenny, looking fresh and beautiful.

'Hey you, did you forget something?' Noelle cupped her face and kissed her – nothing dramatic, just the kiss of two past loves who had made peace with each other.

Jenny stepped in the door. 'Well, I don't know where my Britney costume is, but aside from that I just thought we should have a talk about last night.'

'Good idea.' They bypassed Gabbi and went straight up to Noelle's room, where they sat beside each other on the bed, a little giggly about the night before. But then Noelle grew serious. Jenny's feelings were far from funny to her, and this time around it was important that they both fully appreciated what was in the other's heart. Noelle resolved: no more telling Jenny what was best for her.

'Listen,' Noelle started, but Jenny interrupted her.

'Me first, if I may. I had so much fun last night. It felt like all the resentment and heartache drifted away. Not exactly forgotten, but it'll no longer make me sad, or angry at you. I can now think of you, one of the pillars of my life, in a way that makes me smile again. For that reason, I'm so glad you came back, and I'm so glad last night happened.'

Tears popped over Noelle's eye line – she couldn't have wished for any more. '. . . But?'

'But you know we're not back together, right?'

'I do.'

'Is that okay with you? I just don't know if I want long-distance, and I think we need more time to get reacquainted. Not just in the way we did on this bed.' She patted the duvet.

Noelle reached over and pulled Jenny into an embrace, touching her hair, and breathing her in. 'Yes, I'm one hundred per cent committed to getting to know you again, and also one hundred per cent committed to not making any future commitments. This is a team effort, this time around, and we'll just see what way the wind blows.'

After spending what felt like yonks being indecisive in the pharmacy, Emmy emerged and almost ran smack into Jared's chest.

'Ooo Officer, hello again,' she leered in a completely cringemaking-way without thinking, and then noticed his colleague standing beside him. *Shame!*

Jared blushed a little, and the other police officer indicated he'd go on ahead.

'I'm really sorry, that just came out, I think I might still be just a tiny bit tipsy,' she stammered.

Pushing up his sunglasses, Jared smiled at her and reached out a hand. She did the same, and both of them were in limbo with hovering hands, not knowing which page of the book they were both on. Then Jared rested a hand on her hip and kissed her cheek, while she play-punched his shoulder.

They both pulled apart, sheepish.

'I'm on patrol right now,' he said. 'But I guess we should talk?'

They threw a left so that they moved away from the eyeline of the other officer, away from the main row of shops, and strolled side by side. It was hard to believe it was November already. The weeks had gone by in a blur, and late summer had turned to autumn, and now winter was already making its first presence known. Trees that had held copper leaves in abundance now had just one or two, which were fluttering in the cold wind; the rest of the branches bare and trembling.

Jared spoke up first. 'I just need to say that, on behalf of Jared-the-boy, I am honoured that last night happened. Jared-the-man was pretty chuffed too. But Jared-the-boy just had his life made.'

Emmy felt her heart swell. 'All the Emmys had a nice time too. A really nice time.'

'So, what do you think?'

'I think … I want to know what you want to be?'

Emmy sneaked in there so he'd have to be the one to reveal his feelings first.

'I don't know – you leave in a week. I did like the kissing, though.'

'Good the kissing was!' Oh, why did she have to lapse into her Yoda voice now? 'Maybe we break down the problem and take it one step at a time?'

'How efficient,' he smiled. 'We could start with how we should behave around each other while we work out the rest?'

'Like – awkward, or back to normal or a bit kissy?'

'Yes. Um,' he glanced at his colleague, who had reappeared at the end of the road and was tapping his watch, 'let's go with a bit kissy, and see what happens?'

'That sounds good,' she said, relieved. 'But maybe not too much in front of other people, until we have it figured out.'

'Yes, brilliant, agreed. Good teamwork. Okay, I'd better go.'

They high-fived and went in different directions. 'I'm a Jedi,' Emmy whispered to herself with happiness.

After a bit of fresh air and a ride around, including a lovely long stop at the viewpoint high above the town,

Rae returned to the house with a husband in tow. Emmy was walking back down the driveway at the same time, and she was relieved to see her older sister looking more at peace.

Inside, Noelle had Gabbi sitting on a chair in the middle of the kitchen, her hair (what remained) tied back, a towel around her shoulders, and surrounded by little bowls of water, toilet tissue and what looked like gloopy icing.

'Hiya,' called Noelle as they walked in, and looked up from Gabbi's face. 'FINN!'

Gabbi opened her eyes and smiled.

Noelle dropped the cotton wool ball she was holding and skipped to Finn, embracing him without allowing her hands to touch him.

'Finn came to visit!' Rae beamed.

Noelle stepped back and looked up at him, pleased. 'Rae has been going absolutely loopy-loo without you.'

'That's not true, I don't need him!'

Finn planted a kiss on top of his wife's head. 'She really doesn't, but I'm here anyway. How are you, Noelle? How's the Jenny sitch?'

'Very nice, thank you for asking. We had ourselves a little reunion last night.'

'She is so smug about this,' said Rae, before pointing at Gabbi. 'What are you doing to my friend?'

'I'm still your friend?' Gabbi asked.

'Well, your guess is as good as mine as to what happened last night, so I think we might need each other. Finn, meet Gabbi, more commonly known in these parts as Mayor Reynold.'

Gabbi turned her face fully to smile at Finn, and a chunk of her skin fell to the floor.

'Dammit,' Noelle said.

'Wow,' Finn laughed. 'Nice to meet you, Mrs Mayor.'

'What is happening?' asked Emmy.

Noelle picked the skin up off the floor. 'The henna wasn't fading at all with anything we were doing, so I was looking at YouTube videos of Halloween make-up – you know the kind of thing where people add these huge realistic scars and things to their faces. So I thought it would be worth a try.'

'Isn't her nose enough of a huge gaping gash?' Rae asked, coming closer.

'Thank you,' Gabbi replied.

'I wasn't going to do a scar, I was going to do a second skin, just using the same methodology. All you need is to glue loo roll on the face and then cover it with make-up. But we didn't have any glue, apart from superglue, and I think the mayor has enough permanent features right now, right?'

Finn was circling Gabbi, checking out her inscribing

and trying to make out what it said underneath Noelle's not-so-masterpiece.

Noelle continued, 'So we used cornflour and water. But it didn't really work, I guess.'

'Oh!' Finn suddenly clicked and started giggling like a schoolboy.

'Did you have any luck?' Gabbi asked Rae and Emmy.

Emmy reached into the plastic bag. 'The pharmacy here is pretty small. They didn't have the hair-dye stripper, so I got some blonde dye. I thought that might tone down some of the, you know, Goth, but you can't hold me accountable if it goes a really strange colour. Then I picked up the antiseptic cream, a concealer – there was only one kind – and then I stopped and got the baking soda and lemon.'

Gabbi thanked her and dived straight in for the concealer, taking the handheld mirror off the kitchen counter, wiping remnants of cornflour water from her cheek.

They all held their breath.

She slicked the concealer over the 'M' of 'Maplewood', following the black line carefully and with force.

The colour was so very off. It was as pale as milk, and just looked like she'd Tippexed the word rather than hennaed it. So she tried blending a little, and there was the black again, shining through.

'What about if you put it all over your face and then

didn't blend at all?' Emmy suggested, so pleased this was someone else's balls-up and not her own.

So Gabbi tried that, and then looked at them.

Emmy and Noelle spent a while looking her over, though both were only killing time because they didn't want to be the first to say she looked horrendous.

Rae, however, had no qualms about this. 'Urgh, you look like a waxwork figure. Who's melted.'

'Which is better though: waxwork, or c-bombed?'

They all lapsed into silence.

'Well, thanks, everybody,' Gabbi said, getting up. 'I'm going to go and have my fourteenth shower of the day and then try and make myself look vaguely presentable for when the police come by for a visit later.'

'Help yourself to anything you need from my room,' Noelle called behind her, and when she was out of earshot turned to the others. 'With that thick make-up on, did she remind anyone else of a reverse Donald Trump?'

Later that afternoon, Gabbi was in full-on panic mode, and Emmy was, to be totally honest, getting a little bit sick of her taking up all their time. Which was mean – she could see her predicament – but she would also really quite like to have a quiet evening cleaning up the rest of the mess and then sitting in front of the TV, resting her hands on her boobs for comfort and eating a takeaway.

Rae and her friends' dramas had always seemed so much more chaotic than any dramas she and Jared had faced. Except now that they'd kissed maybe life would be full of dramas. They were both polite people – what if they decided to give things a proper go just because one of them didn't have the heart to say it was just a drunk snog? What if she had to move down to Maplewood and have his babies, and live for ever more crossing the street to keep away from Annette, who was clearly never going to die?

She was tired, and her own brain was scrambling to find things to worry about because it knew she liked to worry, and it knew she needed to drown out Gabbi.

'You can still see it, even under all of this the words still show through,' she was bleating to her hair and make-up team (Rae on the hair, Noelle on the make-up, Finn trying oh so carefully with his big hands and a pair of tweezers to extract the earring from Gabbi's nose). 'I look fifty shades of ridiculous.'

Emmy glanced over. She certainly did.

Finn pulled back and flexed his fingers before going

in. 'Sorry about my big hairy hands right in your face,' he said to Gabbi.

Gabbi shrugged. 'At least they aren't dismembered.'

At this, Finn just blinked at his wife, who opened her eyes wide. *'You don't know the story of the Hairy Hands?!* Settle in, sir, this is Devon folklore royalty, and you need an education.'

Finn looked around at Gabbi and the other sisters, who nodded gravely.

Rae continued, 'Picture yourself deep in the middle of Dartmoor – the sky is ink black, the mist as usual hangs low and cold, and you're out there in your car alone. You have to drive between two isolated hamlets, Postbridge and Two Bridges, and you know you don't want to.'

'Let me guess, the road is called Killer's Way, or Highway to Hell?' interrupted Finn.

'The road is called the B3212. But you don't want to drive it alone.' Rae crept closer. 'Because as careful as you're being, as hard as you squint into that dark night, as hard as you grip your icy fingers onto the steering wheel, BAM – the Hairy Hands will get you!' She shot out her arms and grabbed Finn's shoulders, causing Gabbi to shriek as he was gripping the piercing between his fingers.

'It's no joke, many a motorist has come to an untimely

death on this stretch of road, thanks to these disembodied hands violently grabbing the wheel,' said Rae.

Noelle nodded. 'I heard there was a woman in the nineteen-fifties who was in a campervan nearby and she woke up to the hands trying to break in. Tap, tap, tap. Or rattle rattle. I'm not sure how they were attempting to gain access, actually.'

'But whose hands were they, and why were they so hairy?'

Emmy reached far into her memory. 'Hadn't they belonged to an escaped convict from Dartmoor prison, who died on the road at the turn of the century?'

'That sounds familiar. And prisoners back then were probably very gruff and hairy,' said Noelle.

Finn was trying to follow. 'But why are just his hands floating about?'

All three sisters were silent for a while until Rae spoke up. 'Probably something to do with the accident, it's not important, the important thing is that the Hairy Hands are true and you better watch yourself.'

The team went back to work, suitably spooked, and picking herself up off the sofa, Emmy wandered out of the room and up to her bedroom. She sat on her bed and let out a long sigh. This room was nearly no longer hers, in a way. The yellow walls were gone, and there would be new carpets and a new bed within the week;

it was nearly as if young Emmy had never been here. Nearly – because the glow-in-the-dark stars were still on her ceiling. And although it was very early evening, it was already getting dark now that winter was rolling ever closer; so she turned off the lights and left the curtains open – the moonlight flooded in, and all she could see was the moon and her stars.

She lay for a while, lulled. Six weeks ago, she used to dread coming in here, feeling like she was in someone else's room and like she just wanted to get out. Now it was her sanctuary, and she thought that maybe it always had been?

Her phone rang in the darkness.

'Hi, Jared,' she answered, keeping her voice low so their conversation stayed between them.

'Emmy, we got so caught up talking about kissing earlier that I never said sorry about this morning at the police station,' he said. He sounded out of breath and she presumed he was walking home. 'I just finished my shift. I told them you had nothing to do with any of this.'

'I don't know if you should have said that,' she replied, counting her stars. 'We have a pretty kid-napped mayor downstairs right now.'

He laughed down the line. 'Yeah, I heard she called and said she was at your house.'

'One of your colleagues is still planning to come over

and check up on her this evening. I don't think it's a good idea. Could you fend him off?'

'I can't . . . ' he hesitated. 'I've actually been taken off having anything to do with the case.'

'But it's not a kidnapping!' Emmy sat up.

'The case is more the vandalism to the house and the shop; the kidnapping is just, well, "extra evidence".'

'Why were you taken off?'

'Conflict of interest. After I admitted I was your alibi.'

'Oh. Did you get in trouble?'

'No, although I got a slap on the wrist for insisting I did the first interview with you.'

'Sorry . . . ' Emmy walked over to the window and looked at the den in the distance. A smile formed, whether she meant it to or not. 'So, about last night?'

'About last night,' Jared echoed.

'So we've decided the kissing might continue. How different things would be if you'd gone home early, as planned.' Her heart thudded for his response and she rolled her eyes. It was like teenage Emmy was here in the room, and this was all a big game of Dream Phone.

And, actually, it was just as fun.

'I meant it, though – I was very glad I didn't,' he answered, and she thought she could hear a smile in his voice, but that might be because she was in parallel remembering Bruce, her Dream Phone boyfriend, and his pearly white grin. 'Do you wish I had?' he asked.

'I think I would have died of hypothermia if I'd slept outside on my own, so I was pretty happy you were there.' A moment later she added, 'For clarity, that was my way of saying I was happy you stayed.'

Outside her bedroom, Emmy heard the noise of someone running up the stairs and frantic whispering, followed by the doorbell. 'I'd better go. I think that policeman is here and the mayor's, well – it's a long story, I'll fill you in tomorrow.'

'All right. Night, Em.'

'Night night.' She hung up and walked out the bedroom. Downstairs, she could see the police officer was standing in the hallway.

'Psst.'

Emmy turned and there was Gabbi hiding behind Rae's door. She was dressed in dark glasses, a floppy denim hat that was once a star possession of Noelle's and Finn's scarf, which was wrapped around her face.

'I can't go down there, not tonight,' she whispered.

Downstairs, Rae and Noelle were fending off the officer.

'She's very poorly and she doesn't wish to see anyone,' Noelle was saying.

Rae stepped forward and glared at him. 'Do you have any idea what it's like to have your uterus lining break down and fall out of your vagina *every month*? Have you seen *The Shining*, and that scene with the corridor and the lift doors?'

'Okay, okay,' he said, hushing them with his hands in the air. 'I get the idea. I'm sure she's capable of saying hello for just a minute. According to those tampon adverts, you girls can do anything when you're on your periods.'

Snarky arsehole. *What would Rae do?* Emmy thought. Her sister was a quick-thinking risk-taker, and never afraid to get her hands dirty to help others.

Hands dirty … She grabbed one of the henna-covered towels from the laundry basket, which was now stained with a deep, dark red, and she stomped downstairs. 'Phew, you guys, it's getting really messy up there.' She flung the towel over her shoulder and watched the policeman baulk as he put two and two together as to what the markings on the towel were. Emmy ignored him. 'I'm going to cook her a steak because she needs some iron in her ASAP.'

'Maybe I'll come back in the morning,' he said, relenting, and backing out of the door.

'We look forward to it,' Emmy said, locking it behind him. She faced her sisters. 'And in the morning, we go back to normal, yes?'

# Chapter 22

When morning came, Noelle was sitting on Emmy's bed, waiting for Gabbi to vacate the bathroom. The two of them were drawing up a plan for the day.

'I think the carpet fitters will move furniture themselves tomorrow, we don't need to do it all today,' Noelle said.

'No, I know, but that drink stain didn't rub off the living-room wall, so we need to touch that up anyway, and while we're at it I think we might as well just get on and get the old sofa out of the house.'

'And Dad's chair? What are we doing with that?'

'It's going in Mum's room.'

'I don't think it'll fit, Em. It's ginormous.'

'We can't get rid of it.'

'Do you want to take it home, Emmy?' Rae said,

walking into the room holding on to her fanny. 'How long is she going to be in there? I am busting for a wee. We really should have added that extra loo downstairs.'

Emmy hadn't thought of that. She hadn't thought about having any of her old stuff back at her home – wasn't that the opposite of what she wanted? But her dad's chair ... 'Am I being silly and sentimental? It's just a chair.'

'Stop being so strict with yourself, just take the bloody chair.' Rae twisted herself into a variety of yoga positions in an attempt to hold back the urge to piddle on the carpet. Although it was going tomorrow, so ...

'How would I even get it back?'

'Finn and I could take it back with us and drop it off at yours. We were thinking of going tonight, actually.'

'What?' Noelle and Emmy said in unison.

'For how long?' Noelle asked.

'For a couple of days, you knew about this. I've got the performance the day after tomorrow, and then I'll drive back in time for us to go to Bonfire Night. So, Emmy, just give me your keys and we'll leave the chair at yours.'

'But, but, your car is tiny, and your husband is huge. It won't be possible.'

'He'll be on the bike, he has to return that back home. So I'll be convoying him in the car. Let's just try it, live dangerously.' Rae walked out the room and hammered on the bathroom door.

'Wait a minute.' Emmy walked out. 'You can't just bugger off now, we've got loads of stuff still to do. The house is still a mess.'

'It's not that bad,' Rae replied. 'And I'll be around all day today to help. Tomorrow the carpets are being fitted so it's not like we can do a lot then anyway. *GET A MOVE ON, GAB.*'

'Do you think now is the best time to leave?' Noelle asked. 'Your friend is hiding in our house. The police are investigating you.'

'They're not investigating me, it's a pissing trick-or-treat stunt. Can't you two just cope here in Maplewood without me for two seconds?'

Emmy, as usual, struggled to find the words she wanted to argue back with. This was *so* Rae to up and leave just because *she* needed a break. Instead, she let a dash of her pettiness unleash. 'You know, we were waiting for the bathroom before you.'

'Your monobrow can wait to be plucked, Emmaline, unless you want me to burst.'

The door opened and out came Gabbi. Her nose was bright pink and swollen and she looked like she'd been crying. Her hair had toned down a tiny bit, and she'd brushed it into a side parting that sort of covered the shaved section, if you didn't look closely and she didn't make any sudden movements. The writing was still very much on her face. 'I finally got the earring out of my nose,' she said weakly.

'Yes, girl, high five,' Rae said before legging it into the bathroom and locking the door, a parting middle finger to Emmy.

'So what's your plan for today?' Emmy asked Gabbi.

'Well, I'm supposed to go to work, but I don't know how that can happen, so I'm just going to call in sick. Can I stay here a little longer?'

Noelle and Emmy looked at each other.

'We have quite a lot of house stuff to get on with today,' said Emmy.

'And Rae's actually heading back to London for a couple of nights tonight,' Noelle added.

'I can help clean?' said Gabbi. 'Please? I just can't risk being seen like this. I'm washing my face constantly and I can't tell if it's even fading. But I was having a look online this morning and there's this make-up kit I can buy from Amazon that covers tattoos. If I order it today, it'll be here by tomorrow, and then I can be out of your hair.'

'Ahhhh, that's better,' said Rae, coming out of the bathroom. 'Of course you can stay, Gab. You can sleep in my room and be the extra pair of hands these two are so worried about missing out on while I'm gone.'

This time, the entire gang were ready when Police Officer One came a-knocking. The sofa, which would come in handy one final time before being shifted outside later in the day, was to play a pivotal role.

Gabbi was to lie down on the sofa on her side – the left side, which was the side with the very rude word. She was told *not* to sit up, under any circumstance.

Rae was to sit by her side like she was Mother Teresa herself, holding hot towelettes to her forehead and the other, exposed cheek. Who could suspect Rae of any wrongdoing when she and the mayor were clearly so close?

Noelle was to answer the door and do most of the talking, if necessary, because she was all law-trained and stuff.

Emmy didn't really have a job – in fact Noelle advised her to maybe stay upstairs and do something housy, given her relationship with a certain PC Jones.

Finn was to make tea. He made a cracking cup of tea.

*Ding dong.*

'Battle stations,' Noelle whispered, and went off to answer the door.

Police Officer One stood on the doorstep and nodded curtly at Noelle when she let him in the house. 'So, Ms

Lake, may I see our mayor today or has something else got terribly in the way?'

'I'm in here,' Gabbi's voice called out from the living room.

The police officer did nothing to contain his surprise and walked past Noelle and into the room.

It really was a beautiful scene. Rae cooed and spoke gently and massaged one of Gabbi's hands.

Gabbi's eyes fluttered. 'Good morning, Officer,' she rasped. 'Thank you for your concern, but I'm really all right. We women are strong.'

He surveyed the scene. 'Mayor Reynold, may I speak with you alone for a moment?'

'No, I'm afraid not. I'm off work sick today.'

'This won't take long, ma'am, and it concerns a more personal matter to do with your house.'

'I told your Sergeant I didn't want to pursue any charges relating to the damage of my house.'

'With all due respect, Mayor Reynold, your house is government property, and we also believe the vandalism of your house and that of Annette's Newsagent's to be linked. Therefore, it won't be possible for us to close the investigation quite yet.'

Noelle cut in: 'Taking the mayor's health into consideration, I think it would be wise to ask any questions you might have at a slightly later date?'

'And when exactly will that be?' the officer asked with a sigh.

'Very soon,' Gabbi answered. 'Just give me one more day. To recover. Thank you.'

The police officer nodded, stared hard at each of the players, and made his way to the door. 'Mayor Reynold, may I ask what happened to your nose?'

'. . . No, you may not.'

'I see.' And with that he was gone.

Gabbi jumped up. 'Right then, what can I do to help?'

As much as a small part of her hated to admit it, Emmy found that, with the extra hands provided by Finn and Gabbi, the house was looking back to pre-party state in no time. In fact, it looked better. It was like a new house, a holiday house. The windows were crystal clear, new curtains were up and each room was a stark contrast, colour-scheme-wise, to its previous incarnation.

While they worked together to pivot the sofa out through the hallway and the front door, the three sisters were a little more quiet and reflective than normal.

'Ready to try and put Dad's chair in the car?' Rae

asked Emmy as they walked back inside, leaving the sofa sat in front of the house.

'You don't have to . . .'

'Let's try it.'

It was a strange feeling, moving something that so linked a parent to a home out of that home for ever. 'Are we getting rid of Dad's memory?' Emmy asked all of a sudden, grasping at a reason not to move the chair.

'No,' Noelle said. 'You're keeping it. It'll be closer to you now.'

'But what if he wouldn't have wanted that?' She paused, trying to find the words. 'I didn't come home often enough; I wasn't a very good daughter. I think he would want his chair to stay here.'

Noelle and Rae lowered the chair and came over to Emmy. 'Where's this coming from?' Rae asked.

'It's just . . . Dad's gone, and Mum no longer needs this family home to feel like a family home any more, and we stopped being a family.'

'But we're back here now. We're together again,' Noelle soothed.

'But Dad's gone,' Emmy repeated. 'It's too late. I thought everyone else was to blame for my defences always being up, but I'm the one that ran away and cut Mum and Dad virtually out of my life, and I'm the one who's left it too late.'

Noelle sat Emmy down in the chair. 'Em, kids move away after school. That's life. And Mum and Dad more than anyone wanted us to fly free and be happy. Remember they were hippies,' she smiled.

Emmy nodded. 'I just miss Dad. And I wish I'd spent more time here after I left. I wish I knew him more as a grown-up.'

Rae knelt down next to her sister. 'None of us knew them completely, at least not until we saw that naked photo. But we're getting to know them now. It's only been a year, kiddo, it's okay to be grieving.'

'My walls have all been knocked down since coming back to Maplewood,' Emmy said, feeling deflated.

'I think being here is helping you. With the grief.'

Emmy nodded at her older sister's words. She let some tears flow for a little bit, and Noelle and Rae joined her.

A short while later, Finn walked by, holding a paintbrush. 'Oh no, the chair didn't fit in the car?'

Emmy stood up and mopped her eyes. 'Nope. I think it'll go in the car just fine. Let's go.'

# Chapter 23

The house seemed quiet the following morning without Rae, which she would have hated to hear. While Gabbi was scrubbing herself, again, in the shower, Noelle was pottering about humming to herself, a sweet sound that was peppered with large rips as she brandished a Stanley knife and pulled up strips of carpet. Emmy wandered into the living room with a cup of tea for her.

'They'll do all of that for us, you know.'

Noelle wiped her brow. 'I know, but the less they have to do the faster they'll be done. I'm hoping they'll be able to get the whole house re-carpeted in one day, so I'm just doing what I can to help. Plus, it's very, very therapeutic.' She held out the Stanley knife.

Emmy took it and positioned it against the old threadbare carpet and pushed down, drawing a long line. She then stood one foot on one side of the carpet and yanked the other, and *rrrriiiiippppp.* 'That is fun!'

'I told you! It's been helping me work through my thoughts about Jenny.'

'Uh-oh. Are you two not in a happy place?'

Noelle took the knife back from Emmy for another go. 'Actually, we are. I *really* like her, because she was such a big and important part of my life. Seeing her again, and apologising, and … you know … feels like that chapter got the ending it needed.'

'Does it have to be the ending?' Emmy challenged.

'You know, I think it does. She was my "then", and being with her takes me back, like a sweet drink of nostalgia. And I will always care about her a huge amount. I want us to stay in touch, stay close, but I don't think either of us need to recreate what we had so that we're each other's "now".' *Rrrriiiiipppppp.*

'That's very grown-up sounding. Are you being a martyr or do you really feel that way?'

'No, I really do. I'm happy. I'm happy she's happy.'

'So Jenny feels the same?'

'Yes, she does. I made sure this time – we're on exactly the same page, and it feels really good.'

Emmy took back the knife and had another few hacks at the carpet.

Eventually, Noelle said, 'I've just realised how

insensitive this all sounds. What's going on with you and Jared? I didn't mean to imply relationships from the past weren't worth exploring again—'

'No, I know you didn't. To be honest, I haven't figured out what we're doing yet, and neither's he. I guess we'll just see how the next week goes. God, it's only just over a week until we leave.'

'What do you want to happen with him?'

Emmy shrugged. 'Right now, I just want to enjoy living in the moment. I know that sounds stupid, because he's a blast from my past, but perhaps what I should say is I want to enjoy *enjoying* myself, back here. In conclusion,' *rrrriiiippppp*. 'I'm procrastinating.'

'Do you know what *he* wants?' Noelle asked.

'I do not. Hopefully once the carpets are in and a certain someone is no longer under our feet, he and I can get together and make awkward small talk until one of us admits our feelings.'

Speaking of which . . . Gabbi's voice rang out over the bannisters. 'Noelle? Emmy? Do either of you have any knickers I could borrow?'

'Okay, nope,' said Emmy, putting down the knife and walking into the hallway. She looked up at Gabbi. 'Nope, nope, nope. Gabbi, you have got to go home.'

'But my face! I can't go out there yet.'

'Then you at least have to go and get some of your

own things. There's a reason I'm thirty-one and live on my own and not twenty and living in uni halls any more. And that reason is that this girl,' she pointed at herself, 'does not share underwear. Maybe a bra, with one of my sisters, but not knickers. Nope.'

'Noelle?' Gabbi looked hopeful.

'I'm with her, sorry. You need to go and get yourself some pants.'

'How about if I stay here and you go and buy me some new ones? I'll throw in an extra tenner for you to keep?'

Emmy shook her head. 'As much as being tipped for buying someone else's knick-knacks for them isn't at all insulting, you have to get out of hiding. Not least because there are going to be carpet fitters in here all day anyway, so we – all of us – need to be out of the way. Go on, get dressed, and we'll drive you over.'

'But what if someone sees me?'

'You're the mayor – tell them to avert their eyes or something.'

A short while later and they were all leaving the house, Gabbi in a hat, scarf and with large plasters on her cheeks and nose. She looked like a botched-plastic-surgery patient.

As Noelle drove them across town to the mayor's house, Gabbi stayed low in the seat. 'You are going to take us back to your house afterwards, aren't you?' she asked Emmy from the back seat.

'That was the plan, but if you think you'd be more comfortable in your own bed . . . ?'

'No, no, Rae's bed is pretty comfortable.'

'We won't be offended.'

'I think I'll just come back with you.'

'But our house is so messy, don't you miss your own . . . teabags?'

'I like your house.'

She wasn't giving in. Emmy tried a different tack. 'How good is Netflix, huh? That's something I miss about our mum's house.'

'I actually don't watch a lot of TV,' Gabbi replied.

*Who doesn't watch TV?* Emmy thought with exasperation. 'Let's see how you're feeling when we're back at your house. I think you should consider staying back there.'

'But I'm afraid to be there on my own – the police haven't caught the person who vandalised my house.'

Now Emmy felt like a prime meanie.

'They broke my window, and my door was left hanging open,' Gabbi continued. 'I don't know how they got in. I'm just scared, that's all, but if you'd like me to get out of your way so you can finish painting Rae's skirting boards I'll understand.'

Emmy and Noelle stole a glance at each other.

'Of course not,' Emmy relented. 'Sorry, I didn't mean to make you feel like that. It's just that our house isn't finished so it's not the most comfortable right now, for anyone.'

'The carpets will make a big difference,' Noelle contributed, and at that point signalled left and turned into Mayor Reynold's driveway.

'Bugger,' Gabbi mumbled. The house came into view and looked as good as new. The broken plant pots had been replaced with shiny blue-lacquered ones, a new window had been fitted, already, and was sparkling clean, there was no silly string in sight and not a scrap of loo roll, apart from one short length high up in a tree, waving in the breeze. And coming out of the mayor's front door carrying a bin liner was the scrawny chap that worked with Gabbi, whom they'd seen her with the first time they ran into her.

'That's my assistant, Sid,' said Gabbi. 'What's he doing here?'

'What a nice guy, it looks like he's been cleaning up for you,' said Noelle, parking in front of the house.

'I don't want him to see me.'

'Too late.'

Sid put down the bin liner and waved at the car, a huge beam taking over his skinny face.

'You're back!' he cried, opening up the rear car door and reaching in for Gabbi, like she was an OAP who needed assistance.

'No, I'm not.' She lowered her head, looking at the ground. 'I'm staying with my friends for a few days, I've just come back to pick up a few things.'

'Are you okay, Mayor Reynold? Is your face all right?'

'I'm *fine*, Sid, just a bit under the weather.'

Sid looked up and narrowed his eyes at Noelle and Emmy. 'Did you do this to her?'

'Did we do *what*?' Emmy replied.

'Did you do something to her face after you kidnapped her, is that why you're forcing her to stay with you?'

If Rae were here she would have been quite impressed with the surprising size of this guy's balls. As for Emmy, she went into goldfish mode and struggled for words, so Noelle stepped in. 'Nobody is forcing the mayor to do anything, and no, we did nothing to her face. Now you remember her telling you, several times I believe, that she's just under the weather?'

Gabbi stayed silent, but nodded.

'Fine,' said Sid. 'If that's true, then Mayor Reynold and I will go inside and collect her things. And you two can stay out here.' He added quietly to Gabbi, 'Then you can tell me what's really going on.'

Gabbi looked at Noelle and Emmy fearfully. Why did she have to look so fearful? For crying out loud, she couldn't make them look more like abductors if she tried.

'I'm sure Mayor Reynold can pick out her own knickers,' Noelle said to Sid.

Finally, Gabbi spoke. 'Yes. I'll go on my own. Thank you, Sid.'

'Everybody knows you three are responsible for this, you know, for what happened to her house,' Sid said when Gabbi was out of earshot. 'I don't know why she's protecting you all, or whatever it is you have on her, but she's a nice woman. A great mayor. And she's one of our own, she grew up here, so we won't let you get away with this.'

Emmy found her voice. 'One of your own? *We're* one of your own! We grew up here as well! So don't you dare lecture us like we're outlaws who've ridden into town to cause trouble. We had nothing to do with the house, we had nothing to do with Gabbi's … appearance … and no, we do not have anything "on her".'

Sid folded his arms. 'Well, I've heard a lot of rumours about your family. It must be costing a pretty penny to do all those renovations on that house. Money the mayor might have access to.'

'We're grown-ups – we have careers and bank accounts and savings, and my father died last year so we also have his inheritance, if you must know. We don't need *anything* from the mayor, other than for her to get better and go home.'

Gabbi stepped out of the front door. 'Okay, stop arguing please,' she said, and threw her bag in the back seat. 'Goodbye, Sid, I'll be back at work as soon as possible. Believe me.' She climbed into the car, and Emmy felt herself die a little.

Noelle walked over to the driver's seat, and called back to Sid, 'And none of our family – neither my sisters nor our mother need anything from the people in this town.'

Back in the car, Emmy turned around to look at Gabbi. 'I didn't mean that – you can stay as long as you need. I was just trying to make the point to your assistant that we weren't holding you hostage as some kind of money scam.'

'That's okay,' the mayor smiled, though it hurt her nose to do so. 'I will be out of your hair soon, though. Hopefully the make-up will arrive today, and everything can go back to normal.'

Emmy faced forward and looked at the streets of Maplewood rush past, thoughts of Jared, the house in the woods, her home in Harwell, new carpets, her job, her sisters, her teenage self all running through her mind. And she wondered, what would normal be, after this trip?

# Chapter 24

The next day rolled in and still Gabbi was hiding out in the Lakes' house, her make-up kit unarrived. But the carpets were in and looking fresh and beautiful, just like the day itself, which was full of bright November sunshine.

Emmy was waiting for the delivery of new mattresses, and taking a breather. From decorating, packing, Gabbi, everything. She'd found her old bicycle in the garage – with its basket and its stickers and its Spokey Dokeys that came out of cereal boxes – and was riding up and down the driveway; long, lazy rides in the unnatural squat position of an adult on a child's bike.

She'd had a phone call from Bonnie that morning, filling her in on the gossip levels at The Wooden Café, which were through the roof, apparently. Talk of the sisters had gone from sniggering 'do you remember when's to nastier, accusatory 'I always knew's and 'since they came back's.

Bullying. It sounded like a childish term, something that happened to children and broke the hearts of those that loved them. Not to adults; that was usually given more grown-up terms, like abuse, trolling, gaslighting. But Emmy was sure this constant undermining, this repetitive negativity, this attempt to storytell her family's lives based on nothing but prejudice, surely came under the umbrella of bullying, right? Was it something she could only get away from once and for all if she erased herself from this place altogether?

Up and down she rode, circling the leaves and the trees, until she heard a voice.

'Looking comfy over there, lady,' Jared said, appearing around the end of the driveway.

She stopped cycling and put her feet down, a warm smile spreading across her face. 'Hey, you.'

'Nice wheels – are those Spokey Dokeys glow-in-the-dark?'

'Um, *of course*. What are you doing here?'

He stepped towards her, and she wondered if they were about to have their first kiss since the morning after the party. Should she use tongues? He was coming, snap decision time!

*Peck*. Okay, no tongues. She was okay with that, though it was a little too close to how she used to practise kissing on her hand, and a little too removed from the big fat make-out session she really felt she could do with.

'I have the day off today, so wondered if you might need a rugged man to help you with anything with your house?' he asked.

'Nah.' Emmy put her feet back on the pedals and circled him. 'We don't need no man, we're rugged enough on our own. Although, actually, there is a little of the clear-out that still needs to be done. And I don't want to take the boxes up into the attic.'

'All right, can you give me a ride?'

She laughed. 'Hop on!'

And he did. He climbed on the back of the bike and squidged in close to her, wrapping his arms around her waist while she heaved and hauled them both down the driveway. It was wobbly going, but some much needed tears of laughter and only one muddied knee later, they made it to the front of the house.

Emmy pulled to a stop and stood. Before Jared had a chance to do the same she twisted around and kissed him properly, fully, on the lips. She'd needed that.

In the house, Gabbi was lying on the sofa watching TV. She screeched when Jared walked in, and threw a blanket over her face. 'I'm still poorly!'

'Relax, Gabbi, we're going straight upstairs,' Emmy said.

Noelle was in their mother's room, cleaning up the space around the window for the stained-glass panel to be fitted tomorrow. They'd gone for a simple design so it could be done relatively quickly, with the Triple Goddess' three moons coloured in an indigo blue.

'Noey,' Emmy said, poking her head around the door. 'Jared's here, he's going to help shift some things up into the loft. Can those boxes on your bedroom floor go up there?'

'Yep,' Noelle replied. 'I've done my charity shop runs so all the boxes that are left are keepy-things. Same with the boxes in Rae's room. Thanks!'

Jared climbed up into the loft and then dangled his upper body down, while Emmy passed him a train of boxes of different shapes and sizes. After a while, Jared removed his sweatshirt, leaving his arms bare. 'How many more boxes?' he asked.

'Just a few. There's a beer waiting for you at the end.'

'Ahh, motivation!'

'All right that's it,' she said, handing up the last of Rae's containers. 'I just have one box, but I need to go through it quickly and see if I really want to keep any of it. Do you want to come down and keep me company, and I'll get you that beer?'

Emmy and Jared sat in her room with a beer each and a big bag of Sensations crisps between them, and Emmy pulled her box of keepsakes over.

'You just have one box?' Jared asked. 'Didn't I just move the equivalent of the Amazon warehouse into the attic for your sisters?'

'I might not even have one box, actually,' she replied, and tipped the box on its side, spilling out the contents. Together with her crop top, Baby-Sitters Club book and maths revision guide, she'd also stowed away two teddy bears, a 5ive tour T-shirt, a snow globe from Disneyland Paris that her father gave her, and a handful of toys and jewellery. It was all stuff she really didn't need to keep, if she was honest.

Apart from the teddy bears, because you can't chuck those, they have feelings.

'Do you think a charity shop would want my 5ive T-shirt?'

Jared took a gulp from his beer. 'Doubt it. You used to wear that all the time, though; you can't get rid of that. What if you ever meet Ritchie? He's not going to love you if he finds out you chucked his merch.'

'I need to get rid of it,' she smiled.

'Why?'

'Because I don't care about this stuff any more. It's just stuff. And also, it's not like it's really *me* any more.'

'Is this about the party?'

'No,' she lied.

'Is it about the aftermath of the party?'

'No,' she lied again.

Jared slid down off the edge of the bed and sat next to her on the floor. 'You know this is all very familiar. Classic Emmy.'

'What do you mean?' she asked, distracted by the storyline on the back of her Baby-Sitters Club book.

'Up you get.' He pulled her to her feet. 'You can take a break for a couple of hours, right?'

'Sure,' she answered, confused. 'But why?'

'Good, you haven't touched your beer yet, then you're driving.'

'Not far now … Okay, pull in right here.'

Emmy turned into the parking area, where there were just two other cars. They'd been driving for close to an hour, deep into wild Dartmoor, and as they came to a stop, two sheep glanced up at them and chewed reflectively.

'Come on,' Jared said, jumping out of Noelle's borrowed car.

By the time Emmy had climbed out, done her coat up, found a hairband and locked the car, he was already on the grass.

They were slap bang in the middle of breath-taking British scenery. Green surrounded them on all sides, cobbled with granite tors rising up from the hills. The wind was blowing a hooley, not that these hungry sheep cared, but it whipped Emmy's split ends around like nobody's business. Her eyes watered immediately. She loved it all.

'What are we doing out here?' she yelled over the whistling wind, laughing.

'We're going for a walk – up there.' He pointed to the top of a nearby tor.

She scrambled closer to him and grabbed his hand, letting him lead her on and upwards.

The ground was hard and uneven, and more than once they stumbled. A pair of Dartmoor ponies watched them, their long hair shimmering in the gusts. Eventually, they made it up to the rocks, where they huddled together away from the direction of the wind, and looked out at the spectacular vista.

'You can't beat this view,' Emmy breathed, her cheeks pink and her hair all over the shop.

'You can't?' asked Jared. 'Not even in the wonderful Oxfordshire?'

Emmy shook her head. 'So, can you tell me now how we jumped from my 5ive tour T-shirt to climbing a tor on the moors?'

'Because of this, for one.' Jared pointed out at the view. 'I thought you could do with being reminded that your birthplace isn't just Maplewood. It's Devon. And all this is just as much yours as anyone else's.'

'Devon is Heaven, that's what you always said,' she nodded. He was right as well. She'd stayed in, blinker-visioned, way too much since being back. 'God, I wish I'd come out here earlier, now I only have a week before going back home.' Then she asked, 'Back at the house, what did you mean by "classic Emmy"?'

'Let me take you back.' Jared snuggled in a little closer, putting his arm around Emmy. She wasn't sure what he was about to say, or if she was going to like it, but she felt comfortable with whatever was coming with her best friend so close.

Jared continued, 'There was a time in our lives, we must have been sixteen? Maybe fifteen. And I remember you being so very similar to how you are now.'

That surprised her. 'I'm nothing like I was at sixteen.'

'You don't think? In some ways you aren't, but believe me that in others you are.' He leaned over and kissed her forehead suddenly, sweetly. 'You were having a rough time at school. Not with the work but with the people. The bullying was pretty relentless – in their stupid eyes you were always wearing the wrong thing, doing the wrong thing, saying the wrong thing. Tell me if any of this is too hard to hear.'

Without realising, Emmy's watering eyes had turned to tears. Not sobs, just tears of resignation and recognition of her past. She let him rest his head on hers, and he spoke softly, his breath gentle and warm against her hair.

'You ignored it for so long – you wouldn't tell your mum and dad, Rae was gone by this point, and you began to shut me out. You said we couldn't be friends any more.'

'They were making comments about you to me. About how I fancied you but you'd never be more than my friend because I was too flat-chested and too stuck-up and too poor.'

'None of which was true, as demonstrated by my unwavering love for you.'

Emmy had always loved Jared; he was the kindest person she'd ever known. She didn't quite understand in what way she loved him, she just knew she did.

'So,' he said. 'I came over one day to see what the heck was going on. And you were doing much like you were doing today – packing up all the things that meant something to you, ready to throw it all away. Including me, and including your GCSEs. You didn't want to be clever any more; you just wanted to be cool.'

This was indeed sounding familiar, Emmy remembered the day well. She was giving up. She wanted to give all of it up and just fit in, and she was willing to lose everything just for the peace that comes with being part of the crowd.

Jared met her eye, forcing her to look away from the view and at him. 'But then, and now, you were never the problem that needed fixing. Not a single thing about you needed to change. Teenage Emmy was perfect, and she and her amazing mind and her kind disposition made her go on to be the person you are today. So, I need you to not throw her away. And I need you to stay strong around the bullies one more time, and don't let them decide what happens to you and your memories.'

Emmy inhaled the cold Devon air, deep into her lungs. Maybe she wasn't on edge, or stressed out or upset. Maybe she was on *the* edge, on the edge of something life-changing. Was she going to take flight – or fight?

# Chapter 25

The following day, Gabbi came downstairs from Rae's room at a leisurely ten o'clock in the morning. Emmy and Noelle were already up, working together to hang some natural-finish floating wood shelves in the kitchen. Noelle had found the shelves in Jenny's shop, and they fitted perfectly with their Devon woodland theme. She'd bought dozens of them, to put in every room.

'I've cancelled tonight,' Gabbi announced, helping herself to a bowl of Coco Pops.

'You've cancelled Bonfire Night?' Noelle asked, a screw hanging out of the corner of her mouth.

'Not the whole thing, but I'm not going to be the one lighting the bonfire any more. I've asked Sid to do it on my behalf.'

'But why? Your make-up kit thing will surely come today, and the words have faded a bit now anyway. With a good Sharpie I might actually be able to turn that into "Maplewood is full of dudes".' Noelle tightened the screw in place and then turned around to peer at Gabbi's cheek.

'I don't want to risk it. And anyway, my nose still hurts. Just one more day and then I'll hopefully be back to normal.'

Emmy stood back to admire their handiwork. *One more day, one more day, one more day* ... Considering Gabbi was an elected mayor, she seemed very reluctant to utilise any problem-solving skills for herself.

Her phone bleeped – a text message from Bonnie. '*Ummmmmmmm, you might wanna check the FB page ...*'

'Noelle,' she said, bringing the laptop to the breakfast bar. 'Bonnie just said we should look at the house page on Facebook.' She navigated to the page and scrolled down. There was a photo from the party – quite a few in fact, and Emmy cringed at one of her dancing in the background with ten million chins – but the photo at the top was of the mayor. Not at the party, an official one, of Gabbi, arms folded, smiling at the camera.

'That's me!' said Gabbi. 'Why am I on there? Do people know I was at your party?'

Emmy clicked on the picture and looked at the

caption. 'It says, "Where is our mayor? She is being held captive in this house!!!!!!! She's not coming to the annual Bonfire Night!!!!!! We must save her!!!!!!!" That's a stupid amount of exclamation marks, and you're hardly being held captive,' she added, thinking, *We're trying anything to make you leave.*

'Why do they think I'm being held hostage? I thought it was only the police that thought that.'

'I thought you'd set that right by now?' Emmy answered.

'Well, there's no telling some people … What do those comments say – I haven't got my contacts in yet?'

Emmy read on. 'The first comment is by the same person that posted the photo. It says, "Hardly anyone's seen Mayor Reynold since her house was trashed on Halloween – the same night these sisters threw a huge party that got completely out of hand. They've got her at their house and they're refusing to let her out!!!!!!!!!"'

Noelle was leaning over as well, and read another comment out loud. '"Agree with above – I heard she was seen out yesterday with bandages all over her face and the sisters wouldn't let her be on her own. Do you reckon they beat her up?"' Noelle laughed. 'Why would we beat you up?'

'According to this one, because we're "completely jealous of her making something of her life. These

347

sisters need to get a bloody life of their own".' Emmy sighed. Yet again, judgements based on no facts whatsoever. She read on, picking out bits and pieces from various comments. 'This one says, "Blah blah blah, I heard they were blackmailing her to pay for the house, how else would they afford it", then "My taxes aren't going on that dump", "Mayor Reynold needs to be rescued, she's such a lovely girl", and wait, this one says "Shall we all go over there?"'

'"Shall we all go over there?"' Noelle echoed. 'Over here? What would they all do if they came over here?'

'I don't know, the comments end there. That was about twenty minutes ago. So it could be nothing, or it could be that they've moved on to Messenger or something.'

'I don't want them to come over here,' said Noelle.

'They won't – this is a bunch of wannabe paranormal investigators sat behind computer screens. It's all talk,' she soothed her little sister. 'But Gabbi, you need to get out there and make some kind of statement. As soon as that make-up kit arrives today.'

At that moment, the door swung open and in walked Rae, looking refreshed, her hair still in soft curls from a posh up-do the night before. 'Good morning everyone!'

'Hi!' Noelle zoomed over and hugged Rae, followed by Emmy. 'How was last night?'

'It went so well. I was worried my voice would have got a bit lazy but it was great! I was so buzzing I barely slept, so I got up early and came straight back down. Wouldn't want to miss the last week of renovations,' she said, raising her eyebrows at Emmy and walking into the kitchen. 'Oh,' she said, seeing Gabbi. 'You're still here. Still calling everyone the c-word.'

'That's just what we were talking about, actually,' Emmy said, sitting back in front of the computer.

'I'm just going to go for a wee,' Gabbi said, legging it.

'What?' said Rae, looking from one sister to another.

'She's got to go,' Emmy said bluntly. 'We can't keep looking after her, it's making people talk and she's just getting in the way.'

'For god's sake,' Rae sighed, wandering over to pour herself a coffee. 'It's just helping out a friend for a few days. Aren't you used to people talking by now?'

'But she's *your* friend, and you left. We're telling you we've had enough.'

'You're still angry at me for leaving? I had a job to do!'

'We have jobs too,' Emmy retorted. 'And we took sabbaticals, like we agreed, for the whole time.'

'It was three nights! You do know we're going back to our real lives in a week anyway, you two are going to have to go back to surviving without the mother here.' She pointed at herself. She was loath to admit it – not to herself, and definitely not to her sisters – but she'd actually felt pretty rubbish running away and leaving them this time. It didn't feel as refreshing as it had when she was younger. It felt like quitting, on family.

'It's not about us not surviving without you; it's about you leaving us alone to deal with your mess!' This time, Emmy was fighting, not flighting.

'I'm sorry about that, but come on, is that big a deal? *This is not our real lives.*'

Gabbi came back into the room and rolled her eyes at Rae. 'They have been on my back,' she laughed. 'Glad I don't have any little sisters.'

'Hey.' Rae turned to her, good mood vanished. *Oh hell no, you don't bash my sisters.* 'This isn't about you, Gabbi. My sisters aren't here to look after you and help you cover up your mistakes, they're here – *we're* here – to do up our family home. But they're helping you anyway.'

Gabbi looked a bit embarrassed.

Rae downed the coffee and poured another one, then continued, 'In fact, it's never been about the family home; it's about we sisters being back together and spending time together, and doing something meaningful for us and for our mum. So don't make it about you or say they aren't doing everything you need well enough.'

350

'Fine – sorry, and thank you,' Gabbi huffed, holding up her hands. 'I'm going to go and get dressed.'

When she'd left the room, Emmy walked over to Rae and wrapped her arms around her, causing her coffee to slosh. Noelle joined them.

Rae smiled at her family. 'All right, no need to be a twat about it.'

'I think it's nothing,' Rae said a little while later, after being filled in on the activity on the Facebook page. 'It's all talk.'

The sisters were taking a walk around the outside of the house and the woods, clearing some debris as they went.

'You're probably right,' said Noelle, swinging a rake at her side. 'How did Mum and Dad deal with it, though, all this constant talk?'

'I don't think they did have to deal with it – it was like Jenny said when she was over, somehow the attitude towards them changed long ago. We got the brunt of it instead, I guess.'

'All right then,' Emmy said. 'So how did they turn the town around? How did they change people's minds when they were so intent on a witch hunt?'

'Maybe they did send around that naked photo, with their middle fingers up and the witch's hat, and maybe it so made a mockery of what they were being accused of that people felt silly and just gave up?' Noelle suggested.

Rae kicked a branch out of her way. 'I think we should just ignore them.'

'I don't think we should any more,' Emmy replied. 'We've tried ignoring them, we've tried being nice to them, and still they grab hold of any possible rumour and next thing we know they're threatening to who knows what. Storm the house and rescue Gabbi? They can have her!'

'So what do you suggest?'

'Well, I don't know, actually. I'd like to be more like Mum, but I don't know how.'

'You can't please everyone,' Noelle said all of a sudden. 'Haters gonna hate, and all that. I don't think we need to change at all, actually, or be more like Mum; I think it comes down to just being ourselves, and people can take us or leave us. Let's not wave a white flag, let's go down with the ship. Stick our middle fingers up and laugh it off.'

# Chapter 26

'We're not even having a Guy Fawkes?' Rae clarified, displeasure on her face.

'Nope.' Emmy shook her head. 'We can't; if we're going to have a mini Bonfire Night around the campfire by the den it has to be just that – mini. We don't want the whole woods going up in flames. I got us sparklers, though.'

'Jenny's going to pick up some apples on the way over so we can make toffee apples,' Noelle said, wandering into the kitchen. 'And I also just spoke with Bonnie, who said there's been no further activity on the Facebook page. People have got bored of themselves, evidently. She's going to remove the post as soon as she's home from work. We do need to meet up with her before we leave, though, because she wants a couple more quotes for her article, and a photo of the finished house.'

'Is Jared coming?' Rae asked.

'Yep,' Emmy answered. 'Is Gabbi?'

Rae looked towards the stairs. 'I might make her. She can't hide in my room for ever; I need to finish it off. Even if that make-up thing doesn't show up, I think it's time she just showed Jared.'

And when Jared showed up late that afternoon, Gabbi's make-up still hadn't. But she'd succumbed to sticking the plasters back over her face and graced them all with her presence as they trundled back and forth between the house and the den, taking snack foods, drinks, blankets, gloves and more food out with them.

The sun went down quickly, and the bonfire was up and running before it was even fully dark.

The sisters, along with Jared, Jenny and Gabbi – their pasts – watched the flames crickle-crackle over the wood and leaves. Jared and Emmy clinked their beer bottles together. This was nice. They had one week to go, but it felt like a pleasant ending. A calm ending.

Until there was a snap of branches from further within the woods.

'Do you think that was Vicky?' Noelle asked. 'She is putting on weight . . .'

'I can hear talking,' Rae said, her guard up. 'Is it out on the road?'

'I don't think so,' Emmy answered her. 'I think it's in our grounds.'

Gabbi skittered back towards the house while Jared shifted into SWAT-team mode again, stepping around the campfire and peering into the deepening nightfall. Jenny got out her phone and ducked backwards to make a call.

The voices grew louder, the twigs snapped like machine-gun fire, and out through the trees like a bunch of extras in a zombie movie stepped what felt like half of the Maplewood townsfolk.

'Well, here's a lot of familiar faces,' Rae said, though her heart was beating fast. Despite her façade she didn't actually relish confrontation, she never had. 'Have you come back for another party? Come back to drink our drinks and eat our food and have loads of fun until the morning, when you all pretend you were so above it?'

'Where's our mayor?' said Tom Bradleigh, stepping out from the middle of the group.

'I get it now,' Emmy spoke up. Her voice wobbled a little, but she was determined to find the words. A little squeeze from Jared and Noelle's hands as she stepped forward helped. 'You're here because you *didn't* get an invite to the party, and you're feeling left out? Unpopular?'

'I don't care about your party, we want our mayor back. She's supposed to kick off the town bonfire tonight, and we're here to escort her over.'

'No, you're not,' Rae said. 'You're here on some glory mission based on nothing but bullshit. If the mayor wanted to go to the bonfire she would, but she's . . . sick.'

'I heard you beat her up,' that girl from school, Becky, piped up. 'Show us our mayor.'

'We did not beat her up,' Noelle said. The crowd jeered and all started talking over one another.

Jared tapped a rock against his beer bottle until he got their attention. 'You're all on private property, and have no right to make these accusations. I have seen Mayor Reynold, and she is fine, just not ready to face you all yet. So please leave, and go to the bonfire without her.'

'With all due respect, PC Jones,' Police Officer One appeared, and Jared rolled his eyes, 'you're a little too close to the situation. The people of Maplewood are concerned, and I think we have a duty to listen to them.'

'I'm not too close to the situation, with all due respect,' Jared said through gritted teeth, while thinking what a patronising twat his colleague was.

'Yeah, you patronising twat!' Rae called out, and gave Jared a quick thumbs-up.

'Would you like to repeat that Ms Lake?' he replied.

'Why don't you just go back home and leave us alone?' shouted Annette, barging her way to the front.

'This *is* our home,' Emmy retorted, surprising herself. '*You* go home.'

Annette shook her fist like a cartoon baddie. 'You know what I mean, back where you came from.'

Emmy stood firm. '*This* is where we came from. Our family has lived in this town for thirty-five years; we are not outsiders. Your mayor is also our mayor. This is our home town, just as much as any of the rest of you.'

'Then why come here and trash it?' shouted out Kelvin, without a shred of self-awareness that he was, in fact, more trash than they would ever be. 'Why did you do all that shit at Mayor Reynold's house, and then take her hostage, and then wreck poor old Annette's store?'

'Oi.' Annette turned her attention to him briefly. 'Less of the "old", you.'

'How many times do we have to tell you, we didn't do any of that?' Rae cried. 'Where's your evidence? Why are we always guilty until proven innocent, and even then it's just a matter of finding something else to pick on this family of mine about.'

'Trouble only comes to town when you three are here, that's the problem,' someone shouted.

Jared spoke up again. 'You and I both know that's not true, Jonathon. Some of you could do with remembering

357

your own antisocial behaviours over the past decade – did you want me to bring them up now?'

This only prompted more backlash from the crowd, some of whom shouted to get their voices heard and some of whom tried a half-hearted chant of *Bring out the mayor!* The sisters' voices rose as well, and Emmy was actually blood-boilingly close to picking up a handful of burning sticks and throwing it at them all, when Gabbi appeared out of the darkness at her side.

'All right, all right, may I have everybody's attention,' called Gabbi, not very loudly, and staying pretty much out of sight. Still the arguing and accusations continued, until she shouted, 'Maplewood, *SHUT UP.*'

The noise quietened and everybody turned to face their mayor, who stepped forward so she could be seen.

Her nose was still bulbous and pink, but not too bad. Her hair actually suited her, especially now she'd cropped the rest of it shorter and wore it in a side parting the other side from the shaved bit. And the writing on her face, well, that was still there, and Gabbi had uncovered it. It had faded, somewhat, and she had clearly grabbed a black pen from inside the house and had changed the rude word to 'dudes', as Noelle had suggested.

Annette gasped. 'What did these horrible girls do to your pretty face?'

Gabbi took a deep breath. 'They didn't do anything. Nothing. I did this to myself. And you're just going to have to believe me when I say it looks worse than it is, and it was way worse than that, and the Lake sisters have helped me.'

'They've never helped anyone but themselves,' shouted out another face in the crowd, someone the sisters didn't even recognise.

'Oh, pipe down, Mister, this isn't an audition for *West Side Story*,' Emmy tutted.

Gabbi continued, 'I came to the Lake sisters' Halloween party.' (Cue much gasping.) 'That's right, I was there, and I saw a lot of you there too, quite happy to drink their booze and dance to their music and snoop about their house. Well, I got drunk at that party, and don't you dare gasp at me, Maplewood. I've made no secret of my past, and Rae Lake and I have been drunk together on many an occasion in our youth, *many occasions*.'

Rae, although pleased to see her friend hadn't turned into a total cowardly cow, made a small gesture at Gabbi to indicate maybe it was okay to tone it down a little and move on.

Gabbi nodded at her. 'Anyway, some of you seem to have forgotten that fact, and are pitting me and the Lake sisters against each other, which was never a narrative either of us set out to write – that's on you.'

The townsfolk shuffled in the dark, peering at each other and looking a bit abashed.

'However,' Gabbi said, taking a breath. 'What is on me is what happened after the party. Or more specifically, when I left during the party.'

A hush fell over the audience. Actually, it was already hushed, but Emmy definitely felt this might be the grab-the-popcorn moment.

'The Lake sisters are not responsible for what happened to my house on Halloween. I am.' Gabbi looked at Rae, who appeared confused. 'I asked Rae to go for a walk in the middle of the party, and I led her to my house, because I wanted to get changed. But on the way to my house, in my inebriated state, I'm ashamed to say that I spoke to Rae about how I'd never trick-or-treated anyone. And I – *I* – was suggesting we, um, did so.'

'Oh yeah,' said Rae. 'I'd forgotten that. You were well up for a bit of egging of front doors.'

'Yes, I was, thank you, Rae. Anyway, Ms Lake, Rae, was the one to convince me not to do that, but I was very insistent, and I'd like you to remember here that part of why you elected me as your mayor was because of my strong willpower to stick to my goals. And for that reason, the house we chose – I chose – was my own.'

Annette turned to Rae. 'You plied this poor love with alcohol and forced her to ruin her own front garden?'

'No, she didn't,' Gabbi insisted. 'Rae didn't want me to do it; *she* was the voice of reason. But she also had a kip on my garden swing so I did it anyway. And I might have gone a bit over the top, not sure why I thought breaking a window was a good idea, but at the time I had fun, and it was on my own private property, well – government property, technically, so my responsibility nonetheless – and no harm came to others.'

Rae stepped forward. 'So you knew it was you all this time?'

'Yes. Didn't you?'

'No, I genuinely couldn't remember. You let me be questioned by the police about this, several times.'

'Rae, I'm sorry—'

'My sisters and I helped shield you from this bloody lot for days, when you knew we had a lot of other stuff going on, and the house to finish. And you remembered everything; you knew we hadn't done anything wrong.' And like a shadow lifting, Rae was glad she'd grown up, even if Gabbi hadn't. Yes, it was fun to revisit some of her rock-chick roots, and she would love that version of herself until the day she died, but she would never have done something like this to a friend.

Gabbi looked uncomfortable. 'It was just while I was trying to fix all this,' she waved at her face.

'Yeah, I get it, you were the priority, what happened to the Lake family didn't really matter, it never does. But this isn't school, Gabbi—'

'Mayor Reynold,' Police Officer One corrected her.

'Oh, cock off. This isn't school, *Gabbi*, you can't shit on your friends and expect them to let it just roll off their backs any more. Stand up for us.' She waved at the ground. 'Don't leave it to us to stand up for ourselves. Have our backs.'

Gabbi didn't know what to say, and Rae knew she was directing this at the wrong woman, really. But still she stared her old friend down.

'You're right,' Gabbi said, eventually. 'I'm sorry. I can't make excuses because none of that is relevant to you, but in truth, it felt nice to have a few days off.' She turned to the crowd. 'I love being your mayor, I do, but look at you. You're a handful.'

Someone put down their pitchfork.

She continued, 'I am sorry, Rae, Noelle, Emmy. I took advantage of your hospitality. It was a proper dick move.'

Jared caught Jenny's eye and smiled. He quite liked this version of their mayor. A bit humble, but also a bit sweary.

The crowd began to fidget and the mayor addressed them a final time. 'Please go to the bonfire. I shall join you there. It's about time I left these sisters in peace.'

'What about the shop, though?' Kelvin shouted out, munching on one of *their toffee apples*. 'I reckon that was still Rae.'

Something popped inside Rae, and she started laughing. Emmy and Noelle exchanged a look. Rae laughed harder, looking up at the night sky and inhaling deep, meditative breaths. 'Oh my god, I don't care any more.'

Kelvin shuffled, and everybody just watched Rae, as if waiting for their cue for the next scene.

She continued, 'I don't care about your little games. I don't care about what you think of me. I don't care if you don't like me or my family, because we don't like you either. I truly don't care any more, and it feels amazing. Emmy, you of all people need to get on board with this feeling.'

'You don't like us, we don't like you,' Emmy said, quietly, cautiously. It seemed like an unhappy solution, but it *was* freeing. And why rely on other people's thoughts to make them happy? She'd already found more comfort in her own skin just from being back here. The elements of her personality that she thought were weaknesses had actually proven to be her strengths;

they'd got her to where she was today. And she'd had so much happiness in this house, she wasn't going to forget that any more.

And then the last voice they expected to hear spoke up, one that was deep and confident. 'I'm bored of you now. Get off my property.'

Leaning against a tree, watching the action from the shadows, cigarette in hand and looking like Jessica Lange, was Willow.

'Mum?' Noelle whispered.

'Go,' Willow snapped at the crowd, and waved her hands at them. 'Unless you want me to start revealing a few of *your* secrets as well? Let everybody judge *you*? Ohhh yes, I've known you all for a very long time now. *Go.*' The crowd immediately turned, muttering, and began to pick their way back over the sticks and leaves. Willow opened her arms wide, and in rushed the three sisters.

'What the hell are you doing here?' Rae said, tears pricking her eyes. 'I thought you were still in South America, somewhere near the Antarctic by now?'

'This cruise turned out not to be my cup of tea really. Too many couples. Not enough scandal. So I'm back.' She kissed her daughters on their heads, holding on tight.

'How long have you been back for?' asked Emmy, holding her mum around her middle.

'I got back yesterday.'

Emmy looked up. 'What? ... What?'

'Where did you stay?' Noelle asked.

'With Jenny. Don't look at her like that, Noelle, she's the one that called me tonight when that lot showed up. I asked her not to tell you.'

'Why? Did you know what we've been going through?'

'Yes, but I also know you. I wanted to give you time to resolve this yourself, and finish the house, without thinking I'd come to rescue you. I knew the three of you could handle it, you can handle anything. As just displayed.'

Jenny touched Noelle's arm. 'Sorry for not telling you.'

'That's okay.' Noelle was just so pleased to see her mum – they'd been through so much with this home over the past two-plus months, and now it was like the final puzzle piece had arrived.

'I'm going to head off then, leave you four to catch up.'

Jenny and Noelle shared a brief kiss, on the cheeks, and Jared excused himself also. Gabbi went off to pack her bag in preparation for leaving for the town's Bonfire Night, and then it was just the three sisters and Willow left around the dying fire.

'Mum's home,' Emmy said.

'Yes, I am, and I thought I told you no parties ...'

# Chapter 27

'Are you ready, Mum?' Emmy said, leading her up the steps. 'Ready for the big reveal? It's not completely done and dusted yet, but it's pretty close.'

Willow stopped and looked at the porch. 'Noey, did you do the outside?'

'Yep,' Noelle replied.

'It looks so beautiful, you did a brilliant job. I can't wait to see it in all its glory in the morning.'

'We all helped with replacing the wood.'

The sisters stopped in front of the doorway and looked at each other. This was it.

Rae opened the front door.

'Wow!' Willow breathed and looked around.

Rae began the tour, leading their mum slowly from room to room, the sisters talking over each other to point out changes and the decisions they'd made, and to laugh about tiny flaws like paint drips. Willow remained largely quiet as she walked around, a wistful smile on her face.

The house was exactly how the sisters had pictured it, right back at The Wooden Café on their first day in Maplewood. They'd chosen to go with Devon woodland as the theme, and it couldn't have looked like a cosier country home if it tried. Shades of green and pale, morning yellows coated the walls, chunky wooden furniture and matching accents ran throughout the house, and huge framed landscape photos of all things Devon – from the tors of Dartmoor to the whiskery noses of grazing cows – were hung in every room.

'So you see,' Emmy was saying as they led her along the landing towards her bedroom, 'we tried to keep it really "countryside" feeling, really *Devon*. Noelle checked and The Wooden Café can deliver cream tea hampers every time we have someone stay, as a welcome gift.'

'That sounds lovely,' her mum replied, distracted.

In her bedroom, Willow stopped and looked around, and then moved towards the bed. She sat down on their father's side and looked towards the window at the night outside. She was so quiet; at that moment, even she, Willow Lake, appeared vulnerable.

Emmy watched her, her heart breaking, because she

wondered how often her mum sat like this when she was at home; lost in thought in this big, quiet house. Emmy vowed there and then to come home as often as she could, as much as she could manage, because home wasn't just Maplewood, home was family.

'Mum?' she whispered, selfishly pulling her mother from her thoughts because she couldn't bear to see her sitting here, and yet a million miles away, any longer. 'Mum, what are you thinking?'

'I'm thinking ...' She dragged her eyes from the window, looking up at her daughters, really looking at them. 'I'm thinking that your dad would have loved what you've done to our home.'

Relief and grief flooded Emmy's heart, and she leant against the door frame, letting her eyes be clouded by her tears.

Willow smiled a soft smile. 'You've done such a wonderful job. It reminds me why your dad and I fell in love with Devon. I miss him.'

'We miss him too,' Rae said, and she reached over to put an arm around Emmy's shoulders.

Taking a deep breath, Willow stood up and walked over to the sisters. She wrapped them all in a big hug, the biggest she'd given, or received, in a long time. 'I love it so much, the three of you are very talented indeed. Thank you.'

It had been worth it, then. The ups and downs, the arguments and the rekindled romances, the hangovers and the highlights – it was all worth it to have their mum feel closer to their dad again.

Willow pulled back from her daughters, and even she had wet eyes. 'There's one thing missing, though.'

'What?' asked Noelle. 'We can add anything you need, I'm sure.'

'What's missing are all the physical reminders of you girls. I didn't know I'd miss your crap until it was all gone from under my feet.'

'But Mum, look.' Rae pointed up at the stained-glass window. 'Look closely, we had our initials put in each of the moons, so that we'd always be here with you. Even though that's soppy as hell.'

'That one's mine, I'm the maiden,' sang Noelle.

'And I'm the mother,' added Rae. 'Because someone had to watch over these damned kids while you were off on a jolly.'

'And I'm the crone!' Emmy grinned. 'All right, don't all give me pity eyes; I'm perfectly comfortable with being the crone, thank you very much. I've been reading up on crones, and yes, the official dictionary definition is ugly old woman, which isn't the furthest thing from the truth, but it can also mean wise woman. And I think I'm a little wiser now than I was when we first got here. I like being the old lady, and I like liking being me.'

'Then in that case, my *beautiful girl*,' Willow said, 'nothing is missing at all. It's perfect.'

'And by the way, Mum,' Emmy added, 'if you ever need a little more of our crap under your feet, just open the loft hatch and stand back.'

Emmy and Noelle went up to bed first that night, exhausted, and Rae sat with her mum in the living room, a glass of whisky in each of their hands.

'Mum, I need to talk to you about something,' said Rae, wanting to get this off her chest once and for all.

'I thought you might,' Willow replied, swirling her glass. 'You and I never really finish off any of our arguments, do we?'

'How do you know I was going to argue with you?'

'Because you're my flesh and blood, and I see a lot of me in you. I know when you're about to get heated.'

Rae was about to huff at her mum for being such a know-it-all, when she stopped herself. Pick your battles, Rae. Instead she said, 'So it seems you've been through something like tonight's storming of the troops before?'

'Oh yes,' Willow replied, but a smile came onto her face rather than a frown, or any hint of sadness. 'Unfortunately, it's always been the case that if you rile a few people the rest will follow. Quite literally.'

'But how did you and Dad go from having a townful of crazies storm the house, to them leaving you alone – or at least not being vile to your face?'

'It was simple really, I just showed them I didn't care. I take it you saw the photo in the loft?'

'Of the nakedness and the middle fingers up? Ew, yes. But to be honest, Mum,' and this was the crux of it, something Rae wanted to say now, while they were calm, adult, 'I feel like you should have cared because they were still awful to your daughters.'

Willow sat forward and picked up one of Rae's hands. 'I cared very much about what happened to my daughters, and I am so proud of the women you've become.'

'But you were always in the background. Even tonight, you just let us fend for ourselves. You weren't there.'

'Oh sweetheart, I was always there. It's true, I was in the background. I built up my arsenal of knowledge about everyone in this town and ensured nobody pushed any of you too hard, but you're right. I should have been more front line. In my attempt to give you the tools to be strong, I made the wrong choice.'

Rae considered this. Her mother wasn't perfect – whose was? Could she forgive her?

'Did you feel free tonight, when you finally realised you didn't care?' Willow asked her eldest daughter.

'I did,' Rae smiled.

'You see, I've always been one to follow my own path, and not shy away from the person I am. Your father helped me blossom in that way, you know, so I tried to make sure you girls were raised feeling the same. But it took a while for me to not care what people thought; I worried that we didn't fit in here, that we'd have to move, even though we bought this house – our first house – out of pure love at first sight.'

'How did you find yourselves here?' Rae interrupted.

'We spent several months camping our way around the Devon and Cornwall coast and fell in love – with the place and with each other. On our honeymoon we came back down here, saw this place was for sale, and couldn't believe our luck. It was rubbish and run-down and cheap and we wanted it.'

'You just . . . liked it and did it?'

'Quite right too. I remember the day of the house-storming well; Dad and I had spent the day outside, planting acorns and tree saplings, and we'd talked about raising a family here. It was all very symbolic but then we were raging hippies.'

Rae laughed, and her mother continued, casting a look of fondness over her eldest daughter.

'We decided that very afternoon that we were going to start by having you. We were going to try for a baby. And even though I hadn't met you yet, or your sisters, who we also couldn't wait to have, I realised that I didn't want to waste any of my cares on ignorant people any more. I wanted to use them all on my family, my house, my own life. So when they all came stomping over here full of rage I just thought, *fuck off you twats.*'

'Mum!'

'Please, I know you of all people know words like that. The short answer to your question, my dear, is, as you kids, say "haters gonna hate". Realising that took away my cares, took away their power, and I realised I was free. That's one of the very, very best things about being a grown-up – you realise that if you don't fit in, if people don't like you, then it really doesn't matter. You don't like them either. Now isn't that refreshing?'

'Morning, Mum,' Emmy said, coming down early to put the usual pot of coffee on. Willow was already in the kitchen, wearing a nightie and wandering around, running her hands over the paintwork and the door frame.

'What happened to my door?' she asked, not angry.

'Rae happened to it. And me, a little. Coffee?'

'Tea for me, please. Proper tea, Jenny only had that green herbal stuff at her house.'

Emmy started preparing the drinks, thinking how this was the best time to say what she wanted to say to her mother. She felt butterflies, not because she was worried how her mum would react, but she was worried she wouldn't be able to get the words out.

'Before the others come down, can I just talk to you about something?' she began.

Willow settled at the breakfast bar and smiled at her daughter. Emmy looked at her for a moment. With the morning sunlight on her face and her hair carefree after a night of rest, she still looked like the person from the photo, the one of her and Emmy's dad, laughing and sticking up their middle fingers. Willow's skin was older and the life lines on her face more pronounced, but she was still vibrant, and Emmy loved her so much.

'Mum, I'm sorry I didn't come home more. Before Dad died and after.'

'Hey, what's brought this on?' Willow asked, holding out an arm, which Emmy slid in under.

'I should have made more effort. I left it too late, all because I was a huge coward and cared more about what other people thought of me than about my own family.' Uh-oh, the waterworks were back.

'Shhh,' Willow soothed. 'It didn't matter *where* we saw you, we still saw you, lots. We knew you weren't too happy coming back here which is why we usually came up to Oxfordshire. Besides, you work so hard and we were retired; it made sense to come to you.'

Emmy sniffed. She felt a little better. Even if you don't go home, if home comes to you, does it still count? 'Are you angry at me?'

'Hush, of course I'm not angry at you. You know your dad was incredibly proud of you?'

'He was? Why?'

'Because you made it through some tough times – growing up with us as parents wasn't easy, and neither was growing up in this town – and yet you grew up to be an independent, strong-minded woman. You made a career for yourself, you have your own home and, more importantly, you pushed yourself to be happy. You're a little heavy on the waterworks at times,' she teased, 'but we could all do with taking a leaf out of your book on that front from time to time. You made yourself happy, and that's the only thing we cared about.'

Emmy was a million times lighter. Emotions-wise. Body-wise she'd eaten a lot of crisps these past two months, but who cared? Every single thing had been worth it.

'I heard on the grapevine you and Jared finally kissed,' Willow said, nudging her daughter back towards the kettle to finish making her tea.

'*Mu-uuumm!*'

'God, Mum,' Rae said, coming into the room. 'Just because you're a hundred and four doesn't mean you can sit around in your nightie all day. We've got a house to finish.' She leant over and gave her mum a big kiss on the head. It was so good to have her back home.

A couple of days later, Rae was walking up Gabbi's driveway for what she felt would probably be the last time. They hadn't spoken since Bonfire Night, but Rae wasn't holding any grudges. Life was too short.

She rang the doorbell and Gabbi answered almost instantly, wearing a full, bright-pink face pack, and gabbing on the phone. She grinned at Rae and beckoned her in.

'Jared, thank you so much,' Gabbi was saying into the phone. 'Rae's just shown up, actually, so I'll tell her now. You'll call Emmy and Noelle, yes? They should be kept updated. Okay. Okay, bye.'

She hung up and faced Rae. 'In one minute I'm going to apologise, ask if you want a drink, beg your forgiveness, but before I do, that was Jared. PC Jones. They've caught the person who smashed Annette's shop window. People, I should say. And, well, it wasn't you.'

'Yay!' Rae cried. 'I mean, I thought it wasn't, but I also didn't remember you trashing your own garden so I wondered if I might be guiltier than I suspected. So – who was it?'

Gabbi led Rae towards the kitchen. 'Guess. No, don't, I'll just tell you. It was Tom and Kelvin. They wanted to frame you. Or "prank you", in their words. That Bonnie girl came forward because she heard them boasting about it when she was babysitting last night. I've been bugging the police constantly since Bonfire Night to try and find answers to clear your names. I'm sorry it took so long.'

'Thank you.'

'Don't thank me, it was the least I could do. So, first of all, can I get you a drink?'

'Wine? No, just a water is fine, I'm not staying too long.'

Gabbi nodded. 'Okay. Then I'll say this now – Rae, I'm so sorry. I took advantage of you, and used your friendship for my own gain. I'm not proud – not at all – but I promise I won't do it again. I think we've grown apart, and that's okay, but I hope that maybe next time you're in town I could take you out for dinner or something.'

'In public?' Rae smiled.

'In the middle of the village green, if you want. Sorry for being a mega-bitch. Truly.'

Rae waved her hand. 'All is forgiven. And you were the one that ended up with your face looking like the Tate Modern; you've had punishment enough.'

'Talking of my face, Sid tracked down these face masks. They're fantastic, like paint stripper. I don't even want to know what chemicals are in there, but I reckon three more applications and the writing will have gone altogether.'

'Then you might not need this any more.' Rae reached into her bag and pulled out the tattoo-covering make-up kit. 'It finally arrived.'

Gabbi laughed. 'What fantastic service! I will take it, though; I'm supposed to be going to a dinner tonight with the people from the library.'

Rae gulped down her water and stood up. 'Okay, I'm going to head off. Thank you for the water, and for the sorry.'

'Thank *you* for being so gracious, and thanks for showing me a good time. When are you leaving town?'

'At the weekend.'

'So the house is all done?'

'And looking perfect, if I say so myself. Don't you let any of these mad Maplewood residents storm it again when we're gone, will you?'

'I'll make them outlaws if they do,' Gabbi said. 'You have nothing to worry about. Also, I'm putting anti-bullying higher up on my agenda this year, just so you know.' She stood also, and embraced her old friend. 'It was good to see you, Rae.'

'It was good to see you too, Gabbi,' Rae replied, and she meant it.

At the same time, Noelle was sat on the gleaming new porch, wrapped up against the cold, waiting for Jenny to arrive. She was armed with a letter and a chicken.

'Vicky, we can't keep you here,' she cooed at the bird, who strutted about with her bottom in the air. 'Mum's already got her next trip booked, and I can't take you back to Bristol. Could I? ... No, no, I really think this is the best option.'

Jenny pulled up at that moment, stepping out of her car with a big smile and a suitcase. 'This is your mum's,' she said, hauling it up the steps. 'I've been promising to bring it over for days. Morning, Vicky!'

'You are a star,' Noelle said, taking the case from her.

'Thanks for coming over today. Can I get you anything to eat or drink?'

'Actually, I can't stay that long, I'm sorry. I'm heading over to Mum and Dad's later on to help them out with some flood-defence building.' She stepped back and looked up at the house. 'This place looks truly beautiful, by the way. You're going to give a lot of holidaymakers some very happy memories.'

'Thank you! Speaking of your mum and dad, though, do you think they'd like to adopt Vicky?'

Jenny laughed. 'What?'

'I need to find her a home, and I think she'd like it out by the river. I was going to ask you, but I thought she might poop all over your stock. You can say no, I don't want to be an imposition.'

Jenny stroked Vicky's soft feathers. 'They'd love her. They already have three mad chickens so she'll fit right in. Thank you.'

'Thank *you*.'

'So you're leaving?' Jenny turned to her, but her face was warm.

'In just a couple of days. I wanted to have you over here today because I wanted to say goodbye properly this time. I know we're not together, and I don't mean to suggest you in any way would be heartbroken by my leaving, but I just … Well, this feels a bit cheesy now, actually.'

'Spit it out,' Jenny said with kindness. 'I would love a proper goodbye.'

'Okay. You sit there, on the porch steps,' Noelle got up and faced Jenny. Vicky sat on Jenny's lap. 'I have a letter again for you, but this time I want to read it to you. Is that okay?'

'Of course, I love getting post. Sometimes.'

Noelle cleared her throat and unfolded the letter. What had she been thinking? This felt so silly now. 'Here goes. "Dear Jenny" – don't laugh, okay?'

'I won't, and neither will Vicky.'

'"Dear Jenny, last time you read a letter from me on this porch I'd been a huge, selfish lesbian. Sometimes I still am, and perhaps getting back in touch with you is another example of that, because as much as I wanted to apologise, I also wanted to see you again."' Noelle looked up, relieved to see Jenny listening, smiling.

She continued, 'Um, where was I? "I also wanted to see you again. And I'm so pleased you were willing to see me. You have been a huge part of my life and I wouldn't change that for a second. All I ever wanted was for you to be free and happy, and you are those things, not because of me and what I did, but in spite of me. I know we're not in love any more, and I'm not trying to rewrite history, but to paraphrase what Natasha Bedingfield sang during the opening credits of *The*

*Hills*, our future is unwritten. Knowing we might be in it together, even while apart, as friends, is perfection. Thank you for being you. Love always, Noelle.'"

Noelle's hands were shaking as she folded the letter back up. Closing arguments were much easier than this. She was afraid to look at Jenny. Had it been too 'me, me, me'? Would Jenny be insulted, maybe it sounded too patronising? 'I just—'

'Thank you,' Jenny interrupted. She stood up, holding on to Vicky, and put a hand against Noelle's cheek, then leaned in to kiss her. One final kiss. 'That was really lovely to hear.'

'Really?'

'Really. I'm glad you told me all of that, and I'm glad you came back here for the time you did. It's been nice getting to know you again.'

Noelle pulled Jenny into a gentle hug, careful not to squash the chicken. She lay her cheek against Jenny's hair, just for a moment. 'Right back at you. Goodbye, Jenny. See you again soon.'

# Chapter 28

And then it was Emmy's turn to say goodbye to Jared.

What did she want from this goodbye? Did she want a goodbye at all? The answers didn't come as easily as if they were black and white. Because, no, she didn't want a goodbye – not at all – but she was her own person, perhaps now more than ever, and she didn't know how to join the two things together.

'Nice weather for a duck,' she used as a greeting when Jared joined her in the bus shelter on the edge of town. The November rains were back; heavy, quiet rain that gave everything a soft tone and nothing a shadow. She'd originally thought a nice goodbye would be meeting at her den – their den – but this weather would have, literally, made the idea a wash-out. And inside, her house was too full of people. So she asked him to meet her here, and bring her a coffee.

'Loving the romantic venue choice,' he replied, and leant in and kissed her over the sweet-smelling coffees. Just a light kiss. One that knew not to push things in case it hurt their hearts even more.

He settled on to the plastic seat next to her, and she was, as usual, at a loss for the right words. 'When do you head up to Oxford?' he asked.

'Tomorrow.'

'It's gone quickly.'

Emmy nodded. *Say something! Tell him how you feel! Also, how the bloody hell do you feel?*

'Do you know when you'll next be back down?' Jared asked, braver than her, like he always had been.

'Really soon,' she replied honestly. 'I want to make a lot more effort to visit Mum from now on, whenever she's not off on her trips. And, um, I don't know if you'd want to meet up again when I'm next down, but that would be quite cool too.'

'I really would,' he answered, and Emmy felt quite simply happy. He meant a lot to her, he made her life better, more fulfilled. Time would tell if that would be because of anything romantic, or just because he was a true friend.

'I got you a present,' he said all of a sudden,

handing her his coffee to hold while he reached into his coat pocket. 'You've had a lot to focus on since being back, and there've been some bumpy times, and also, some really nice times.' He sneaked her cheeky smile. 'So I thought – and disagree if you want, but only if you still make it sound flattering because I'm quite sensitive – I thought maybe before we try and make any kind of decisions about long-distance or whatever, we could start out by just aiming to stay in touch more. You know, breaking down the problem and solving it piece by piece.' He handed over the gift.

Inside was a pink plastic phone case. Garish and childish. She looked up at him and laughed. 'Thank you?'

'This way, you can pretend it's all just a fun game of Dream Phone, until we're ready to become, I don't know, grown-ups.'

Emmy grinned at the phone case. What a thoughtful gift. Who was she kidding, she knew what she wanted, she was just so used to hiding behind indecision, and hiding her feelings in general. She wanted this – friendship – with Jared. And she wanted that to work long-distance. And if it did, she wanted *him*. Not just because of the boy he once was, but because of the man he was now. Funny. Kind. Courageous. And he didn't want to change her one bit.

'So you'll call me sometime?' he asked.

'I'll call you all the time.'

That night, the Lake sisters sat around their fireplace with their mother. The new sofas were comfortable and cosy, and the carpet was as clean as it would ever be, with four bags of crisps being passed around and wine glasses threatening to topple over at any minute.

They were passing between them photo albums that chronicled their childhoods. Emmy aged five, fast asleep in the den with a cardboard box on her head. Noelle's first day at secondary school, the highest pony-tail you'd ever seen. Rae in the school play, not joining in with the dance routine.

Willow laughed and held up the photo album she was browsing. 'Look at this one – do you remember your dad building you that tree house? I took it down the next day because Noelle had fallen from it, and Rae was so angry at me.'

Rae chuckled. 'We had a pretty great childhood growing up in this house, didn't we? We were actually very lucky.'

There had been tough times – there still were – but they wouldn't change their family for the world, because it was who they were. They'd all found an awful lot of happy in this hopeless place.

It was leaving day, and it had come way, way too soon. Willow helped them move their belongings to their cars, trying to load them up with things from the fridge (or things from the attic).

Before they left the house for the last time, Rae, Emmy and Noelle huddled together in Emmy's old bedroom. They embraced each other in turn. 'We did it,' said Rae. 'It was a tough road but we did it.'

'I'm so glad we did,' Emmy agreed. 'I was so nervous coming down here, but it's been the best couple of months ever.'

'Better than sitting in your lab?' asked Rae.

'Better than if I was flying to the moon,' she confirmed.

Noelle breathed in the room. 'I feel ... light.'

'You always feel light, hippy,' Rae teased. 'But I do know what you mean. I feel like layers upon layers of heavy, shitting armour have finally fallen off.'

'What would we have done without you and your smart mouth, Rae?' said Emmy.

'What would I have done without you two?' she replied.

Emmy wanted to tell her sisters about something she'd been thinking about. Something she might have benefited from when she was growing up. 'I'm going to join a mentoring scheme with the Women's Engineering Society. I'm going to help more young girls get into this profession.'

'That's amazing!' Noelle cried, and they all squeezed in for one more hug, before they broke apart and joined Willow out on the decking.

'Mum, I finish at work on the twenty-first of December, so I'll come down the next morning,' Emmy said, wanting to get Christmas locked down. 'Rae has a Christmas Eve performance so she and Finn will be driving down on Christmas morning, is that right, Rae?'

'Finn'll be driving; I'll be probably wrapping your presents on the back seat.'

Noelle pushed a box into her car. 'I think I finish on the twenty-first too, Em, so let me know closer to the time if you're still okay to pick me up.'

'Thank you again, girls,' Willow said, coming to a stop. 'I can't say it enough. I almost feel bad that I'm not going away again until January and nobody else gets to enjoy this house.'

'It was our pleasure,' Rae said, going into her mum for a final hug, of this trip at least. 'Despite everything,' she laughed, 'it really was.'

'Wait!' Emmy yelped. 'We need to take a photo of us with the house, for Bonnie's article!'

'Actually, I'd like a copy of that too; good idea,' said Noelle.

'I've got the perfect idea ... We just need to get a couple of things down from the loft.'

And then, after ten minutes of faffing around in the loft, ten minutes of faffing around inside the house, and another ten minutes trying to get Emmy's phone to balance in a suitable position to get both them and the house in the shot, they were ready.

'This is going to make such a lovely photo,' Emmy said, jiggling about with excitement.

'Is the timer on?' Rae screeched as Emmy ran back to the group.

'Yes, stop talking!' Emmy took her position and they held their pose, the laughter spilling out of them without governance, for three ... two ... one ...

They say a picture can tell a thousand words. This one told of a thousand blissful memories.

# Epilogue

Bonnie was pretty chuffed with her article. She was tweaking and rewording and thesaurusing it to perfection, when an email notification flashed up on her phone.

It was from Emmy Lake, with the subject line, 'Here's the photo!' Bonnie opened up the attachment with excitement, and nearly spat out her Diet Coke (laced with a tiny splosh of whisky).

The photo that filled the screen was flawless. Two generations of Lake women – Willow, Rae, Emmy and Noelle – stood facing the camera outside the house in the woods. Noelle in an awful tie-dyed dress covered in plastic mirrors; Emmy wearing a 'Girl Power' crop top with pride; Rae with masses of eyeliner on, her tongue out and holding her leg up in the air, ancient-looking Dr. Martens on her feet;

Willow, stark naked, concealing her lady parts skil-fully with foliage.

And all four women of Maplewood were laughing, holding up their middle fingers, with their heads held high.

# Acknowledgements

Hello! Thanks for reading until the end; much appreciated. For being such a bloody good person, you can have the first thank-you, reader. I hope you had fun hanging out in Maplewood with the Lake sisters. Come back soon; watch out for the Hairy Hands.

Thank you to the big scrumptious team at Sphere: Jennie, Thalia, Clara, Amy, Bella, Bekki and Lucy who designed the cover, and all the others in Sales, Production, Rights – the list goes on. And most of all thank you to my first and second Sphere wives (editors), Manpreet and Viola. I think I'm actually in love with both of you DON'T FREAK OUT but I think we're all going to be best friends for ever.

My next giant thank-you must go to the lady with the lovely hair, who is probably sick to death with me banging on about her hair, Hannah Fergalicious (Ferguson), my fantastic agent. She and the crew at Hardman & Swainson are such a joy to work with – thanks for letting me be part of the family!

An agent and an editor are a flippin' dream team, I tell you. I wish they would organise and advise my whole life.

I've got a dog! And I'm going to thank him next, because he's just inspired my next book. Thanks Kodi-Bear, you humongous Bernese Mountain Dog.

Thanks Phil! Thanks Mum! Thanks Dad! Thanks family and friends!

Thanks to Devon for being the bestest county and for holding some fabulous writer pals in your bosom – Emma, Holly and Belinda, here's looking at you, kids.

Thanks TV and pizza. I love you.

Thank you to all my sisters around the globe who make us laugh, make us strong, and make the world a better place.